A Maroon Star & A Silver Thread

Written by

Caroline Sophia Hamel

To request permissions, contact the publisher at caroline@carolinesophiahamel.com

ISBN (Paperback Edition): 9798986273952
ISBN (eBook Edition): 9798986273969
ISBN (Hardcover Edition): 9798986273976
Library of Congress Control Number: 2025903765

Cover Art by © mihaellustrates
Edited by © I.O. Scheffer

First printing edition 2025

Place of Publication: Bellingham, Washington

A Two-Part Dedication:

For every trans girl and trans woman who feels they can't do it, that you aren't valid (you are), or that the world is against you. I love you. This book is for you.

For Tasha Edwards,

Thank you for helping me grow my wings and encouraging me not to shrink down for anything. Thank you for believing in me and believing I could grow and blossom. Thank you for sticking by my side and supporting me these past few years. You made my transition much easier and I'm grateful for that.

~

A Brief Guide to Pronunciation

Eu is pronounced like "Yew" or "You" (hard "U" sound)

Ei is pronounced like "air," "heir," or "their"

Veiria is pronounced like Vuh-air-ee-uh

Neihdria is pronounced like Nay-dree-uh

Noctine is pronounced like Noct-een / Nock-teen

Acellia is pronounced like Uh-sell-ee-uh

~ Trigger Warnings (Spoilers) ~

Transphobia, Internalized Transphobia, Deadnaming, Misgendering, & Gender Dysphoria ~ "Mirages of Memory", "The Curtain of Mourning", "Chills in the Night", "Bejeweled in Love & Belittled in Spite", "Specters of Darkness ~ Tears of Love", "Crescendo in the Theater", "Deep in Her Heart" (& general dysphoria throughout the book)

Violence, Serious Injuries, Blood Loss, & Stabbing

Three Fake Out Deaths (No Characters Permanently Die, I Promise) ~ Decapitation (Illusionary): "Chills in the Night", Burning to "Death": "Sweet Dreams"

Light Horror, Some Disturbing or Unsettling Scenes & Imagery, Suicidal Ideation, Suicide, & Self-Harm Imagery

Mental & Physical Torture (in Nightmare Scenes, Mostly Related to Gender Dysphoria)

Three Kisses without Consent and / or with Unclear Consent (There are five kisses in total) ~ "Perched on Heaven's Staircase", "Bejewed in Love & Belittled in Spite", "Crescendo in the Theater"

Brief Scenes with Sexual & Erotic Content (within the Confines of YA) ~ Erotic Scene (Non-Explicit / Semi-Vague): "A Garden of Pleasures", Clear Sexual Thoughts: "Mirages of Memory"

Internalized Homophobia ~ "The Crush of a Schoolboy", "Perched on Heaven's Staircase", "Bejeweled in Love & Belittled in Spite"

CisHeteronormativity (Internalized & External)

5

She's dreaming in a cage of stars

If she wakes, it all falls down

But if she stays in bitter dreams

She'll lose something, her precious wings

Table of Contents

Amnesia of a Lost Soul

Veiria

My eyes flutter open to the warm touch of the sun, a breeze whispering across my face. I sit up, purple blossoms falling soundlessly around me and scattered across the land.

Frowning, I raise my hand and watch the dim sunlight flit through the sea of falling petals.

I stare at my hand as it trembles, reaching up with the other to trace it with disconcerted awe, my skin is fair, soft, and strangely flawless. Coming to my feet, I notice the beautiful, silver-white silken dress falling gently over me.

I startle at the sound of a crow.

My breath catches and I shift around in the fabric, turning a few angles. This lovely sensation kindles a warm and light feeling in me.

I glance up to see the petals part and a flock of crows take off, disturbing the quiet scenery.

I bite my lip, glancing around only to see deep purple and a paper white sky.

There's nothing here but the sound of silence.

Tentatively, I take a few steps in my bare feet.

There's the odd sound of chains and crumbling stone and I whip my head backwards.

Behind me is a grassy hill and what I take for a stone tablet, shattered to pieces.

Strange.

I kneel, running my hand over a scattered piece of stone and feeling its cool surface. I frown some more when something catches my eye. It looks like a side table. There's a music box and a cracked photograph.

I pick up the music box first, pressing it to my ear and feeling a hollowness in my heart when nothing happens. It makes me want to cry. I know there's a melody I want to hear—need to hear. But it's not there ...

Then my heart drops and I grasp the picture frame. The music box puffs away into thin air as it falls from my hand, but I only see the frame. My fingers tremble as I gaze at the three indistinct faces of a family, and I suddenly jump back, yelping and dropping the photo as it shatters into a million pieces at my feet.

I clutch my hands to my chest, taking erratic breaths and looking around wildly until my heart settles a little.

"Veiria," calls a voice on the wind.

My heart steadies a little more and I smile nervously. Yes, that's my name. I may have nothing more to go by, but I know that.

My name is Veiria.

It's perfect. At least, I think that sounds right.

The rest of my mind may be startlingly murky, but I know that one fact and, for now, that's enough—even though my heart pounds; even though I'm scared.

I turn away from the broken stones to find a crow staring at me with beady eyes that render my heart cold. It feels like it's peeling at my flesh.

I back up. "Can you tell me where I am?" I know it's a bird that means no harm. It could be lost, but suddenly it's frigid and I grip my arms close around my middle.

The crow bursts into a cloud of feathers.

I don't understand. What's going on?

Sweat drips down my forehead as I try finding an explanation for the impossibility my eyes witnessed.

The crow multiplies. I turn my head and stumble backwards in fright. A black, feathery swarm flies towards me, an inky cloud bleeding from the white nothingness.

I scramble over myself and run, my heart pounding as the darkness licks at my hands and ankles, until I come to a precipice.

Desperate for another escape, I whip my head around. My eyes widen as the cloud forms a shadow-like hand that wisps at the air behind me.

The wind picks up and chills, withering the purple blossoms to a deathly gray within the hand's shadow.

It comes closer. Without thinking and ignoring my heart, I jump and the world stops, the birds and the darkness and the hand. Frozen.

I squirm in confusion, suspended in air, before I'm sucked up, screaming into inky black water above me.

I clutch my throat, indiscernible faces and harsh thoughts aimed at my neck. There's a strange feeling of wanting to disappear as the water strangles me, yet I can't discern what it speaks of, just that it tosses me, tangles me in violent disgust. I cover my ears, letting it play me as a rag doll as I try to take myself to silent waters.

Veiria, a voice echoes, cutting through the turbulent, hateful thoughts and finally silencing them.

There's a tautness in the water and a burst of pitch-black feathers that cascade through the depths around me, barely distinguishable in the ink. Crow feathers.

Veiria ... it's not time. Stay ... stay where it's safe.

But I'm scared, I think like a murmur. *Where am I?*

In the place I had to keep you. You weren't ready. I'm sorry.

Sorry? Why should you be sorry?

The voice lets out a sigh. *I can't stop you. You've already broken the seal. Be safe, until we meet in flesh. You have friends here, Veiria. Trust them. I wish you luck.*

But what are you? Who are you? I think loudly as the feathers spread like tar to a black sheet. *Who am I?*

Someone who scares you. Though that was never my intention. In my confusion, I can't make out if the voice is ominous or comforting, but their answer leaves me recoiling in the depths of the darkness. *Who you are is something I can't answer. Only you can.*

Then there's a glimmer and a flash of silver and the strange sound of something like a lock clattering.

I collapse, drenched, down an incline of a hill. The murky water above begins to shimmer between a disgusting inky black and calm blue. Petals settle on its surface.

It's a strange thing—water where the sky should be.

I rub my eyes, squeezing them shut, and suck in a breath.

"Let me out."

I open my eyes, startled as the ground falls away a few feet from where I'm lying to a silver stairwell.

I frown. Odd.

Tentatively, I crawl towards it, grabbing my chest and breathing heavily at the seemingly endless dop below.

My breath grows labored, and I scoot away. Where else can I go?

Wincing, I get up on my elbow to scooch over to the rail and grip it until my knuckles are white. Resolute, I force myself to stare into the forever blue abyss. With my eyes on the bottomless pit below, I take my first wobbly steps, hand to my chest. "It's okay," I breath in a feather-light voice that nearly makes me jump. But I close my eyes and breathe, pushing my fear down and hugging the railing tightly, because when I look up, there's nothing above me but the murky depths that whisper of a nightmare.

I hear a creaking sound as I glance up at the watery sky, now a deep, ocean blue slowly descending towards me.

I feel my stomach plummet. I guess there's nowhere to go but down, so I wind my way around the spiral stairs into the infinite sky, nothing but blue, with occasional clouds and tiny specks below that are impossible to make out.

I look furtively for a noise or something, suddenly feeling like I want to shrink and hide myself, even if there's something that feels more homelike in my steps and the lightness of my body. This feels wrong, and that picture makes me know it.

As I descend on trembling feet, the watery sky above creeps ever downwards. My hand traces the railing in wonder at the infinite sky, forgetting my fears for a moment and wondering if I could fling myself off the railing and fly into the distance—away from troubles and pains and the throbbing in my head. I'm aware that something's wrong in some way or another with me being here, but since I can't remember, I can't place what that is.

Hours seem to drag by until something white and tiny sails towards me and unthinkingly, I extend my hand to a beautiful, pure white dove that settles on the rail and nestles into my palm.

I smile a little, stroking it with a tiny bit of peace entering my mind. I think I like gentle things like this. I have no clue as to why, but I can't take my eyes off it. It's beautiful and my chest beats in affection as I stroke it and smile at it with tender eyes, my lips strained. "Are you lost too? If you are, you're just like me," I whisper softly to it.

It lets go a beautiful, low call as its eyes close and it brushes its head against my hand. Both the bird and my hand that strokes it are too perfect. Too beautiful.

It ruffles its feathers suddenly and takes flight. I reach for it desperately. "Come back ..." My chest cracks as a loneliness creeps back in.

I sigh, my heart aching. It's lucky. It can fly off wherever it wants—leave this place and be free. Not like me. I'm stuck here in this weird place that just leaves a heaviness in my heart. The open sky now feels oppressive and too wide.

I bury my face in the bars and hopelessly sink down to the steps. Do I even want to go on? But I glance up and know the answer. The ceiling of water will follow me ... perhaps forever.

As I descend, huge chunks of rock come into view, suspended over the nothingness, gnarled roots protruding from their undersides and patches of grass and wavy, bright orange coral-like structures on top. Shimmering gold birds flit between them and strange, coiled dark creatures whiz off in the distance. Far below me, something ominously red flits into view from behind an enormous mass of rock. It bathes the world in an eerie, dark glow.

I open my eyes wide.

It's a huge flaming ball of what seems to be a deep maroon shade, floating strangely below me at an angle in the blue sky. And that makes no sense whatsoever.

A shiver passes up my spine as I'm bathed in that light. It's ... so surreal.

I don't like this.

For a moment, I wonder if I can do something about that, but when I squeeze my eyes shut, it's still there.

I stop for only a moment, descending cautiously and gripping the railing harder as I watch it flit between the land masses at a distance, sometimes encroaching on the stair, but never close enough to touch. The eerie light of the star still rests below me and at a slight angle to the side, casting long strange shadows, but oddly not the only light source.

Eventually, I grow used to the star, instead casting my gaze towards the landmasses of sparse trees and grass, finding a refuge for my loneliness in the occasional long, anguished calls of birds echoing in the huge, open space. They're rare noises amid the quiet.

Until finally, the spiral stair stops on top of a land mass and I step into a pool as thin as cloth. My foot sends forth a ripple. The maroon star and clear blue air vanish in an instant, swapping for a moon and stars, reflected to infinity around me as beautiful pinpricks of brilliant light—below, above, reflected on the water—everywhere in endless beauty. And the moon rests above me in the sky, yet below the far-stretching waterline that reflects those stars further to infinity.

As I turn in wonder in the middle of the endless sea of stars, the silver stair behind me shatters and I step back a pace reflexively, as it swirls towards my hand in sharp, delicate pieces. My eyes go wide, mouth open, as I reach out in awe to touch one of the floating shards. In an instant, they coalesce in my hand into a sword of flawless, mirror-sharp silver.

I blink, tentatively running my fingers over the new weight and feeling a strange sense of familiarity as I gaze at the sword that looks made of glass—delicate and cold as it is, it's comforting.

I give it a reluctant flourish, a dread and joy taking form in my chest simultaneously. It's a beautiful, deadly thing and I find as much as I want to hate it and as revolting as it is, I feel safe.

My lips tremble into a smile and I breathe a deep sigh. "Okay." I close my eyes. "Neihdria." Intuitively, I know its name. I have no idea as to why, but I don't need to. Having it is enough. As cold and cruel as the thing is, it's something real and familiar.

I breathe in again and take a step. Neihdria suddenly shatters and I screech, falling to my knees outside of the pool and swiping at the shards as they swirl around me, just out of reach. It's suddenly day again, the maroon star twinkling off the shards in deadly, rich maroon.

The shards seem to gloat at me as I let out heavy, erratic breaths, hands to my chest. I shake violently as I look up at the sky, endlessly blue again. I move to cover my face. "Why?" I feel weak and helpless. I want to feel that silver in my hands again, even if the concept of it terrifies me. Even so, I force myself to stand, wincing tiredly and following them until they form a silver stair at the edge of the land mass that I subsequently proceed over.

It leads me to a covered path on the exterior of a spiraling rock and I follow it slowly upwards until, finally, exhaustion catches up with me and I collapse under the cliffside.

In my dream, I'm chained to a cliff face, surrounded by the feathers of a crow.

I remember a young woman I can't quite make out crying, a young man next to her, holding her close for comfort. He looks to me with something like pity as the sky darkens and lightning cracks. Thunder rips at the air and she screams for me. It's a wild, raw scream as she looks up and the last light of hope seems to fade from her eyes. Seeing her sink into despair for me and hearing those dismal cries makes me ache inside. It feels like I'm missing something fundamental. I feel tears running down my cheeks as the wind buffets me against the cliff face. It's almost like I miss her ...

Then there's a voice.

It's done, Veiria. It's time. The world is in shambles and much as I have regrets, I promise to save your loved ones.

I see the outline of a dark figure with midnight bird wings and crow's feet. They look at me with pity and sorrow in their violet eyes as they extend their pale hands and the chains tighten, making me scream.

Trust me, Veiria. Close your eyes, and it'll all be over. Close your eyes and your world lives. It's for your benefit, so you can return another day.

They smile gently and I struggle against my chains, feeling a confusing sort of comfort and fear at once.

This place is precious to me, I think. I don't want to go.

It's just for a little while. I was glad to try to preside, but I see I missed something dearly.

As the chains tighten and my eyes grow weary, I notice that weird maroon star in the distance fluctuating, seeming to shrink as the darkness grows.

They disappear and I'm left with their last words. *Say goodbye to them. I know they'll find you again one day, but for now, it's too late. All I can do is render my judgment and await your return.*

I open my mouth to the feel of blood on my lips, but before I can utter anything to the two people I'm told are precious to me, the vision fades and all I'm left with are the girl's frightened eyes that are such a familiar shade of brown.

I wake up in the dark, huddled under a cliff face. Neihdria lies in my open palm, solid and comforting. Beads of water float through the air. I brush them aside and get up, moving to the edge of the path I had taken so I can stare into the void. I get splashed in the face from below and release my first laugh I can remember.

I frown and clutch my head, feeling almost nauseous until I recall the cool metal between my fingers. I stand there for a moment, gazing at the upwards rainfall. The edges of my lips tingle with barely a smile. It's an odd sort of weather and I close my eyes and listen to the patter below me as I walk down the winding path, not knowing where I'm going, apart from the tug of Neihdria in my grasp.

The path wraps around the column of rock. It's thin, the overhang forming a continuous ceiling above me. Roots stick out from the bottom. I look to the side. There are trees growing on most of the cliff faces.

As I walk, I suddenly stiffen, glancing around as Neihdria heats in my grasp and without thinking, I clutch its hilt harder.

Then, BAM!

In an instant, I shriek, tumbling into the air as the rocks below me shatter into fragments.

Another explosion, and I lose my grip on Neihdria. It shatters once it leaves my grasp. My heart plummets to my throat.

The wind shrieks by as I try to correct myself, straining my fingers towards the shards. They stream towards me and my face contorts in concentration, forgetting that I'm falling who knows how far up in the air.

So close ... I narrow my eyes. I can reach it. My fingers tremble with the effort.

Another explosion and the shards are blasted apart into dust.

My eyes go wide with shock, and I cry out. The world flashes sporadically in color. My mind is desperate, but I'm losing focus, plummeting through the endless chasm of air. A moment later, my vision turns black.

You will begin again, Veiria. It's time to live. This is the same voice from earlier. A cold voice.

In the darkness, I see a flickering light of hope and reach my trembling fingers out to it as I swear I hear another voice, far quieter and more touching …

I'm almost there, Veiria. You'll be home soon. Just, don't do anything stupid …

I miss you.

It's the warmth of that admission that drowns out the other voice. Gives me something solid. The light is snuffed out before I can reach it.

I'm doomed, aren't I?

Yet, something in the last voice rejuvenates my spirit.

Am I really this dramatic?

Beware of Neihdria. Be cautious of your fears, Veiria.

And this time, it's the cold voice that speaks.

The Kindness of a Stranger

Veiria

I rub my eyes as I sit up in a bed as soft as feathers. Sunlight streaks through the window in what I take for mid-afternoon.

Glancing up, I notice an elderly woman, her hands extended comfortingly by my bedside. "It's alright, dear."

She smiles at me, kind wrinkles forming around her hazel eyes and I smile weakly back, ignoring the throbbing pain in my skull.

"You had a nasty fall. Goddess knows from how far up. Several sphere lengths, at least. Thank the Goddess of the Skies my husband found you. You can thank him later. In the meantime, young lady, how about I make you some soup to help your fever?"

I hesitate for just a moment, but my thirst and exhaustion get the better of me. "Yes, I'd like that a lot." I bring my fingers to my throat cautiously as I speak. My voice sounds angelic, like it's not mine and it catches me off guard. "Thank you ... so much."

The dark skin around her eyes crinkles into a warm smile. "What's your name, dear?"

"Vuh ... Veiria." The name seems somewhat unfamiliar, but I recognize it as mine.

"It's a beautiful name."

"Thank you."

"I'll be right back with your soup." She smiles again, getting up quietly for my privacy.

As she shuts the door quietly, I lay back, my eyelids drooping and my vision still blurry.

What just happened to me? I don't remember much of anything. A tiny thread seems to pull on my fingertips, as if something is missing. I curl them slightly against the edges of the sheets.

All I know is that I fell from the sky, and I'm being cared for by this woman. How can I possibly repay her generosity?

And how does one fall from the sky? I scrunch my brow. I don't know what sphere lengths are.

I shift my hands from my throat, staring at them without blinking and turning them to look at my arm. My hands are fair, not calloused, and my arm looks unnaturally pretty. I look away from it, feeling suddenly nauseous.

The woman comes back with a steaming bowl of soup that she sets at my bedside. "It's still hot, so be careful. I hope it's to your liking. It's Norsica Grass and Miilyum."

I eye it for a moment in bewilderment at the strange ingredients, but I don't feel like questioning her kindness. "Thank you. I ... I didn't catch your name."

"Bell. Simple, I know."

"It's lovely." I start again at the sound of my voice, but I hide it under my compliment, instead studying Bell. She's a sweet-looking old woman in what looks like a hand-knitted shawl, her hair held up in a beautiful clasp of a strange bird. Her hands and skin appear frail.

"I'm glad you think so. Sometimes simple is best. It always bothered me a little, but others always seemed to like it."

"It suits you," I say truthfully. She is sweet, like a bell.

"You're a sweet girl."

"Th—" I almost thank her, but I stop myself. I'm not sure I've done anything deserving of that praise. "Is there anything I can do for you? You've been so kind."

"Get better for me," she says simply, hands set modestly in her lap and those kind wrinkles illuminating the goodwill in her eyes.

"I'll try." I'd feel indifferent about recovering if she hadn't requested it. I'm indebted to her, after all.

"I'm going to the market. If there's anything you need, tell me. My husband and I will be back in the evening." She gives me another sweet smile and then leaves.

Evening? Something about that doesn't sound right. I shake my head. It's morning now. I know that, yet something feels odd about what she just said.

Colors seem to flash almost imperceptibly behind my eyelids. I try to blink them away. They're gone before I know it. Was that maroon?

I feel groggy and I reach for the soup bowl. It's delicious in a tangy way—not that I normally like that, but I feel like it's made with love, and I feel some energy returning to me.

Bell exits the room quietly, hugging her shawl to her hunched figure and leaves me be as the oak door creaks behind her. I glance around the room once she leaves, finally taking more note of the surroundings. It almost looks like a cabin—ruffed wood and logs along the wall and thick beams set into the sloped ceiling. Besides the earthy wood and smell of thistle and lavender, there's a fair amount of vivid mint green.

I smile at a stuffed bunny next to me in an embroidered pink-and-white top hat. "Hello there."

Suddenly, I'm hit with a wave of nausea and sit back into the white and rose-pink pillows behind me, the wood of the bedframe creaking from use.

I clutch my stomach, feeling wretched as I fight against my sudden panic.

It's just a little pain, I think, wincing. Okay, maybe a bit more than a little?

I sit back, observing the room as I fade in-and-out of consciousness for the rest of the day. The mint green and pleasant rose pinks are pretty against the authentic wood, logs, and old-fashioned tasseled lamp and nightstand.

At one point I think: *Maybe this is a little girl's room? Or was?* I sigh deeply. That sounds so nice. I spend a minute thinking about what it would be like to grow up in a cute room like this before fading into a half-sleep again as I'm lulled to peace by birdsong outside the open thatched window.

I'm awoken later by a second voice and a light knock on the door. "Veiria"—Bell's voice—"we're home."

I clear my throat, bringing myself away from my comfy position against the girl's pretty pillows and the bunny I'd subconsciously cradled while I'd slept. On the nightstand is a flute-case labeled "Melody." That must be the owner of the room. I smile, overjoyed at the thought of someone playing the flute. It's a beautiful-sounding instrument.

"Come in." I notice just how tired I sound, but at least I feel a little more rested now and surprisingly at home.

"You must be Veiria," Bell's husband addresses me with that same warmth. His eyes are a bit lighter, but just as kind, and he shares a similar dark complexion, wearing a modest work vest.

"Yes. Thank you for bringing me back to your home."

"Of course. It's my pleasure to do what I can to help."

"If you want to rest some more, the two of us can make you dinner," Bell offers.

"Are you sure you don't need any help?" I reflexively start to pull the covers off at the thought of being useful, despite how sore I am.

"That's nice of you, Veiria," Bell's husband says with a smile, "but you need your rest. Bell says you slept for a full day."

"I did?"

"Don't worry, dear, just rest. The two of us have been doing this more years than we can count."

I eye the name "Melody" on the flute case. Is *that* what they mean? Or do they help any strange girl who falls from the sky? I wonder if this is normal here. I'm alive, after all. "I forgot to ask your name?"

"Diel. Diel Liis." He tips a fedora in his hands. It makes him look like a grandpa and I want to laugh.

"Thank you, Bell, Diel." I squeeze my covers. I really don't want to be a nuisance. It really is a lovely home. If anything, it's probably lovelier than where I live, not that I would remember that.

I walk down the hallway, the dull orange light of twilight casting hazy shadows through the open windows. I glance out of them, seeing what looks like a small, pretty garden outside, but I can't tell because of the lighting. I do try craning my neck, though. I approach the end of the hall, entering the kitchen as Bell and Diel are preparing dinner.

"Hello?" I stand awkwardly in the doorway.

Bell and Diel smile warmly at me. "Have a seat, Veiria." Diel motions to a counter island with two high seats centered in the wrap-around kitchen.

I pull out a chair, glancing around at the compact kitchen with spotless cabinets.

Diel eyes me, cutting a loaf of bread. "Sleep well?"

I rub my eyes, hesitating for a moment. "I think. I mean … it was a lovely bed …"

Bell frowns at me in concern. "Dear, you look exhausted." She's turned to me from the corner, a boiling pot on the stove next to her. She approaches me. "Let me see."

She smiles and I nod at her outstretched hand. She places it against my forehead, feeling my temperature. "Well, then. Nothing a little soup and rest won't help with."

I nod. "Thank you so much. But …" I glance around in distress. "You didn't have to. I'm fine."

"Nonsense, dear. You're our guest and you had a nasty fall."

Diel looks up and winks. "It'll do you good," he says, firm and soft. "You need looking after."

Bell looks at him with approval.

Meekly, I nod. "Can I help though?"

"My dear, you're exhausted." Bell laughs a little. "Look at you."

Reluctantly, I look down and bite my lip. They're right. I know that. I barely have the ability to stand.

"Just sit tight."

I watch Bell and Diel as they work in tandem, chopping, stirring, and consolidating ingredients. Despite their age, they're quite nimble at cooking. And they're a cute couple, affectionate in old age. The sight of them makes me feel at home and I smile a little, despite my discomfort.

When they're done, they lead me to a table, lighting a few candles.

Diel leans forward on his elbows, assessing me with a friendly smile. "So, where are you from, Veiria."

My voice feels dry, and I tentatively reply, "I don't know."

"Anvi? That's our town," he adds. "It's about a sphere length from Jespaira. Any friends in the area? Family?"

I shake my head stiffly and whisper. "I'm so sorry. I really have no clue where that is. I ... I know I'm just a burden." My brain is annoyingly foggy and suddenly I just feel so worthless in their presence.

"Oh, you poor thing." Bell's eyes crinkle with sympathy. "We'll help you. Don't feel sorry."

I smile weakly. "You're too kind. I'm sorry that's not much help."

"Veiria. It's the right thing to do. When you get to my age, you find that every little thing counts."

"In the meantime, you should eat. Don't feel bad," Diel nods at my food.

I squint at it curiously—there's a little bowl of silvery broth with odd red stems sticking out, plus a small plate of greens and white meat. Beside it is a glass of a bizarre, electric-purple liquid.

"Thanks. So much." I really don't deserve this kindness, but I take a small sip of the deliciously sweet beverage, pursing my lips.

It's like nothing I've ever tasted, and it lights up my taste buds like warm cream. They tell me it's from something called a Juthoe berry that supposedly rejuvenates your spirit.

I soon find out that the meal is the same sort of deliciously strange.

Bell and Diel ask me occasional questions that I try to answer through my murky brain and they try to fill me in on their small life with their garden and the nearby Anvi market.

"How about we take you into town tomorrow? You can stay as long as you like," Bell says in a comforting voice, patting my hand. "You've had such a rough few days for being such a sweet guest."

I open my mouth to protest, and Diel simply adds, "Stay."

I look to Bell's inviting eyes and cave, my shoulders relaxing. I guess I like it here. Something about them feels so ... so peaceful. "I really appreciate your hospitality. That ... might be nice." And perhaps I'm a bit curious to see where I landed, too. It wouldn't hurt to go into town with them and go from there. At least I can be out of their hair. Though, that is a strange phrase, right?

I look out the window again at the strange sky of clouds and floating land barely standing out in the stars twinkling and growing brighter outside. They're beautiful, but I think I would recognize a constellation or two. I haven't forgotten that, have I?

Something feels wrong, I just have no idea what. Without realizing it, I notice I've been scratching at my hand.

I can figure this out tomorrow. And with that thought, I focus on eating my food and pleasing Bell and Diel.

As I finish and they promise to clean up, despite my protests that I should do something to repay them, I thank them again, once again feeling useless and undeserving of their kindness, but nevertheless, I collapse instinctually into the feather-soft bed and immediately pass out, a light, cool breeze, twinkling stars, and silver moonlight leaking through the open window by their garden.

Sentiments & Companions

Veiria

In the morning, I'm greeted by a new turquoise dress Bell had laid out—slim, v-neck, and knee-length. I trace my fingers over the silky material, turning to the mirror I hadn't paid much attention to during my recovery.

I drop the dress in shock, shaking at my reflection, and I hold my hands to my heart. I don't match the reflection I see. My vision goes blurry for a moment, my mouth dry, and I feel like I'm going to have a heart attack.

My knees threaten to give way. The person I look at is beautiful. I swallow several times.

This *can't* be me. I touch my face. Her skin seems to glow. It's fair, smooth, unblemished and everything ... everything I would want to look like. Her frame is what I would imagine a beautiful young woman would have.

She's ... *everything.*

Her legs are perfectly shaped and gorgeous, her eyelashes sharp, her face pretty in a simple way, but one that stands out, and her lips full. She's well taken care of. She's thin, but still has a perfectly defined figure. She looks like a girl from high school I'd wish to look like. Her breasts are rounded and full, and she has shapely hips, enough to be noticeable that they're real and she ... well, just that she's clearly a young woman. Her hair is a straight, golden blonde in perfect care and her eyes are a depthless sky blue, like the heavens. She has a modest style, but at the same time, she's striking.

I lift my hair through my fingertips, a bit clumsily. *Should it really be blonde?*

That girl can't be me. She's flawless and delicate.

I nearly faint.

My fingers shake as I undress and feel too breakable, too angelic.

High school? My mind comes back to the words in my head. This is what I wished to look like in a far-off world. I forget it as I look back at my reflection.

The only thing that doesn't match is the girl's eyes. They look scared, but even they are a tender, gorgeous ... Blue? Or is that silver?

I fumble with the straps of the bra. I feel confused for a second. I want to hide a little, yet there's this tiny ghost of euphoria I can't place and my fingertips tingle against my too-soft, silky skin. My breasts are far too full and perfectly rounded for someone like me and they fill the cups perfectly.

I feel the smallest shiver of goosebumps at the slightest amount of ... wonder? Yet there's some fragile longing there too—something close to joy, but too bitter. I feel tears in my eyes that I wipe with my hands. Something isn't right, but I know the image in front of me is something I want.

I feel light. My mouth is dry as I try to move it, still stunned. But at the same time, I shiver. It's like the reflection is mocking me and I don't know why. I feel so close to happiness, as I struggle to even touch my skin—to feel that this is real. For a moment, I almost remember something.

I can hardly look at myself and turn away as quickly as possible, stumbling off to breakfast in the gorgeous turquoise dress that's halfway between modest and revealing, knowing I'll feel more at ease when I see Bell. I loosen my smile a little, doing a quick spin in front of the mirror, but a frown creeping back. Something is so off, but so right. I bite my lip as I open the door more reservedly again, glancing around the corner down the quiet hall.

I breathe out. Just another day. I do admit that there is a rightness in this body, if it were really mine. I hardly notice as my dress shimmers momentarily to a silver-white from recent memory, before returning to turquoise.

I head down the hall, glancing out a window at their garden and a few bluebirds that make me wonder if my voice would sound as pretty singing. I resist, because I'd probably be a bit awkward and I don't particularly want to shame myself in front of Bell and Diel if for some reason it comes out awfully deep or something like that. At the door of their little home, I witness Diel fixing a button-up work shirt and kissing his wife goodbye. He turns and waves at me with a smile. "Good luck with Bell today, Veiria."

"Thank you, Sir," I say, crinkling my forehead at wherever the 'sir' came from.

He chuckles and heads out the door. "The same, ma'am."

I rise on my heels at 'ma'am,' feeling strangely giddy and reining myself in from a hop. Instead, I shift on my feet awkwardly and smile self-consciously as I glance down in flattery.

Bell and I head into town—her dressed in her knitted earthy brown shawl, lime green blouse, casual boots, and carrying a basket for goods under her arm.

As we approach the market, I'm greeted by a sprawling expanse of green, dotted with brilliantly colored tents and stalls. The sky is mostly a clear blue, with a few clouds above and below. The ground seems to drop off after a mile or two. Beyond the tents lies a town that looks vast to my eyes. All around this isle of rock lie towering cliffs, separated by a vast expanse of blue. And the star in the sky … is yellow?

"Bell?" I frown, perplexed.

"Yes?" Bell replies sweetly.

"Why is that star yellow?" I ask in confusion, staring hard at the star until my eyes water and I blink away the afterimage. I have no idea what color it should be, but yellow feels wrong.

"That's Yelyaa." She seems to sense my confusion, speaking in a soothing voice like a parent. "Maybe yellow is a strange color, but as far as I can remember, that's how it's always been."

"Yelyaa. I don't like it," I whisper.

"What was that, dear?"

"It's nothing really, just a thought." I'm still squinting at Yelyaa, though.

"Venah ..." I whisper again to myself. That name sounds more familiar, yet I can't place it.

Bell lets me head off on my own for a while. I still feel ... strange in my own skin, but despite feeling a little on edge, there's the barest of thrills.

I try to enjoy the market, but there's this nagging sensation as I catch sight of something of interest out of the corner of my eye.

Smiling a little, I approach a stall of beautiful crystalline jewelry and pause to glance down at the assortment of stones. A little shopping couldn't hurt ...

My hand drifts over a red stone—a deep maroon color that catches my eye. It's startlingly gorgeous, prompting me to stare entranced for what seems like eternity. Yet, despite that, I can't bring myself to touch it. I frown, coming out of my rapture, then I glance briefly at the store owner and swallow. I look over my shoulder as well, but no one seems to think me anything out of the ordinary.

I try to shrug off whatever discomfort that is, my gaze traveling to another piece, this one an empty silver pendant.

"You like them?" the shop owner asks, looking up from his work polishing another beautiful stone.

"Yes ..." I say, jumping a little at his voice as my heart hammers.

"Pretty pricy, but they're worth it. What do you think?"

"No thanks," I laugh a bit nervously. My voice catches in my throat with indecision, and I ponder that for a moment as I bite my lip. "How much?" I ask tentatively.

He smiles with a hint of charm. "How about this, miss? I'll lower the price for you. It'll look good on a pretty girl like you."

I feel my cheeks turn a bright red and I avert my eyes. "I'm sorry, I don't"—I reach into a small pocket in my dress—"have anything ..." I pull out a large handful of silver coins. "Never mind, I'll take that gorgeous maroon piece ... and that empty pendant. Could you fasten them together?"

"Why of course. Thank you, miss."

My chest lightens up as I hear 'miss.' An odd sort of levity that makes me want to soar.

"Give me a while, why don't you? You're welcome to stay and watch."

"I'll do that." I feel the corners of my lips twitch up, satisfied that I somehow have the money to buy the brooch and overjoyed at the thought of giving myself something so beautiful. I feel my cheeks warm from a small smile. It's something I want desperately. Something for me.

The shop owner gets to work right away. It's fascinating, watching his craft. And maybe my eyes linger a bit too long on his muscles flexing as he tightens the brooch together.

"What's your name?" I ask curiously, both for the sake of small talk and I like how he's treating me.

"Heeni. And yours, miss?" He glances up, giving me a quick smile amid his work and I feel that same levity fall on my cheeks—breathless at the simple word, like it'd never been uttered to me before.

"Veiria. Your art is beautiful," I say sincerely.

"Glad to hear it, miss."

"Um ... Are you sure about the discount?"

He shrugs, grinning at me toothily. "I told you. For someone like yourself, it doesn't cost me a thing. I already lowered it. Those stones are too pricey anyway. Mordria, they're called. Rare. You got the last one I've been able to get my hands on. It's a shame nobody else wants them but you. They're lovely. I reckon no one buys them as they're rumored to be a curse of the Sky Goddess. Pity," he muses, massaging the alluring gem with his thumb, before handing it to me. "She was said to be kind and beautiful beyond compare before she went berserk."

I'm silent for a moment as I stare at it in fascination, a chill running up my spine. "Sky Goddess?" I say quietly, my lips dry. Odd. I glance up at him with a question.

"Try it on, if you'd like." He waves his hand encouragingly. "It's yours, anyway, and I'd like to see what it looks like on a beauty like yourself."

I smile self-consciously, my insides burning as I pick up the brooch and place it delicately around my neck. It may just be my imagination, but it's like it pulsed on contact with my skin. My eyes get lost in its beautiful depths. A vision flashes through my head of a red star. "Venah," I whisper.

Heeni doesn't seem to notice. "Take care of it for me, young lady."

I give him a smile, doing my best not to look shaken. "I will."

"And come back any time. I enjoy the company."

I laugh nervously and wave, feeling flattered. "I will! I'm glad I met you, Heeni." All the attention and the compliments feel somehow new. A little unnerving but thrilling at the same time. It's strange.

I turn away from Heeni's stall, tracing the surface of those maroon depths.

Where did that image come from? I can't link it to anything else. My mind is a wall, shielded off from myself, like I'm not allowed to reach it.

"Ouch!"

"Huh?" Without realizing it, I'd crashed into someone ... and knocked him over. "Sorry ..." I say, but my voice trails off. My eyes catch on his; they're a beautiful cinnamon color. I scramble up hurriedly, feeling awful for being distracted and bumping into him and preparing to reach out to offer help.

"Don't apologize. Everyone loses themselves occasionally. I'm Eu," he says, good-natured, while rubbing his forehead.

"Eu…" I lose my voice for a moment. I know I'm staring at him, but he's so … so … beautiful, pretty, and handsome. He's lean, with gorgeous light golden-brown skin, curly black, messy hair, and such a kind-looking, smooth face with a handsome jawline. More than anything, though, I can't stop staring at his pretty, cinnamon-colored eyes. "Sorry—Veiria!" I resist clapping my hands over my mouth and instead, force myself to calm down. "I'm Veiria. I'm sorry for bumping into you."

He laughs at that. "Veiria. Don't apologize, remember?"

"Right …" I'm not sure I quite mean that.

"I'm glad I bumped into you, anyway," he says, clambering to his feet and dusting himself off with a smile before I can even reach down to help him.

"Really?" I pause. He doesn't make any sense. "But I bumped into you."

"That's beside the point." He clears his throat, as if he's a little nervous. "I'm glad because I met a great person today. Wonderful. Truly stunning." He flourishes his hand up-and-down in front of me. "I just know you are." He beams dreamily.

"Oh …" A lump seems to form in my throat at my surprise and I feel myself thoroughly blush.

"Veiria." My chest tingles at the way he says my name. "I would really like it if that great person would accompany me through the fair. Would you?" He ducks his head a little to let his curls hang cutely over his eyes.

I giggle just a bit, flailing my arms laughably. "I would!" God, I feel like a schoolgirl. A *schoolgirl*?

His mouth curls up into such a preciously cute grin that also brings out some very cute dimples. "With that settled, I think we can be on our way."

I do giggle into my hand as he motions to me invitingly. I like this boy very much. Strange or not, he's immensely charming and likeable. He has to be the prettiest boy I've ever seen. He's exactly my type.

I swoon inwardly. Why couldn't I run into a boy like this where I came from every other day? I mean, he does look slightly familiar, but I chalk that up to fate and destiny. In every storybook there's a pretty boy to whisk you off. Maybe he'll be mine?

We lead each other around, weaving through the colorful tents and stalls waving in the breeze and I can't help smiling delightedly. I probably look crazy in love.

And his smile is just as senseless—a charming type of lopsided I dreamed of receiving.

"You're right, it's the biggest town for five sphere lengths. I was raised here, all my life. I can't bring myself not to like it. My parents are farmers and artisans. I help out while attending school. A teacher is what I'd like to be. I love little kids."

He really is so precious. Kids—I jump giddily in my shoes at the thought. He's my dream boy! "I hope you make it someday. I think you'd be an amazing teacher!" I try to reign in my excitement at this boy of all boys—or rather, any boy, really—talking to me in a way I think could be considered flirting. He does keep staring at me for awfully long seconds and it makes butterflies dance in my heart.

He gives a pretty laugh. "You haven't known me that long. Maybe I'd be a horrible teacher!"

"I guess not, but I don't think so." No one this pretty and charming would be terrible with kids. I'd trust anything out of his mouth.

"Hmm ... Well, I'll trust your judgement. You never mentioned where you're from."

"I don't know." I shrug, trying to pretend I don't care, when the truth is, I'm not entirely sure. I suppose I could forget all about it with him. He has exactly the type of personality I like. I sigh out. I'm doing *that*. Do I always get this immediately enamored with a person?

"That's a problem," he says, without even a hint of surprise showing.

"So is your reaction." I smile broadly.

"You think so?" He arches an eyebrow, and my breath catches in my chest.

No, I *think it's charming*, I think to myself. Oh my God, I swear I've never had this much attention from a boy who treats me like this. I breathe a bit heavily. Like ... like I'm a normal girl who he likes *because* I'm a girl and because he finds me attractive. I mean, Heeni was nice, and he complimented my looks, but he wasn't my age—a bit too old—and Eu is just way more casual and someone I can actually *talk* with.

"Maybe it is ... Anything else you do remember?" He puts a hand to his temple, stopping momentarily as he ponders.

"No to that, too," I grin slightly, ready for his unsurprise.

"I thought so!" he exclaims, snapping his fingers.

"Now I definitely think you're odd." In a good way, of course. I sort of understand it. I'm still warming up to him. Maybe I'd join him if I weren't still self-conscious? Instead, I flit my eyelids at him and laugh between my words. "But I like it ... *and you*." I stifle a snort. *You're embarrassing yourself, Veiria.*

"Not one little tiny thing?" He pleads with those gorgeous eyes of his.

"Um ... well ..." I sigh and shake my head. "Not a clue. I'm so sorry."

"That's fine. We'll figure it out, I'm sure of it!" He gives me a thumbs up.

Except, that isn't all. I can't shake the vision of the maroon star, especially after buying my brooch. "A maroon star ..." I whisper barely audibly, subconsciously tracing the stone of my pendant for the millionth time that day. I glance down at it. It's only a little more fascinating than Eu.

"Maroon, like your brooch?" His gaze travels to it too, and he thumbs his jaw curiously.

"Yes," I reply softly. "I think that's right. But, why are you asking?"

He takes a step closer, inspecting it like it's the most interesting thing in the world and I forget to breathe for a moment. "It's just so curious. You're fascinating, Veiria, and I'm very interested in fascinating." He tilts his head, eyes narrowed in concentration on it. "Is that why you liked it?"

"I don't know, I just know I wanted it, but I can't figure out whether or not I like it. It's so confusing." I realize I'm pressing my fingers to my temples. "I just know whatever star is in the sky shouldn't be yellow."

"That's odd."

"Says you. I just know it's wrong."

"Well, this time I don't know what to say."

"Good, then," I say jokingly, shaking my head as if to shake myself out of the slight frustration that there's an important connection I'm missing.

He shrugs. "Let's keep walking, shall we? I ..." Eu looks at the sky. "I think I may have some time to kill."

I smile coyly. "Are you bored of me yet, Eu?"

"What?" He scrunches his face in confusion, then smiles. "Not at all! I think you're infinitely wise and pretty!" He motions to me extravagantly.

I snort, for this girl has no thought in her head right now but the boy in front of her—well, other than my brooch and my visions of the star that I am *trying* to ignore right now to focus on pretty, handsome boys that give me attention and are funny. "Thank you," I look down and smile at my embarrassment. "So, I can accompany you forever?" I swivel back-and-forth on my feet.

"I wouldn't have it any other way. Just don't fret! You're an angel."

I feel my cheeks heat crimson. "Thanks, Eu." I stare up, just under his feet. "Just so you know, I think you're wonderful."

He stumbles over his words, hand rubbing over his shoulder. "Thanks. Any girl like you"—he laughs nervously. "Person like you. Woman, rather. And beautiful, at that," he mumbles, then laughs it off. Is what I would say is: 'A blessing to the skies.' That's what mom and pop refer to as good things in life," he adds.

"I'm a good thing in life?" I ask nervously, looking down. I couldn't be. Not to him.

He shrugs again, looking away. I wonder if his cheeks are red. "I'd say so. Yeah."

"Hey, Veiria?" Eu says casually as we walk. We had spent a minute or two in silence, before Eu started working up cheery conversation again. He has his hands shoved in his jean pockets and he's looking clumsily cute, walking, taking glances at me, but also seeming deep in thought, like he's trying to figure me out.

"Yeah?"

He creases his brow, kicking his feet a little on the grassy plane. "You said you can't figure out if you like maroon, even though you bought it. Is there a color you do like?" He stops, glancing at me more openly.

A color that I like? Cinnamon ... like his eyes, but I'm too nervous to say that. So, instead, I give the most boring color ever, looking around sidelong at the colorful tents to distract myself from being a terrible liar. "Brown."

"Brown? It's a little ... Well, I suppose it's nice, just a little ... shall I say, unexpected."

"What's yours then, if you think brown's so boring?"

"Not sure."

"Liar," I say accusingly. "I think you could give a boring answer too, like sludge!" I beam. *Perfectly normal, Veiria.* I swing my arms around myself as I wait.

"Blue's nice, then again, I see it everywhere. I suppose maroon is too. But right now, I think I'd go for silver." He poses thoughtfully, his delicate hand tracing his jawline. "Your eyes ... I can't tell what color they are. Like silver swirling in green and flecks of red ..." he muses.

I blush. "What was that for? And my eyes are blue!" I pout, hands on my hips. "Aren't they?" I cock my head, a little uncertainly. I swear they've been green. But I shrug. I'm imagining things.

"We were talking about colors." He laughs. "My bad. They're a beautiful depthless blue. Eternal, like the soul of our creator!"

"Well, I'm definitely no one's creator," I mumble. I purse my lips, then blurt, "Yours are cinnamon!" Then I add in a small voice: "They're pretty."

I could almost swear he blushes a little. Do boys blush? Either way, he's cute and I like being around him. "Thanks," is all he manages to say. "I appreciate it."

I move on after a moment, turning my head to study this strange world and the other islands floating in the distance. It's like something from a ... a book? "Eu ... I feel like I'm missing something ... about myself. I don't feel whole ... like my mind is blocked off."

He's silent, frowning slightly.

"The world feels wrong, too ... and I don't like it. I know I sound crazy right now."

"I don't think so. After all, we all view the world differently. Maybe we're all a little insane?"

"Well, not you ..." I say slowly. *Maybe me*, I add in my head. "But ... something is definitely wrong." My hands tingle for the touch of something to comfort me. "I just know it."

"We'll figure it out. I know we can!" Eu gestures to the two of us, then to the tents. "We have all the time in the world to adventure!"

"We?" My heart skips. "You can't be serious, Eu." I'm just a nothing girl you just met.

"Or you can," he adds helpfully.

"Forget what I said." I pause, lip quirking up nervously. I feel incredulous that he would involve himself with me. I mean, I'd like to think he likes me, or that we're at least friends, but this is too good to be true. "So, what now?" I honestly expect him to leave me. That's what I would do if I were him. I just don't see why he's sticking around.

I shift on my feet. It's not like he has better things to do.

"Hey, you know what?" he says with a thoughtful expression on his face. It looks a bit odd. I honestly have no idea what he's thinking.

"I don't know what. But, what?" I fiddle with my fingers, glancing up at him.

He shrugs casually, grinning. "How about a bite? Niya and Druna's place, The lofty Inn. Shall we go?"

"Excuse me?" I blink, not registering what he just said.

"A little something for an astounding friend. On me."

"A friend?" I lick my lips, then I grin and break out in a smile. "If you really don't think I'm trouble."

"Not at all, Veiria." He sticks out his arm. "I think you're wonderful."

I glance back-and-forth from his arm to his meaningful gaze and shrug with a stupid grin. "Why not?" Still, I find myself squinting at him after a moment as my nerves settle down, trying to figure him out. He looks so pleasant, just going along with everything.

I sigh and shake my head. *Why are you dragging him into your heart, Veiria?*

"There's nothing here, Eu. Is this a joke?" I say, looking over the cliff face and into the open air.

"Nope! My jokes are uncommon, but I wouldn't say they're intentionally misleading. So, I would say ..." He brushes his cheek thoughtfully with his thumb. "Probably not." I can't help looking at the small action, which is another thing that looks cute on him.

"Right; of course, you're too odd for that. Now, where is it?"

"That!" he exclaims, pointing to a covered structure near the cliff's edge.

I frown. On closer inspection, I see a staircase leading down. It's strange that I hadn't seen it.

"It's on the side of the cliff face. The view is spectacular, I would have to say!"

"Eu first," I say with a sly smile.

He grins. "Why of course. I am honored by the compliment! I really wish I would have thought of that."

I'm a little proud of myself for that.

Eu goes in first. I pass under the overhang. Ivy hangs down from it. It almost appears to be glistening, but it's too bright at this point in the day to tell.

We come out into a restaurant made of old-fashioned wood and to the far side of us, a wall of glass looks out into the open air. Balls of fire circle in the suspended hearths, like miniature stars. Shards of glass suspend from the ceiling, catching the glint of the sunlight, and I suppose, the sunset. Outside the window, Yelyaa rests close to the watery horizon. Twilight should be here soon. I stand transfixed at Yelyaa again. I look forward to the sunset, but part of me is still on edge.

"Veiria?" Eu pokes me. "What is it?"

"Nothing." I flinch.

He frowns but doesn't comment further. "Why don't you find a place to sit. I'll go see if I could get us a special."

I shake myself out of it and grin. "No, I'm coming with you, Eu." Eu-Eu—that's a cute nickname. I'll have to remember it.

"Of course. It was utterly stupid of me to offer," he pulls off a face of exaggerated sincerity and good humor.

I stick out my arm, locking my elbow, "Let's go then."

"Why of course," and we walk cheerily over to the counter, locked arm-in-arm. I think we are both enjoying this new friendship too much. Besides how attractive he is … More than that though, he is just so fun to be around. This almost feels like … a date? No, it couldn't be that … not with me, but I feel incredibly lightheaded with adrenaline next to him.

We get to the counter. "Hello, Niya!" Eu greets a woman with pretty, silky-black hair and green, almond eyes.

"Eu! It's good to see you. It's been so long."

"Yeah. Has," he agrees. "How's business?" Eu leans forward on the counter with his elbows. He looks incredibly relaxed and open with these people and his smile is casual. I study him thinking that he must get along with everyone. My heart drops a little. Maybe I'm not *that* special.

"Nothing out of the ordinary." She smiles just as warmly at the young man in front of her as she arranges some glasses behind the counter.

"Glad to hear. Is Druna here?" Eu inquires, craning his neck a little and frowning.

"In the back. I'll tell him you're here for him." She turns her smile to me. "And who's this?"

"I'm Veiria, Eu's friend. I met Eu a few hours ago. And he, erm … wanted to show me your nice restaurant." I do my best to phrase that as casually as possible, swinging my leg nervously and looking away as if something has caught my eye.

"Well, I'm very grateful for that, Eu. Nice to meet you, Veiria. I'm Niya, as he said. And this is my husband, Druna," she motions to a slightly heavyset man approaching the counter from the back. Both him and Niya are in their late thirties, from what I can tell.

He also gives me a smile. "Veiria, it's nice to meet you. And Eu, it's nice to see you!" He grins broadly. "How're your parents?"

"They're doing very well. Excellent, actually. They were hoping to catch up soon. Business is booming, in a sense," he grins a bit cockily. "Mom sold some of her clothes and one of pop's finest knives at the fair last Harp Moon. I'll tell them you asked."

"Are you putting up with him all right?" Druna says, his eyes crinkled in mischief.

I feel a little caught off guard for a moment, before an unusually wonderful feeling lights in my chest, and I look between us. "Yes. I can see why you'd ask, though," I give him a mischievous look back.

Druna winks and Niya gives Eu a gracious smile. I hug my arms around myself, feeling a blush on my cheeks as I glance down slightly and smile with some unfathomable sense of joy. Okay, did I know what I was getting into? No. But, I'm glad. Just, it feels nice ... the attention and the warmth and the thought of a date. "Is there something we can get you, Veiria? I would recommend the special," Niya asks sweetly. "I'll give half-price for your first visit."

"That's generous of you, but I'll pay in full. Thank you. And I'm paying, Eu," I say, as I set a handful of coins on the counter. It's a bit unfair how nice everyone is. It wouldn't feel quite right to keep accepting. It's not like I want to brush off their kindness. It feels so nice. And I mean, I do want a boy to buy me a meal, but that seems a bit too much like taking advantage of his kindness. I had better act now before I lose confidence.

"I guess I shouldn't argue with that. Next time, we'll split it."

"You two go find a seat. We'll have it ready shortly," Niya tells us, picking up my coins and placing them in a silver engraved box.

"Thanks, Niya. Both of you, feel free to join us if the restaurant slows down."

"Always a pleasure," Druna replies, while Niya gives us a smile in return.

"Let's find a window seat." Eu motions me to the left, gesturing to a vacant table as we pass several groups of couples, families, and friends. I admit, the atmosphere is immaculate enough to warrant it. We slip into seats across from each other, making me feel somewhat embarrassed as I'm forced to look straight into his cinnamon eyes. His tawny skin looks really pretty against the sunset—almost golden or glowing. He has this youthful brightness about him that I find so cheery and appealing. "The sun's starting to set. You won't regret coming here." As I look, I see the star Yelyaa dipping into the horizon.

"Where does it go? Yelyaa?" I ask curiously, hand on my palm, as I gaze at it entranced.

"No one knows for certain. People say Yelyaa is engulfed during the sunset, extinguished, you might say, and then reborn in the morning. There isn't a clear-cut answer."

I purse my lips. That's not quite what I was hoping for.

"Anyways, it's starting. I wouldn't miss it for a second."

He's right. As the sun rises into that mass of blue, the light cascades into the room in oranges, reds, and golds. "Wow," I whisper in awe. The inside of the restaurant gets bathed in a twilit orange.

"Never seen it?"

"Not until the other night ... and not like this," I murmur, a bit distracted by the sight.

"It's worth it. It's like a god's paintbrush dipped in the water to spread such rich colors."

"What did you say?" I whip my head towards him, startled.

"Like a god's paintbrush. It's brilliant in a heavenly way."

I clutch my head slightly. My mind feels jumbled. I try to bring myself to poke fun at his comment, but I just can't concentrate right now.

"Are you okay, Veiria?" Eu seems to reach forward, then stops himself, his voice set with touching concern.

"I'm fine." *God* ... The word rings in my head. God? No ... *Goddess.* But where did that come from? I feel like I'm reaching for something that's so close, yet hidden beyond my grasp.

Eu looks at me quietly. "Tell me if it gets worse."

I just nod.

Our food comes shortly after. By then, I'm feeling better, yet I can't shake a concerned feeling.

We both get a special: a noodle bowl in a thick black broth, interspersed with steamy vegetables and what I take to be a bird, though it seems to have four wings instead of two ... Eu labels it as a Neisel, a bird that sticks close to the water in the sky above.

"Some people say they soar into the water sometimes. It's almost crazy, but I think I can imagine it." Eu talks quickly and I listen in fascination.

I find myself looking up there, my palm on my cheek and my elbow on the table, almost slipping into a daydream. "I don't think it's crazy. I can imagine it too."

"Do you think anything is up there?"

"Hmm?" My vision blurs, his words sounding oddly slurred in my ears.

"Veiria?" Eu's voice perks up a notch.

I realize I'm not responding to him. I want to talk, but my gaze is transfixed on something ... a flash of silver from beyond the window. My mind seems to fog up in a trance and I reach out my arm.

"Veiria?" His voice sounds muffled, but I can hear his concern as clear as day.

It's nothing more than a speck, like a grain of sand. It seems so familiar, like a fragment of something precious ... It melds through the glass and my vision goes fuzzy, before flashing erratically. For a second, I see stars and a moon and then it's gone, replaced with a blindingly bright and close red star. "Venah," I whisper, my eyes wide and my voice intimate.

"Veiria!" Eu calls to me desperately, running to my side as I collapse sideways. *Where did that shining piece of silver go?*

A Brief Goodbye

Veiria

A quiet voice slowly fades into my conscious as I crack my eyes open and groan quietly. "Veiria." Niya holds a warm cloth to my forehead. As I come to, she reaches for a glass of some type of dark, cherry-colored liquid.

Behind her, I see Eu's apprehensive expression. "Is she alright?" he asks hurriedly, taking a step forward.

I smile at that and open my eyes fully. "I'm fine," I mumble, the star still imprinted in my mind.

"Drink this." Niya holds out the cup to me reassuringly. "You'll feel better."

I take it shakily and bring it to my lips. It tastes slightly bitter, but in a matter of moments, I feel almost normal again.

Eu lets out a sigh of relief, placing a hand over his heart. "You had me worried."

"Yeah; I'm sorry, Eu." My voice sounds despondent.

"What's the 'I'm sorry' for? Just let me know when something's wrong, no matter how small. Okay?"

"Okay," I agree halfheartedly.

"There doesn't seem to be anything wrong with her, from what I can see." Niya says uncertainly, still assessing me. "But it could come back ..." She draws a hesitant breath, glancing at Druna. They seem to share a silent conversation, before she turns back to me. You can stay here tonight with Druna and I, if you'd like. I think that would be best. We agree on that."

"No, thank you. I'm fine, really. Whatever this is, I don't think you can help me." I pause. "Eu?"

"Yes?"

"There are some people who've been taking care of me: Bell and Diel Liis; do you think you could walk me there? I feel bad for being gone so long." I like Eu a lot, but it's no reason to forget Bell and Diel's kindness.

"Sure … Of course, Veiria." He seems to shake himself out of his shock at my sudden collapse, extending his hand like a gentleman to help me up.

I take it, ignoring the spark of his touch as I lean on him, and he does his best to support me.

"Is there anything you need before you go?" Niya asks concerned, still gripping that strange liquid that's already making me feel more lucid.

"No. Thank you for your help, Niya, but I should be going."

She nods her head, her face still a bit gaunt. I feel terribly sorry for startling all three of them and whoever else witnessed my apparent demise.

Eu leads me out, frowning at me in heavy concern and seeming to support me like I'm immensely fragile, which I do appreciate, but … "Are you sure you're feeling okay?"

"Fine. It's all gone." My voice is quiet, but it almost feels a bit snappy, and I surprise myself at that. I'm still a bit shaken.

"You saw a vision, didn't you?" He asks.

I stare at him, unsure of what to say.

"I saw it when I touched you—a maroon star, just like your brooch. It was huge."

"You saw that?" My mouth gapes at him. How could he have? At least … I don't know, for some reason, I thought it was just me. No one else reacted to it that I'm aware. Niya and Druna seemed to think I just fainted for no clear reason.

"Apparently." He seems surprised himself, of course. "I don't know why, but I did. It makes no sense to me of course, but it fits." He snaps his fingers, a tired, yet encouraging smile on his face.

"Fits?" I'm confused by his sudden connection.

"You were attracted to that pendant, right? We can go somewhere from here."

Go *where*? I clutch the pendant to my chest. "But I'm still not sure how I feel about it …" I whisper. "What did you feel?"

"Honestly, I wasn't sure what to feel. Scared, in a sense, but … there was also something … calming about it, strange as that may seem …" He trails off, seeming far away for a moment.

"Calming," I deadpan. "You're saying a huge ball of fire is calming?" I pause, deep in my own thoughts. "But yes, that's what I felt too. You described it almost perfectly. It was both right and wrong. Eu ..." He turns his attention to me, and I look away. "Can we forget about this for now?"

"Veiria," he sighs and gives me a small smile. "As much as I'd like to forget that terrifying vision of death ... I don't think we can right now. This is important to you in some way, and I think you should know why."

I gulp in nervous resignation.

"But I can set it aside ... if it makes you feel better."

"It does." I remember not to thank him this time. I'm just grateful that he goes along with my hesitation and doesn't question me.

I can tell he's still worried, but he gives me an encouraging smile none-the-less. "Please don't faint on me again. I don't know what I'd do without you!"

"You just met me!" I giggle into my hands, shaking my head.

"I did, but my life has been permanently and irreversibly changed!" he exclaims dramatically.

"I'm glad I mean so much." I almost call him by his new nickname, Eu-Eu, but think better of it, not that he'd care. I figure I'll save it for later.

"Now, where were we?" he muses.

We've reached the top of the landing, where the entrance is, and I finally notice the ivy, which I had noted as slightly-glistening earlier. Now it's shining in a sparkling gold over the entrance and along the stairway. Dazzling and pretty, it's worth seeing as it is now.

Eu's eyes follow mine. "Niya has good tastes. It's a pity they weren't up for our grand entrance, but they shine all the brighter at night. I'm glad you got to see them."

I stare in wonder at them. We sit on the top of the landing for a few moments in silence, while I try to erase the visions from my head and catch my breath. The light of the ivy in front of me helps ... along with Eu's presence. "We should get going now."

"You sure?" *You're alright?* That's what I think he wants to say, but he said he would try not to bring it up.

"Yeah, I really am." I think that's a lie. I still feel shaky, drawn to something inexplicable.

He nods, as if reassured, then rises to his feet. "Well, I suppose now is as good a time as any."

I sit for another moment, staring at the lights, entranced. I seem to fade out of the moment, forgetting Eu's there.

He looks down at me. "Veiria?"

I shake my head decisively. "Yes, let's go." I stand, a bit surer of myself now, and I push aside my trailing thoughts. I take his hand and motion to the outside with my other. "Lead us out," I say theatrically, a way of speaking I've started to adopt around him, though it seems pretty normal to me. Did I find my perfect person?

"And where am I going?"

"Well, I guess I'll have to take us there." I give a knowing grin like a mad woman. Maybe we're both mad after seeing that star. Who knows? I shrug.

We walk back to Bell and Diel's home. The moon, Nytiel, hangs below the waterline, the stars encircling us in their light. It's quiet, except for the low droning of an insect Eu labels as a Gentyr. I think he's trying to break our silence. I'm not quite in my normal mood, yet of course, he manages to bring me out of it.

"A Renel ... I think you'd like it. I'd show you if I could, but they don't live in this area. I've only seen one once."

"What are they?" I ask curiously, shaking myself out of my stupor.

"Perhaps I'll leave that to your imagination." He grins.

"I think I'd rather know."

"It's a bird, basically, or at least that's the best way to describe it. Trust me, I can't. Think of it as an exquisite bird with the most dazzling indigo and golden plumage scattering in the air behind it. It's said to shift the clouds around it and bless your dreams and friendships. I'm afraid my description pales, so I guess I'll just have to show you!" Eu says playfully.

"I'm afraid you will," I say in mock irritation. "And remember, I'm not staying for the company, I'm staying to see this majestic Renel." Though, I find I can barely hold that tone with him.

"I'm hurt."

"Promise we'll see it?" That really is what I want right now.

"I wouldn't break it." I see what I take as honesty in his eyes and he crosses his heart. "Swear on the Goddess above." That makes me wince imperceptibly for some strange reason.

"Really?" I raise my eyebrows.

"That's a yes, isn't it?"

"I'd say it's close enough ... And we're almost there."

A spasm of pain fills my head for just a moment. Pain ... not confusion. I do my best to shut it out, pursing my lips and digging my nails into my palms. Fortunately, Eu doesn't notice. That's a new sensation.

I open my eyes after a brief few seconds. "It's there." I raise my hand and point.

"Quaint," Eu murmurs absently.

I decide I should knock and do so. "Veiria." Bell greets me worriedly, looking Eu up and down as if for approval. "We were wondering where you were. And who is this handsome gentleman?"

I almost choke at the gentleman part, though it's true, it just sounds funny having someone call him that. It's too formal for him. Though I do wholeheartedly agree on the handsome part. "This is Eu. I met him today at market."

"Pleased to meet a sweet old lady." Eu somehow says with a completely straight and friendly face. I think he means it.

"Eu," I scoff incredulously.

"It's all right, Veiria. He seems nice. I find it flattering." She winks at us.

"I'm just bringing Veiria home. She passed out for a few minutes and asked me to bring her back here." Eu once again flashes a look of concern my way.

Bell looks at me with similar concern, then gives Eu an approving look. "Well, I'm glad you did."

"Please don't worry about it, I'll be fine." I swear I'm whining, and I know I must sound a bit irritating, like a broken record. The truth is that I love them taking care of me, I just feel a bit too self-indulgent for my own comfort. It bothers me.

"That may be true but get some rest for us. We're happy to have you longer." Diel appears from behind Bell.

Their kindness never seems to falter, and I feel a familiar smile to be welcomed back to such a loving home. If they had kids, they must have loved it here when they were young. I bet they want to come back.

"Eu?" I turn to him expectantly.

"Yes?" comes his attentive silky-soft voice, lined with a largely inaudible lower tone in a layered sweetness. Yet it still reaches that grand extravagance when he means to. I squeal a little. I *love* his voice.

"Could you come back tomorrow?" My voice is expectant, wanting, but I'm ready for him to say no, though I have a feeling he won't. While I don't want to drag him into whatever this is, I like joking with him, and I can't help feeling giddy at the thought of him protecting and caring for me. His concern makes me happy. I don't remember someone treating me this way before.

"Of course. I wouldn't miss the pleasure of your company. That is, after I finish some work, then I'm sure I could come."

"I look forward to it." I give him a mischievous smile.

"Well then, I'll see you tomorrow," he says with a brilliant grin and a flourish of his arm.

Beaming, I turn back to Bell and Diel.

"Is there anything you need, dear?"

"Thank you, Bell, but I just need rest."

They nod in understanding, as I move into the house and shut their door behind me.

Whatever my uncertainties, I can't help feeling excited for tomorrow.

I bury my face in my pillow once I get into my room, thinking of Eu. But before I realize it, I'm asleep, my vision of Venah flashing behind my eyes.

The Perplexities of an Absent Love

Veiria

I wake up to a crisp morning breeze blowing in through my open window, catching on my silver-gold hair like magic. I gaze at it, entranced, reaching up to smooth the beautiful length of it between my fingers. A calm feeling settles over my heart as I do. This is nice.

I'm certainly beautiful …

I purse my lips. Aren't I? Then I sigh and lower my hand. I wish I felt that way. It helps that Eu sees me that way. If Eu thinks I'm beautiful, then I must be.

My gaze travels to a note by the flute case and I pick it up and open it.

Veiria,

We'll be gone until supper today. You're welcome to anything in the house.

Take care and treat yourself today,

Bell (& Diel)

I sigh and set it down despondently.

They're nice. Too nice, especially for me. I still don't get why they're going so far out of their way, but I really appreciate it. I'll think it a million times, but it's nice being taken care of by kind people, and I'm strangely starting to expect that.

I glance around and out the window. Eu isn't here and I feel oddly empty about that. I wonder about him. I still feel more than a little guilty and embarrassed about last night's predicament. I wonder what Eu must be feeling after the girl he went to dinner with fainted on him. I wonder just how long he'll actually want to stay with me. Will he still find me interesting today? Will he find me clever? Flirt with me? Greet me as a friend? Or maybe he won't even show up and I'll just waste my day thinking about what could have been.

I try to shrug off my thoughts. He certainly seems to have plenty of friends who aren't me, which is *fine*. I smile tightly.

I just adore his attention, his charm, our banter, and his good looks. Gosh, I'm blushing. I wonder what he'd look like shirtless. Probably hot.

I shake my head as I feel my cheeks burn, bringing myself back to my predicament, which I'm looking forward to much less. Still, I reach for my pendant. It's familiar weight is soothing in my hands. I let it dangle for a moment, catching the morning light. Its maroon depths seem to absorb all the light from the room around it, appearing eerie and cold next to the sunlight. And yet, there's something comforting in that.

I fasten the maroon and silver pendant around my neck, as it falls across the swell of my chest. I clutch it for a moment, looking down with just the slightest bit of satisfaction and wonder at both it and this vessel of a body that's like a dream come true, before I gaze absently at the room. I eye a bookshelf and, walking over, I trace my delicate fingers over their spines until I find one that interests me. "Mary's Book of Poems." It looks familiar somehow, like something from a dream. I flip through the pages, my mind tingling with something like nostalgia. I decide I might as well read it and move out of the guest room into Bell and Diel's small garden, a cluster of deep green on the edge of the sky. I flip it open and start reading, my mind greeted by a lush world interwoven by poetry.

A few hours later I glimpse the obvious shape of Eu on the horizon—skinny, sharp, lightly muscled, and remarkably attractive. My back rests in a knot in the roots of a gorgeous old tree on the edge of Bell and Diel's garden. A bunch of vivid red roses twist to my left. I get up, arching my back a little and taking the book from my lap.

"Eu!" I shout, waving at him.

"Yes, I have finally shown up! Hello, Veiria. Is that a book? You looked very comfortable as you were. Don't get up for my sake." He grins apologetically.

"Yes, it *is* a book. A very good one to you." I extend it to him a bit nervously, glancing at his face and wondering if he'd think very highly of poetry.

"Mary's Book of Poems," Eu reads the cover from my hand.

"There was something familiar about it, so I grabbed it."

"Huh ... Is that so?" He looks contemplatively at the book, stroking his cheekbone with a perplexed expression.

It's such a pretty movement that I want to swoon over. If only he wasn't so hard to read.

"Eu?" I ask, wondering what he's thinking.

"Maybe it has to do with your past? Where you're from?"

"Maybe ..." I trail off doubtfully. It's not like I don't want to know ... Something is holding me back. "Or I just wanted to read poems."

"So, where are we off to today?" Eu says, still concentrating on the book, before looking up at me with an open smile and shrugging nonchalantly. "I'm all yours."

All mine, huh? But even though I like that, I'm terrible at making decisions and get a bit quiet. "I think you should tell me that."

"Well ... seeing your inclination, I suppose. Let's catch a view. In other words, a walk."

"To where?" My voice rises curiously.

"Around, as in literally. Some simple sightseeing could be nice. You never know what you'll find."

"Great!" I close the book, getting up and joining Eu. "By around, do you mean ...?" I eye him questioningly, my voice trailing off again. But sightseeing sounds nice.

"Around the island. At least, I think." He shrugs. "It's not the biggest island ever, but getting your bearings might help."

With that, I take the book back inside, setting it on my nightstand to pick up again later, and come back to join

Eu as he takes me casually to some new place. I think he's being a bit too optimistic about my past and I doubt I'll find anything by looking at my reading habits, but I won't spoil Eu's good mood. Maybe he's onto something?

"Eu ... What's that?" I ask tentatively as I stop in my tracks, my gaze set on something glaringly out of place, even for this world.

Eu squints in the direction of my gaze. "Veiria, I don't see anything. If you could be a bit more specific."

I purse my lips. Out in the open air, just slightly below us and ahead, lies what looks like a castle of light. And of course, Eu conveniently can't see it. He can't see it, but I can.

That's it! I think suddenly at what I view as a remarkable thought. "Grab my hand, Eu. Please," I add shyly in afterthought, looking away.

"As you request." Eu places his tawny hand palm up and I take it in mine. His hand is surprisingly soft for someone who works on his parent's farm, but that feeling is laced with smooth callouses. His grip is gentle and warm, and it makes me feel at ease and protected.

"There it is! I'm afraid!" Eu remarks dramatically, taking an exaggerated step back.

"It's truly horrific," I quip back.

"I admit, it's remarkable. Strange that I never noticed it."

I motion extravagantly to the bridge of light that had formed before us. "Eu first."

He grins, tilting his head. "Why thank you, Veiria. You're quite considerate." He steps onto the bridge, making not a sound on the glowing surface.

I keep a firm hold on his hand. I don't know what'll happen if I let go and I'd rather not find out. I assume Eu feels the same.

"You know, I wonder if we're just walking on nothingness," Eu muses. "Not that that makes much sense, as we're clearly walking, but just an idea."

"I hope not." I gulp, looking down nervously as my knees shake and I cling tighter to Eu's comforting hand. The light bridge doesn't look solid exactly, but it seems to take that form at each step. Internally, I'm just whispering: 'It's not so bad. It's not so bad.'

If Eu weren't here, I'd probably faint from fright.

We reach the end of the bridge and I breathe out a short sigh. Except when I stare daggers at the door for sanctuary from the height ... there is no door. I turn to Eu, who has the most insane toothy grin.

"When in doubt, walk through it!" he exclaims confidently.

"Through?" I gape, my disbelief palpable.

"It's light, isn't it?" He taps his brain.

"So is the bridge," I mutter.

"Well, it wouldn't hurt to find out. Let's try it!"

Big brain, Eu-Eu, I guess.

I puff up my cheeks, thinking. Maybe we should, but if I wasn't with him, would I enter, or am I just being risqué for his sake? I glance at him sidelong and bite my lip. I guess it's worth a bit of fun and friendship.

"Logic makes no sense, which leads me to the simple idea: we walk through!" With that, he takes a step.

I prepare myself to laugh when he falls back from the wall, but he doesn't. I almost forget to keep ahold of his hand, not that I'd ever want to stop.

I close my eyes and mentally brace myself, then take a step after him.

"That ... worked," he says, blinking back disbelief and staring around as if he didn't think it actually would.

"Yes, unsurprisingly," I reply ironically. "Good job, big-brain."

He rubs the back of his neck with a timid grin.

Then I too glance around the room with a strange feeling tingling at the back of my neck. Suddenly I feel a bit jumpy.

The entry room appears deserted, filled with a dull, warm orange glow. It seems to fade at the edges into eternity. An orange tide of flame appears, sweeping into a wide staircase to the landing above, covering the far side of the room.

"Well ..." We look at each other. I don't know about this ...

Eu shrugs. "Why not?"

"I …" I purse my lips, hesitating until Eu looks back at me questioningly. I nod for some reason, feeling like this is something I should do, gripping his hand tighter as we ascend.

Before us lies a glowing throne of yellow-orange light and upon it …

"Veiria …" comes an expectant voice from the throne, seemingly with an air of calculation, but besides that, I can't read the intentions in it.

They appear middle-aged, in deep purple robes that billow around them like shadow and eyes of amethyst that seem to assess me coldly. Their hair is a shoulder-length midnight black and their skin a pure pale white, their expression unreadable. Their ankle rests over their knee in a way that captures an almost tense tranquility.

A chill goes up my spine and suddenly a plume of black crow feathers appears hazily in my memory. My nails bite into my arm. *Do I know them?*

They continue to address me with a voice of cold clarity. "Goddess to this world, returned once more." They tilt their head slightly. I've been awaiting your return."

"Goddess?" I say uncertainly, my breath catching.

I glance quickly at Eu. He's staring at them with a funny expression on his face that I can't make out and seems strangely unfazed by the goddess greeting.

They stay quiet for a moment, their eyes narrowed on me, before leaning forward. "Perhaps I am wrong …"

They smile bitterly. "No, a century may have passed since last we met, but I recognize your presence. There's no mistaking it." They fix me with that unblinking gaze. "What are you waiting for?" they murmur. "You got out."

"Out?" I furrow my brow in confusion.

"You have no memory. I would tell you that it's fortunate. You know me, Veiria. You were and are a goddess. The question is: What are your intentions for this world?"

"Why do you keep calling me a goddess?"

"Because you are."

A thin silence stretches over us. Eu grows tense next to me. "Do you mean to harm her?"

"No, but I will not help her either, or rather, I will not harm her unless it becomes unavoidable."

Eu relaxes slightly. "How does she find her lost memories?"

"That would make her my enemy, in a way. Do not look for the things that will hurt," they say almost consolingly, their expression seeming to soften a fraction for just a moment.

"Enemy?" Eu looks startled, taking the slightest step back.

"Counterforce is a more appropriate term. Veiria as a goddess is ... dangerous."

I wince, trying to shrink myself from the conversation and let Eu do the talking, as he seems very inclined to do. I look at him oddly, then to the strange person who makes my hair stand on end ... but at the same time feels strangely, unnaturally familiar.

"Why is she dangerous to you?" Eu furrows his eyebrows.

"Not to me personally, but I do have a purpose. Those memories of hers are better sealed."

I squeeze my eyes shut. I can't be a goddess. That's not right.

Eu looks like he's about to say something, before turning to me. "What do you want, Veiria?"

"I'm not a goddess," I state, as if reassuring myself.

"I know," Eu breathes reassuringly. It was the answer I was looking for.

"But I want my past, if I can have it. I ..." A flicker of a vision flashes in my eyes: a young woman screaming my name again. I swear I saw that vision in my daydreams and for some reason it makes me pause in shock. "I ... only want part of them, though ..." The good parts. The parts here, in this place. I glance up at Noctine pleadingly.

"That is something that I cannot give you," Noctine says with just a bit of sympathy. "Memories aren't something to give."

I close my eyes and smile a frail smile. I expected that.

"Veiria, start over and I will look past you. I wish you a happy life." I can tell that they genuinely mean that.

I bite my lip. I do want that. I don't have much, just a few days, but I'm happy—Bell and Diel are kind to me, and Eu is a good friend and definitely the something more I was looking for, if I can have him. Yet, I still yearn for my past. I know there's something I don't want to know, but ... I feel like an empty shell like this.

"Will it hurt anyone?"

"Yes. I know you as a goddess are near to awakening, and if that happens, those memories will inevitably surface. You weren't ready for yourself last time and it cost those closest to you."

"Thank you," I say softly, not sure what to make of that. My lips feel dry, that hazy memory sticking in my brain. I want to know who that young woman was. I want to remember her ...

"Be careful, Veiria. Of yourself." They lean forward slightly, enfolding their hands. *Is that a threat or a blessing?*

"I will."

I want to trust them, and I do in this moment. I might have poor judgement sometimes, but I think they're sincere.

"One more thing. Your sword, Neihdria ... Stay away from it." Noctine casts their gaze slightly to the distance, as if sensing a presence.

"My ... sword." I hear slight shock in my voice, but my mind is strangely at ease. *What sword?*

"You do not have it with you, and you do not want to. Keep that in your thoughts."

"Why does a goddess need a sword?" Eu asks softly, almost threateningly.

"That is something I will not answer." My blood runs cold, and I clutch my chest.

My hands are shaking. I know that feeling. I've held it and something dreadful stirs within me.

I *should* be holding it. *Neihdria*, I think, suddenly zoning out as I continue clutching my chest. I'm safe with Neihdria.

"I advise you to leave now. My residence is open as an offer of isolation. I anticipate your decline and therefore, I ask you to leave. Know that I mean this as containment, just as much as protection."

I take a shallow gulp. "Thank you for your hospitality and your warning. We'll go now." I have the briefest memory of an endless expanse of white, purple blossoms scattering in the light breeze, and of crow feathers in inky depths slowly suffocating me. I blink. Was I there recently?

They dip their head, as if in respect and I suddenly remember their name. Noctine.

Eu nods to Noctine as well. "Thank you for your kindness and your tolerance." Yet, I can't tell exactly how genuine he is. His jaw is set tightly, like he's grimacing.

Noctine's eyes seem to hone on Eu. "Do not thank me. I pity your future. Take care of her if you choose, just know it will cost you."

"It is what I choose, along with its cost." For once, Eu sounds truly serious—unnaturally so.

I stare at him in wonder, feeling a thrill at the sentiment. I like him helping me, but why would he go so far as to say that?

As we pass out of the glowing hall, I fall silent, wondering what Eu's thoughts are and keenly aware that Noctine's eyes are still on us.

"Eu ..." I begin hesitantly.

"You're just a girl, Veiria," Eu says, looking straight ahead as we pass soundlessly through the light wall and over the glowing bridge.

"So, you don't think I'm a Goddess?"

His eyes turn to me. "You're Veiria. Even if you were a goddess, you'd still be the Veiria I know."

"When I said I wasn't a goddess, you said 'I know.' Why?"

"It's what you wanted, and I'll believe it until you think otherwise. Goddess or girl, you're still you. That's what I choose to believe. You are what you choose to be."

"Your response is uncharacteristically philosophical ... Yet you're still so predictably absurd. But thanks, Eu. And don't tell me not to thank you this time," I say at the turning of his lip. "If I were a goddess, would you follow me?" I mean it to sound offhand, but I want him to say 'yes.' I feel like I'm prying a bit.

"You don't want to be one," he says with maddening calm.

"Fine, I don't, but if I did ..." I trail off with a timid suggestion, turning my eyes down in embarrassment and crossing my ankles.

"I'd follow you anyway," Eu interjects.

I feel a rush to my cheeks. That's comforting—well, more than comforting. I can't be a Goddess, but at least I know Eu would still be by my side if I were. I mean, I'd rather just be an insignificant girl without control of her own fate—something modest—take care of him and a family and all that. Some hazy part of my mind seems to hide unbearable sadness, and I have a notion that it's rooted in a power I can't fathom. I want to live as me.

Interlude 1 ~ Noctine

My face remains impassive, even after they leave, my existence swirling like a tired flame.

I had hoped. Staying would spare her suffering, even if she had to pay for it in solitude. I fear for her ... Just as I fear to fight her. I will avoid that outcome if I can.

Beyond all hope, I hope Veiria will spare herself pain. Her power is as immaculate as her fear. And as long as she's in her current state, she knows no control. For that, she sacrificed the world to burn. She's a tormented soul.

I pity them both.

Interlude 11 ~ Telvin

"You don't stop, do you?" I say tiredly, even as I worry. I want to reassure her that she doesn't have to do this. She's taking out her anger recklessly and she's well-aware of it.

Meren ignores me.

"Don't you think that's enough?" I watch as Meren blasts every speck of the silver dust into bits.

"She betrayed us and now she's back!" she shouts, her voice wavering, her eyes narrowed on the silver dust.

"It wasn't her." My response is consoling. I understand her pain. It's something I've tried not to harbor in myself.

"I know." She turns to me with tears in her eyes. "I know what you think, Telvin, but she went along with it and now she's back …" I can sense that roiling, heartfelt confusion in her. I bear it too. "You still believe in her. I want to, but I can't. She betrayed us of her own will. Whatever you say won't change that. She was like my sister."

"Our sister … and she still is, Meren." I put my hands down, trying to act understanding and reasonable as I soften my voice.

"That's why it hurts," she says with a deep pain in her eyes. "She's chosen her path." Meren drops her shoulders.

"We can help her," I offer, knowing her response. Except her expression softens.

Her eyes still burn. "Just once … Just, not yet."

"Her memories ..." It strikes me as both a blessing and a curse. "She'll remember." But part of me knows it might be best for her not to. What she needs is a guide. Meren would be mortified to meet Veiria with her amnesia. It might break her more than her current pain already has. We didn't leave Veiria in a good place ... Meren never got her closure.

"Shall we keep this up?" Meren stares emptily at the scattering dust, lifting her fingers, inches apart as if ready to send the dust to the darkest realms.

"It bothers me to see you like this, but I know how stubborn you are." I sigh. "I suppose we have to anyway." If we want to save her, save Veiria, the girl who was a sister to us both—then we need to protect her before something much worse than Noctine drives her to madness. Meren needs her, even if she won't admit it. I can't bear seeing Meren like this much longer and Veiria's my friend. Somewhere deep down, I know Meren's right about her, but even so, I must help her—even if it's accepting a different role as a person she doesn't recognize. I can do that. But for Meren, it might be too hard ...

Meren's grief is tearing me apart. She'll realize she needs Veiria. I just have to hope ... to believe in Veiria, even if that belief is irrational.

I send a silent prayer her way, towards the heavens and the Goddess of Venah and the Skies, that we can find her, befriend her, and console and guide her before she can awaken her full power and lose control again.

Eu

As I walk back with Veiria, I ponder the day. Glancing at Veiria, I can see she looks a bit zoned out.

That has to be the strangest day of my life.

Noctine was clearly powerful. I felt like nothing in their presence, like the air was being drained from the room, but Veiria seemed ... I don't know, unaffected?

I purse my lips. I feel a bit like an idiot. I don't know what I was doing in there. I was just reacting on impulse and protecting this girl I just met, probably because she's beautiful.

I glance at her and look away quickly as she notices, staring at me obliviously with a furrowed brow and unasked question.

I chuckle nervously on the inside as I remember her collapsed in my arms last night or taking my hand today.

Yes, I definitely do *like-like* her. She's not the only girl I like right now—there's Veronica, too, but Veiria just, I don't know ... She's weird in a good way. And besides that attraction, I feel a strong urge to be her friend. She's like a magnet. I don't know if I mean that in a literal or figurative sense, but her mere presence is intoxicating.

I ruffle my hair in thought, relief and familiarity filling my lungs as the tents and houses on the outskirts of Anvi come into sight.

As exciting as today was, I find myself thinking of my sister, Lizzie, and my family. The thought makes me smile.

I'll wish Veiria well and give all of this some more thought tonight after I help my parents a little and spend some time helping my sister become the bright little prodigy she is.

The Goddess stuff is too much. I mean, I know of the 'Goddess of our Skies,' but she hasn't been seen in a century. I don't recall hearing her referred to as Veiria—at least not here.

I glance at Veiria, who seems off in her own little world, humming and looking around obliviously.

Nah, I think. *Couldn't be.*

I roll my eyes. That Noctine is nuts, all-powerful and intimidating or not.

I feel a bit embarrassed I was so adamant about protecting Veiria. I probably looked absurd and hot-headed. Noctine is a deity from the myths of Acellia—their patron deity. I knew a little about them, but I left the rest to the Cellites. They're not a deity I thought I'd meet.

I'm not terribly religious. Yes, I believe in the Sky Goddess and the Goddess Mallorn of Jespaira and the patron Deity Noctine. Magic isn't exactly new to me, even if I'm not personally gifted with any, but ...

I snort, shaking my head. What am I doing? Veiria's not some all-powerful, secretive being.

I'll protect a pretty stranger and my new friend with my life if that's what being her friend means. She seems immensely frail and prone to danger as it is.

I chuckle. That's Veiria.

With that, I kick myself out of my on-edge mood, pushing the threat of Noctine and the strange happenings around my new friend out of my mind.

Because she's just that: a friend. Maybe a friend that I sometimes think about kissing, but a friend first.

Veiria

I lie in bed later that night. Eu is long gone. Sometimes it's strangely lonely having so little memory. What time I do have has been happy, but further back, there's nothing, just a misty haze. My personality is there, but what made me who I am is gone—just glimpses of longing and bitterness and occasionally fleeting words from dark beings and a desperate pair huddled on that cliff edge I'd seen so many times, but that's it. Occasionally there are silhouettes of a place that looks more real than here and feelings of loss or anger.

I feel like I'm missing something. When I'm alone, there's so little in my head and I'm just grasping at something to fill the void, something I don't have.

Sometimes in my head, I can almost make out two figures—laughing around a fire or leaning out on a ship under a sky filled with stars, but they never come into clarity. There were people I was close with, closer to than I am with Eu. People I knew much longer. It seems hard to comprehend that I've only known Eu for two days, because those two days have been everything for me. I miss Eu now, because he's almost all I have and he's my friend. I can't possibly tell him what he's meant over so short a time. I hope he stays, and I know he wants to. Plus, I find myself attracted to him, though at this point, my friendship with him far overshadows that. But just thinking of his hand in mine makes me tingle.

I wonder what he thought about today. Truthfully, I would have been too terrified without him. Noctine doesn't seem necessarily unkind, but not friendly either.

I really don't want to see Eu risking himself so much for my sake. I like him defending me—well, a boy defending me—but I'm glad it's Eu, because I feel a kindred to him beyond my attraction. But if he wants to be my knight too, that'd make me happy. Just, I know I'll cause him harm at some point and that scares me. It's just a feeling I have and it's a very unsettling one.

I shiver.

I think back to what Noctine said. What if I am a goddess? I don't want to believe that, but it rings strangely true. Is that really so bad? Yet I cling to Noctine's words. I'm happy as I am. The fact that my mind is blocked gives me a strange foreboding.

That I can see things others can't makes sense now though, if my being a goddess is true. I've come to terms with the day-night cycle now, though it still feels wrong. This entire world feels slightly off, like there's something just below its surface. Sometimes when I close my eyes, I see that brilliant ball of fire. I do now.

I grimace and sigh, turning and cuddling the bunny in the top hat and looking out the window at Nytiel.

But whatever I am, a part of me is missing, and even more than my memory, I miss that part.

Of Farmgirls & Teachers

Veiria

Eu leans on the fence as I lie in the crook of the little tree in Bell and Diel's yard, light birdsong around me and flowers in bloom being pollinated by lazy, buzzing bumblebees that make me forget the world is turning.

World turning? I thought these were floating islands, I muse distractedly. As Eu said, the sun sinks into the water above and then poofs, extinguished—end of story.

"Whatch'ya reading?" Eu asks curiously, trying to lean his head over the cover from a distance.

I turn the book around. "A children's book. You said you were a teacher. I was thinking of you."

"'An Inded's Shell.' Swell! I remember that book from when I was a kid."

"You do! You must have been adorable." *Hehe,* I think, imagining cute little Eu-Eu.

"Well, I was a little!" He grins, lopsidedly. "My mom always said I was a special little devil."

"Devil?"

"Er-erm." Eu clears his throat. "Yeah, I think they were some weird shadow beings? I don't know ... brain foggy.exe."

"Exe?" I raise my eyebrow.

Eu looks to the heavens. "Something is wrong with me today because random terms are invading my mind."

I frown at him, but don't comment, even though there's a strange tingling in my brain. "So ... teaching?"

"Right, right. I'm an established, honorable, delegated assistant." Eu sweeps into a bow, then he leans across the fence on his elbows. "Little Arnold wants to go to the Lunar Sea. I told him we'd work on that. A lot of preparation, that takes." Eu taps his finger against the wood, a knowing look on his face. "Little Elizabeth is learning to count, though she's quite horrendous with her syllables still."

"You'd bully a child?" I ask, my eyebrows quirking up.

"Not in the ever slightest. She's wonderful! It's just a spiteful joke at a friend. She stole my lunch one day and fed it to the worms with Julliette." Eu whispers sidelong, a hand beside his mouth, like he doesn't want anyone to hear. "Maybe it was a bad idea to get the class earthworms ..."

I snort. "Funny."

"Yeah, yeah. I'd say they bully me. Anyway, anyway, Maria told her first lie, but she also solved a quantum equation. Quite talented that one."

"Really?" She sounds way smarter than me. Eu has his hands full.

"Oh no, but she did solve a rather complex equation with all the signs—you know, the four signs of MATH!"

I nod. "I do know MATH." I imitate his exaggerated word.

"I'm proud, Veiria, as a dignified, studied professor. Anyway, then she wrote a story about her cat, Buttercup with her partner Ethan. It was quite charming that I almost forgot they were off topic, but English is English, so I gave them a gold star anyway."

"You're really good with children." I smile, shifting over in my tree trunk to get a better look at his, well, good looks and charm?

"Well, assistant Eu Ledora has a job to do."

"And you shall never fail," I complete that thought, leaning forward further. I think about poking his cheek, but that would probably be too weird.

"Precisely. My dream is to give children hope so that they may follow their silly little ... well, not silly, really." He frowns, then his face lightens in compassion. "Their dreams. Kids are life. They have a lot going for them and I want to sow the seeds of KNOWLEDGE, CREATION, INGENUITY, and CURIOSITY." He lists those four terms a bit overly-proudly and I snicker-giggle at his dorkiness.

"Uh-huh." I nod, lulled by his sweetness.

Him getting along with children and teaching them is honestly so precious. It makes me swoon.

I gaze at him dreamily, my hand on my chin and my head sagging. My mind drifts away with his words, though I try to focus on the present.

I wonder what it would be like staying home with our kids as a stay-at-home farmgirl wife, cooking him meals and lunches as he went off to teach. Maybe some days I'd miss him and come visit, watching him with a loving affection for all the knowledge and care he poured into those kids every day. He'd be a patient husband, who'd be silly and sweet to our kids, and he'd treat me like his treasure, his confidant, his lover, and his high school sweetheart. He'd show me off like a proud husband and I'd blush and say how much I love him. He'd show our children and me so much love. At night, I'd tuck the children in and then retire to bed with him under the covers next to me until we grew old and died in each other's arms.

As I reminisce, I find my eyes tearing up slightly at the happy, far-off notion and I wipe at them quickly while Eu-Eu's not looking, because thinking about our future is a bit too presumptuous and I don't want to scare him off.

I may be a bit sentimental. Can't a girl dream? I must have been stupidly deprived in life to have a bland dream like that, but something so simple feels like it should have been an impossibility. Yet, I'm here.

I frown. I do have everything, so should I really be yearning so hard for Eu? Maybe I need to befriend another girl here so I can gossip about Eu. Or something else? I know it's stupid to just talk about a boy.

Veiria, you're helpless. I pout my cheeks, sitting up a little. For now, we're just friends …

I wonder if that'll ever change, or if I'll just sit here listening to him till the end of my days … or until he moves on and finds another girl. One way or another, I know he'll move on to something better—that he'll just think of me as that silly girl he met one day and nothing more.

But at least I'd be happy with that, because I'd be somewhat myself and in the company of a person who wanted me for how I actually felt at heart, if only for a fleeting moment.

And of course, he doesn't stay long today, but it's fine. Bell said she'd be home early today for something she planned and that gives me some encouragement as I wave goodbye to Eu with a dreamy smile, finding a pond where I attempt to braid my hair as I listen to birdsong and quickly wince in defeat at my terrible attempt that leaves my hair in a beautiful pigsty—I tell myself not to break down now, you'll try again later. I lie down, curled on my side, a book held in one arm as I play with some grass and hum an almost familiar tune that sounds a bit melancholy and lonely as a fluffy, almost quill-like ball thing rolls up to me.

I squint at its odd form, resisting the urge to shriek in surprise. Instead, I reach out my arm welcomingly when I've judged that the strange creature looks pretty harmless and cute. It rolls up my skin, making me giggle at the prickly touch. "Stop that!" I snicker.

It deflates at the top of my shoulder like hissing liquid, and I smile, stroking it as I look up at the clouds drifting across the sky.

"You know, you look like a scary little thing." I smile at its numerous pinprick eyes between its barbed hair. "But really, you just want to live. You're like me. Weird and different." It croaks, wrapping around my neck. I hate things around my neck, but I'll let it pass, as I resist clawing the fuzzy thing off my neck, instead itching at my collarbone. It's cute when you aren't paying attention to the things humans label as horrifying—whether animals, or other humans. If people weren't always so quick to judge, they'd have something precious—something that loves.

It wriggles against my skin, and I laugh again—quite uncomfortably, but I'm not tearing away this thing's joy. "Alright, alright." I stroke the weird, shapeshifting animal with my finger. *I get it, you like me*, I think.

I lean back, my arms braced behind me on the grass and smile toothily in the middle of Bell and Diel's garden. It probably likes Bell and Diel's garden because they're kind. And maybe it likes me because we're kindred souls—not so much different.

I imagine me looking like the creature and what people would think about that. I have no clue why I'd look like that, but who knows?

I'll have to ask Eu the name of this cutie, as I try to ignore my brain screaming 'IT'S CHOKING ME!!!' Instead, I gently transfer it around my wrist a few minutes later and breath out a sigh of relief and a "sorry." Apparently, I have a comfortable neck for little monsters.

Things I Always Wanted

Veiria

I smudge the lipstick across my face in an ugly gasp and nearly cry. After failing at my hair earlier, this is even worse.

Bell knocks. "Is everything alright, dear?"

I jump, startled, clutching my chest, my heart beating rapidly.

"Yes," I reply, a tremor in my voice.

Bell pushes the door open gently. "Oh no, dear. What's wrong? Let me help you." She looks at my poor attempt at makeup with pity. "No one taught you how to do that, did they?"

I shake my head in quiet dejection.

"Well ..." she smiles kindly. "Then I'll just have to show you, dear. There's always a first time for everything."

"Thank you," I say, my voice full of breathless gratitude, even if I'm embarrassed handing her the supplies in my hand. I turn to face the kind wrinkles of her face as she gets to work.

"There. You can turn around now. It's been years since I last did my daughter's makeup. I miss those days dearly." Her gaze turns distant, and she turns me gently to the mirror, her hand on my shoulder.

I cover my face, sobbing into my hands.

"What's wrong, dear?" Bell asks, concern laced in her voice.

I shake my head, trying to collect myself. "I'm sorry. I'm not sure what's wrong with me."

"Shhh ... shhh," she consoles me, patting my back. "It's okay, dear. You look beautiful."

I nod into my hands again. "Thank you." I feel a surreal sense of leaving my body as I gaze at my reflection—the soft accents and blush compliment my features delicately. Bell leaves the room as I touch my face gingerly and smile with a sheepish, child-like joy.

It's the next night that Bell leaves a present on my bed with a note.

There's a handsome suitor waiting for you. He's awfully flustered, and I think he's a little taken with you. Don't think I don't know. There's a star ball tomorrow. I know you want to go.

- *Bell (+ Diel gave his well-wishes for your happiness too)*

I set down the note, running my hands over an ornate white box with a rose pink silk ribbon. I gently tug off the ribbon and lift the top of the box and the vivid gold and green wrapping, pulling out a truly beautiful dress, that I run my hands over reverently. Rushing to the mirror, careful to keep the dress unharmed, of course, I slip out of my pink bottoms and tank-top and then into the dress, being extra careful not to tear the fine material.

My heart stops and I think I nearly have a heart attack. I hold my hand to my chest, turning to either side, then I swish from left to right, giggling a little at the surrealness of being able to wear something so stunningly expensive and jaw-dropping. My hand to my mouth. I look beautiful, almost, and even better: Eu will love it. Or, at least, I really, really hope he does. I put a hand to my thundering chest and swallow, spinning for a moment in wonder, all the while admiring all the fine details and the way it impeccably compliments my skin and hair. I'm impressed and I admire Bell for the thought. I bet she was an amazing mother. And what she picked out is precisely my style—like really my style! I don't care if that's unsettling, because I don't for the life of me know how she'd know that.

It's a turquoise dress with a heart shaped boob window on the chest and an adorable, but still very stunning and attractive, jellyfish style puffy sleeved, with white trailing lace vertical down the sides and horizontal on the hem. It looks like it bobs and swishes when I move, like a cute jellyfish. My pendant hangs in the center of the window, and I hold it for a moment, as I look into my eyes, which look so ... my gosh, they look full and bright, even to me.

I hear a light knock after several minutes of staring at myself and smiling.

"Yes?" I say, somewhat startled, but still staring in the mirror like a young woman in a trance.

"It's Bell dear."

"Come in." I try hiding my smile as she does.

"Oh, dear, you look stunning—maybe a little sexy, if I can say that." She comes up next to me, giving me a reminiscing look. "To be young is a gift, so enjoy it."

"Thank you," I say breathlessly, turning once for her, my grin coming back. "This must have been expensive. You really shouldn't have gone to the trouble for me."

"Nonsense. I was young once too. Something tells me you've been missing out on pretty things like this."

I gaze at my reflection again, my lips trembling in delight. She's right. I know there's something sad there, but I can't face it, nor deny this dream, because sometimes dreams don't come a second time, and I don't trust my luck. I shake my head at the thought. "Who's the suitor?" I almost forgot, but I can feel my ears turning red.

"Now, now." She holds my shoulders. "Don't worry, you look stunning, and he'll fall hard. It's a nice surprise. I wouldn't have asked him if I weren't sure you two like each other. So, I thought I'd set you up and get you both over your feelings. Break-the-ice. And he's good for you; you picked well.

"Thank you," I say in gratitude, my eyes swelling up again, because I never thought I'd have the chance to look this beautiful and that it'd be real. "For everything. I don't think I could ever repay you."

"There's no need." She smiles kindly. "You were a lost little bird when you came to my home, and I just want to see you smile. Okay?"

"Okay ..." I say, as I cover my face in my hands. "I'm sorry, you're being too kind to me. Um ..." I peep through my fingers. "Is my suitor here?"

"Your prince is waiting. I'll give you a moment to calm down and go get him, if that's what you want."

I put my hand to my ear. "I do want that." With all my heart I want this not to be a dream, but I feel too light for it to be fake.

"Okay. He's being quite the scoundrel getting into his tux, but he's doing his best to be patient. He's a polite young man, if clearly out of his element. You should be able to handle him."

Eu

"Now, young man" she finishes combing out the knots of my disheveled, curly hair, patting down my tux with a critical eye—"You're going to want to go to this dance with Veiria. It's every young woman's desire to go to a ball with a handsome gentleman such as yourself." She gives my tailcoat a last straightening. "Now go to her and make her happy. She's still in the bathroom, crying. You show up and I'll hand her the corsage to pin on you. It'll match her dress. And I'll give you this one" she turns open my palm and places the roses in them—"to place on Veiria's wrist. You'd do well to be delicate for her." I glance down at my palm and the crystal blue rose in it.

I squirm uncomfortably in my stiff, sweltering tux. "Are you sure this is what she wants?"

"Oh, trust me, hunny." She winks, patting my wrist. "I know a young woman's heart well enough. She's going to love tonight."

"Well, I suppose I'm honored to do this for a friend." I take a bow.

The corners of her mouth lift in an amused smile. "You two do make a good pair, whatever the case. Give me a moment. I'll afford her some privacy from your prying eyes."

"Trust me." I cross my heart. "Back is turned. Eyes are closed. I'm as silent as a Chinta."

"Well then. Thanks, Eu, for going through all this trouble, but I know you're a real charmer to her and she appreciates it."

She ruffles my cuff one last time and I make a mental note to stay extra still, before she's out the room and to Veiria.

Honestly. My heart picks up a little as I turn in my tux. If it'll make Veiria happy, I'll welcome it, but it's quite the hassle. Does she really want to go with me? Still, I feel a twinge of excitement in my veins for no discernible reason.

She's just a friend, I repeat in my head, but I keep picturing her in an honestly, um ... compelling dress? Sexy, even. Running my hands weird places ... and some other things that give me the ick, because she's my friend. I mean, she *could* be more than that ... I ponder the thought, really think on it. If she wanted me to kiss her, and I wanted to kiss her, what's stopping me?

I squirm, slapping my face to disrupt my weird thoughts. "Ugh." I make a puking face in the mirror, sticking my tongue out in disgust at myself. What is wrong with me is something not even a goddess herself could answer—which Veiria isn't one—definitely nothing like a Goddess, no matter how unearthly beautiful she is—nope, just a normal, ordinary girl, who I have very, extremely platonic feelings for. *Definitely nothing else*, I think sarcastically. Woman, I guess is more appropriate. I think Bell would scorn my manners for the thought and I find myself seeking out her approval a little too much in this moment. I turn one last time in the mirror, wondering just maybe what it would be like if she watched me ... "Huh, huh, very funny, Eu." I laugh nervously. "What a joke! An absolute scam! And I'm off to see Veiria." Now I smile broadly and practice my bow once more, hoping she'll get a kick out of it ... or something like that.

Veiria

"Um ... hi, Veiria," Eu says, tongue-tied as I stand in the doorway. He looks me up-and-down, and I feel my heart thundering incredibly loudly. I feel like my face is going to melt off from embarrassment. "You look ... um ... nice?"

"Eu." Bell gives him a gentle look.

"Oh, right." He rubs his chin and shoots a finger gun that makes me turn my face away in embarrassment. "Truly breathtaking. Surreal. What a sight in my eyes! I promise I'm blinded," he says, covering his eyes.

"Thanks, Eu." I twist my hands in front of me, glancing at him shyly in return. Bell is right that he looks incredibly handsome. The black tux, the white cuffs and collar. They blend nicely with his smooth, brown skin. His hair is nicer, but still a familiar youthful pound of boyishly charming curls. His cheeks have these adorable dimples. He's in some shining black shoes that I think would be great for dancing. And his smile has that same effortless charm, plus his eyes—oh, his eyes. They're so beautiful …

I realize my mouth is gaping and I'm dangerously close to drooling, so I force it shut as quickly as I can so as not to make too much of a fool of myself. That's not very ladylike to be drooling over a guy, now is it? Maybe it is???

He's honestly so hot, though.

I wonder what his body would feel like against mine as he took my hand and then held me close to him in a trance, his hand around my waist in a slow dance and our eyes locked. And then he took me home later and maybe we … did a thing that wouldn't be entirely PG. I try not to giggle, instead thinking that maybe he'd kiss my hand or something chivalrous as a form of greeting.

"Oh, right," Eu jumps to saying, looking at Bell and laughing, his hand over his shoulder nervously as he steps closer and fumbles with a beautiful blue corsage. I remember watching something like this before in a past life … but not from this perspective … He takes my hand and I quickly forget that bitter, hazy thought. I can feel my hot breath slowing down. He slips it onto my wrist. "For you, Veiria. A token of our silly days unending. Yeah, but like, I hope you like it."

"I do," I say softly, looking between us at his lips, but he steps back before I can even consider what it would really be like for him to kiss me—to take my cheek delicately in his hand and place his lips gently to mine and then me wrapping my arms around his neck and standing on my toes.

No—hold on, Veiria. Just—calm. Breathe. Stay sane in the presence of this beautiful boy in front of me.

So, what if he doesn't want to kiss you? It's too good to be true either way.

Eu walks beside me awkwardly, seemingly not knowing what to do with his hands, his feet, or his eyes, as he periodically looks at Bell and I hope that's his face turning scarlet when he occasionally sneaks a glance at me.

"How are you doing, Veiria?" Bell comes up next to me.

"Me?" I jump at her words. "I ... I guess I'm nervous. I know you said some things earlier, but I don't believe them."

She smiles kindly at me, patting my wrist. "You don't need to believe them. Just have fun. And who knows, maybe you'll have this day forever? You might get lucky."

I look at the ground. "I don't think luck was ever on my side where I came from."

"Well then, maybe this is a sign that it's different now." By now we've stopped, leaving Eu to stop a few paces away, trying his best to ignore our conversation as he whistles into the night, scratching at his cuff. "You're wonderful, dear. Ever since you came to me you've been this soft, gentle young woman who thought too much about how you'd mess up for others. You're plenty worthy of him or whatever you want out of life. You just have to start living like you're worth it."

"I don't think it could ever be like that ..." I squeeze my eyes shut. "Things never fell into place." My voice picks up, trying desperately to get something important across to Bell. "I know I couldn't live like this ... can't live like this. People don't want me to. I shouldn't."

"What people, dear?" Bell searches my face in concern.

I blink in confusion at my words and the concern in Bell's tone. "I don't know. I really don't ..." Or maybe I just don't want to. "I'm sorry, Bell, you're just the kindest person I've ever met. "I squeeze my eyes shut, waiting for some sort of embarrassment or pity or just anything that proves me wrong. But when I open them, I just see her pained, compassionate smile.

"Thanks, dear. It breaks my heart, but just know you deserved more people caring about you the way you needed."

"Thanks." I swallow. "I think I felt alone for the longest time. Not necessarily 'alone, alone,' but there's this weird sense that I never want to see where I came from ever again. Somehow, I know that things were ugly where I came from. I'm scared ..."

"Dear?" She clasps my hands. "I don't know what you mean or how the world failed you, but I'm always here to support you, if you ever remember."

"I wish I could do something for you back." I know I'm worthless, though. I couldn't help Bell like she's helped me.

"Nonsense." She turns me gently, a hand on my back as she positions me towards Eu. "Now go to him. He's your future, after all, whether as a lover, or as a friend in your heart."

I reluctantly walk away from her and back to Eu, trying to feel the confidence of my dress that in some moments, makes me feel a bit worthy ... a bit desired ... a bit beautiful. But not enough that I can feel like accepting the love and desire my way, or even contemplate the same desire towards myself. It still feels like a terrible burden, that I'm just not suited for.

Eu's gaze is playful and inviting. He makes me smile. He makes my heart race. He gives me goosebumps. He makes me laugh with my full chest. He makes me feel safe. He lets me be silly and free and the me I could never be. Not in the way that was truly authentic—truly real.

In that way, he's like forbidden fruit, giving me something I know some day will be denied to me again. I'm afraid that if he takes me, I'll ruin him. I won't be enough. How can someone like me have a life so beautiful just handed to me?

It's just too ... sudden.

But then he takes my hand, sweeping me off my feet as I forget it all and we turn to walk to a sphere of transparent 'air' sitting in the starlit field.

Well, when I say air … erm … I don't know what I'm talking about exactly. "Erm … Eu? What is this? Is it safe?"

"Sure," he says in a long voice. "Now let's experiment. Would you do the honors?" He motions.

I hesitate for a moment, then reach my hand out as the surface ripples and I jerk my hand back, yelping as my stomach turns inside out and I turn around panicked to find myself inside the sphere. I rush to the boundary. "Eu! Eu!" I reach up to the membrane.

He touches the outside, right in front of my nose with a mischievous smile, then he vanishes and my heartrate spikes.

"I'm right here, Veiria."

I jump, screaming.

"Woa! Woa!" He puts his hands up. "Pleased to make your acquaintance. It's me, ghost Eu."

"God, Eu, never do that again."

"I'll haunt you as much as I like, thank you very much."

I place my hand to my chest, my lips quirking up in a grin. "I'd like that very much." Then I look down and almost faint, because we're … a little high for my liking.

Eu rushes over and grabs my arm and I feel blood rushing to my cheeks, which makes me feel even more faint. "It's okay, Veiria. We're rising. You'll get used to it. This is the only way to get to the Star Ball."

"You must be joking," I say breathlessly.

"Cross my heart that it'll eventually be fun."

"And I'll cross my heart that you wish you never said that." I grit my teeth.

"Gosh, Veiria. I didn't know you were afraid of heights."

"I can't conceive of anyone who wouldn't be."

He shrugs, rolling his eyes. "Well, I live with it. I better not be scared if I want to herd the Mislerime."

"Mislerime?" I stare blankly.

"Now I know you're definitely not from this world. Ever seen one fly?"

"Maybe you could show me?"

"Honored." He suddenly turns flustered again, pulling me up and quickly dropping my hand as we continue to rise.

We gaze at the starry sky in silence, sparks of color popping not too far off in a display that reminds me of ... *fireworks*? Except they're completely silent. One of them forms a heart, and I find myself looking sidelong at Eu's eagerly pleasing face. I decide to be bold for once and stand, moving to sit down next to him on the transparent bench across the aisle ... while very conscious of being in an invisible bubble, thousands of miles from the ground.

I sit close to him, but not too close, and I yearn hopefully for that distance to close. It doesn't, and I don't know whether to be relieved or hurt.

Then Eu sighs. "You know, I realize I've told you almost nothing about me."

"No, you haven't," I say quietly. I shift a little closer, my eyes turned to him. "Go on. I want to know every last detail of the mysterious Eu." *Eu-Eu*, I correct in my head— the mysterious Eu-Eu. That's his better name, I want to giggle.

He looks away from me, out at the fireworks, and I watch them reflect in his eyes. Then he looks back more calmly. "I have a younger sister, Lizzie. She's a reading prodigy!" Eu grins broadly. "If I do say so myself."

"Did you teach her?" I nudge him.

"Why, I did!" He puts a finger up. "Good observation, Veiria." Eu's voice grows fond. "She comes home every day, and we sit together on this old rocking chair in the corner. I teach her to read in the evenings, after we've had our family dinner. She's a bright child."

"She must be your favorite sibling."

Eu looks at the space between us with a soft smile. "Don't tell my brothers that, but yes. She's my favorite family member, that is. My little princess. I brush her hair, and she practices her singing with me."

"You sing?" I ask, intrigued as I try to imagine what his voice sounds like.

"A little." He laughs nervously, rubbing the back of his head. "You should forget I mentioned it. I'm a terrible singer."

"You're just being modest." I truly doubt anything out of his mouth could be terrible. He must be lying.

Eu clears his throat and continues. "Then my mother bakes the most delicious pie. She also makes some clothes to sell at the fair. My father's a blacksmith—very skilled, and quite handsome, as my mother would say."

I laugh lightly at the comment.

"My brothers are both athletes. I, um … don't take after them."

They must be just as handsome, I think. "Because you're a twig," I tease and when he turns away, I say, "Sorry. I didn't mean that. You're an um … very *attractive* twig."

Eu scoffs. "You're a truly great complimenter."

I feel my cheeks grow red and I mumble, "Yeah."

Eu goes on, looking out the window again, as I glance at his leg and try to resist touching it with mine.

"They're both starting their own families. They're older than me, so it was mostly my sister to keep me company and for me to teach and to take care of with my parents. They've both married their local school sweethearts."

I want to 'awe' at the adoring notion, while something simultaneously sinks in my heart—something empty gaping in my chest, like I lost something precious. *Did I miss something?*

"Then my grandparents ..." He grows quiet.

"Yes?"

"They're bedridden. I'm taking care of them with my parents."

"Oh, Eu ..." I say comfortingly. "I'm sorry."

"It's okay," he says, and I swear I hear him choke up.

"Well, you sound good for them," I say quietly in the silence, hoping those words are even a little assuring.

I look forward, suddenly awkward and all of a sudden awfully conscious of our height once more as I nervously look down, wishing I hadn't. I gulp and try to hold down the contents of my stomach as I lean forward and groan.

Eu turns back to me from his far-off gaze as he hears my far-too-obvious distress siren. "Veiria, you look pale. What is it?"

"Just ... sick." I feel my stomach heave and cover my mouth.

There's a ripple through the bubble and I'm jolted into the safety of Eu's arms—not gently. I scream into his chest and gratefully, he puts his arms around me, which silences my trembling quickly enough. Now I'm just trembling from his body heat.

"It's okay, Veiria," he says, his arms around me awkwardly, like he doesn't know where to put them.

I take a deep breath and sit up as he adjusts me in his arms, leaning against his shoulder, which hopefully he likes. I close my eyes, hardly containing the happiness of feeling his body touching mine. "This is perfect, Eu." *Eu-Eu.*

He's stiff at first, but eventually he loosens up, his hand awkwardly on my shoulder and looking out the bubble.

It doesn't ripple again. But that doesn't matter, because I feel calmer.

Suddenly the bubble clears a set of misty clouds that part like a tapestry, enclosing the bubble.

"Well, I think this may just be our stop."

He takes his hand off my shoulder gently and I pull away reluctantly. He eyes me again, giving me that adorable boyish smile and I feel my face go red, covering it from his view.

"Veiria, you don't need to hide. It's just us. And ... you really are beautiful." He says it a little tongue-tied, but his words are softer than before and more genuine. "I've got you." He extends his hand, and I take it, my eyes never leaving his.

We meld through the membrane, stepping onto misty cloud and I gasp.

"I know." He turns to me and grins. "Crazy."

"This is wonderful," I say breathlessly.

Eu seems to stand up straighter, more gentlemanly and more handsome than I thought he could be, and we literally glide through the clouds, until a wall of them parts before us, revealing the moon and a starry, floating dance floor.

We make our way through, and I gaze around, entranced.

There's dull, but powerful balls of light floating and shining across the dance floor, flowing in waves and bumping into each other. Glittery trails form constellations that look all too familiar, so much that they're on the tip of my tongue, but I can't place them. Several flecks of stardust flow in lavender purple currents around the dance floor like trails of magic. Some ethereal light pools and forms nebulae and galaxies that make me feel like I'm alone in a miniature, beautiful universe. A few paper stars flutter and then pull back to strands of butterfly fairy lights lit in soft white and pink, suspended in thin air in front of me. They read, "Be mine, Veiria," with a huge heart following it.

"Did you do this, Eu?" I say, almost speechless.

"No. I'm sorry, Veiria." I look back and he's looking away with a regretful expression. "I wish I had." He's still holding my hand, though, and he suddenly pulls me closer, until I'm looking up slightly at him into his cinnamon eyes— his handsome chin tilted down, his dark eyelashes gorgeous, mass of curls beautiful and making me long to run my hands through them.

"Hi," I say.

"Hi."

I take a shaky breath in and look down, knowing I'm not worthy of kissing him, but finding myself looking back to the lights. I don't know what prompts me to say it, but it feels like it's a part of my heart that's important to tell Eu about. "When I was younger, I loved constellations, I think," I say in a trance, watching the spiral of a blinding galaxy and feeling the edge of a whole universe in my eyes—one I could only dream of once. "I wanted to be an astronomer." I look back at him, eyes shining with a deep clarity and my voice far off and here all at once. It's the first time I almost want to remember—to feel something real. "They were always so beautiful and bright." I close my eyes, digging for a memory that feels nearly sacred—real. "I ... I think they made me feel comforted—at home. Even so far apart, they were so bright—so breathtaking. Serene. I'd look out sometimes and make a wish that I could have even a bit of their magic. I think I wanted them more than anything. Have you ever wanted something like that, Eu? I felt at home wishing for something so far away, and now they're here."

I turn my gaze back to Eu and I'm caught off guard at the tenderness that's suddenly in his gaze and he ... he looks like he's about to kiss me, his hands now on my waist and a breath on his lips, inches from mine. "Eu?"

"That's a wonderful memory, Veiria. I ... I hope this moment is special."

I lean forward. "It is, because you're here."

He turns his head away as soft music pools in the air and my shoulders sink in disappointment.

"The dance is about to start." He guides my waist, smiling gently and I almost forget about the near-kiss, because it doesn't matter—just that he's here and real and with me. "It's really something, you know?"

His right hand stays on my waist and his left grabs my hand as we start moving and rocking, fumbling with the steps, accidentally stumbling on each other's feet a few times, and laughing nervously at first, but then we're less and less guarded as we lose ourselves in each other's arms, the newness of unpracticed, embarrassingly awkward steps and random unsure gazes that make both of us grin and smile sheepishly, gliding through lights rippling around us like waves on a calm sea.

We slow in the sea of them, my arms around his neck, his encircling my waist, the lights rising and falling around us like slow breaths.

Once more I'm lost in him, and he's lost for speech.

His hands are gentle, but firm and safe. He doesn't make any moves, doesn't say anything, we just gaze at each other in quiet silence, rocking in circles, until he pulls me close in a tender hug and I rest my head on his shoulder, closing my eyes in peace and feeling something aching and raw in my heart.

He pulls me closer, and I sniffle in his arms, something small and broken feeling cradled in his arms until I quietly start sobbing and Eu squeezes me.

The glow fades from the balls of light and they disperse from us along with the clouds, until all there is is us on an empty dance floor, surrounded by stars, me quietly sobbing in Eu's arms, as I bury my face in his chest and clutch his shirt for just his comfort, or something that I crave.

He starts stroking my back, my hair, as I let out the last of my small sobs, staying in his arms and trying to force a smile.

Eu strokes my hair with a protective, comforting touch, the warmth of him a blessing. I can't move—I don't feel like leaving him, but I also just feel so lost. Empty. Alone, even though Eu's right in front of me and I have everything I've asked for.

"Are you alright?" Eu looks dazed and unsure.

I push away from him, turning to the fading stars and taking a few steps as if I can follow them. I stare away into the distance, my hands behind my back and Eu behind me as my heart feels awfully heavy. "Thank you."

A cold breeze blows across me and I shiver. I smile quietly at the dress and my perfect skin and the corsage and the feeling that I should feel like I belong and be at ease. That I'm in a better world.

I don't look at Eu anymore as I face into that cold breeze, my eyes stinging.

Eu comes up to me with a blanket that I could swear he didn't have before and drapes it over my shoulders.

"Thank you. You're a fine date," I say, trying to make my voice sound okay and regain its color, but there's something scared and small in it.

Instead, I lean into Eu and ignore that hollowness in my chest as I retreat in on myself, even as I gaze at Eu wistfully again.

I stub my toe against the solid ground at the heavy silence between us—the dance floor and the bubble transport behind us. "So, um ..." I tuck a strand of hair behind my ear, then twirl self-consciously, holding my hands in front of me.

"Um, indeed," Eu chuckles with a strain in his throat.

"You gonna take me home in a gilded carriage, or what?" I look up from my lashes at him with earnest expectation.

Eu shifts uncomfortably on his feet. "Nah." He studies his beautiful hand for a moment and laughs nervously. "Strict parents. They have the wrong idea."

"Oh. Pity." Something sinks in my chest and my words come out flat.

"But I'll see you later." He gives me awkward finger guns again.

This time I palm my face in embarrassment, before giving incredibly awkward finger guns back, which prompts a huge grin from him, and I can't help my insecurities fading away with his smile. It's almost like his words didn't sting right through my heart, before he turns his back, and I sigh. "Eu," I say quietly, but loud enough for him to hear. "Could you at least take me home?"

"Sure thing, Veiria." He looks a bit weary, and it makes my smile drop even more.

"Veiria, is something wrong?"

I hesitate. "You had fun, didn't you?"

"Of course," he smiles brightly. "All the best for my very dear friend."

"Well … then, I'm glad you're at least happy."

He furrows his eyebrows, before sticking his arm out and I take it with a tired roll of my eyes. "At least you're still a silly gentleman."

"I do my best." He starts skipping a little and I join him. "And we're off to some random, inconsequential adventure! Strap in!"

"Strap in?" Doesn't that sound a bit strange? It sounds familiar, but I can't place the meaning. Is he referring to some sort of belt?

"It's an expression, I think? It just popped into my head; I don't know. It wasn't there before, but clearly it wants to be heard!"

"Strange …" I trail off.

He shrugs. "Things like this happen all the time. Forget about it and enjoy the ride!"

And so, I do, trying to ignore that strange doubt that I know that phrase doesn't belong in this world, but for some reason, I can't shake the feeling.

Eu

I sigh as I strip out of my tux, massaging my eyes.

That was ... I wince.

Look, I have a feeling Veiria wanted more, but ...

Jeez, I messed up. I squeeze my eyes shut. I couldn't go through with kissing her.

I don't even know why. Maybe it was the whole pageantry of everything. I panicked, okay?

It's like ... I don't know. I sit on my bed and peel off my socks. If I'm going to be with Veiria, at least let me do it on my own time, you know?

But still ... seeing her cry against me. It's messing with me. I wanted to do more for her than just cradle her awkwardly. I wanted to kiss her. I really did. Just not there.

Ugh? I lean forward. Do I want to be with her or just friends?

Next time, Eu. I breathe. They'll be a next time and then you'll take her lips in yours. Taste them.

I smile nervously, laughing.

I mean, I like that, but it's getting harder and harder to see her as someone other than a friend.

Maybe I'd rather be with Veronica—that dark haired girl I met at the fair. I don't really want to hurt Veiria's feelings ...

Don't worry. It'll be spectacular.

Maybe I'm just a coward and don't want to be wrapped up in this Goddess stuff when I have my grandparents to take care of.

Look, I told Veiria I don't believe she's a Goddess and that's true, but I still have so much to take care of without her ... Is it worth it to act on my feelings when I still have so much on my plate?

And sometimes, I have these weird feelings I've pushed to the back of my head for years ...

Feelings that don't make sense, that I've never been able to sort out or reason with.

Maybe that's holding me back too? I can't make sense of them.

Traditions & Nerves

Veiria

"Com'on, Veiria. We're friends, right?" He looks at me with overwhelmingly cute concern. "Tell me what's up."

I hunch over, staring at his shoes—he's standing in Bell and Diel's doorway, leaning against the doorframe in a way that makes him look extra hot. "I don't want to remember. Please, Eu. I want to keep this one thing to myself, but last night was more magical than I ever thought it could be. It meant the world to me. Thank you for all of it," I say softly.

"Of course, Veiria. You just seem so glum and I'm sorry I didn't really stick around for you last night. I was in my own world, having my own issues. I want to make you happy." He taps his forehead and grins. "I have pancakes."

A corner of my mouth lifts. "You're sweet, Eu. I'll dump syrup on yours in retribution for making me cry."

"Well, I am deeply and thoroughly sorry and troubled for whatever I did. I apologize." He crosses his heart. "I swear."

"It's not your fault." I sigh. "You're a pushover." I stick out my tongue and Eu-Eu laughs merrily—it's a warm laugh, and the sound of it lights up my heart and makes my body relax again. "Give me some," I demand with an arched eyebrow. I hope I look extremely, positively serious. "Or beg for your life." I cover my mouth and shake my head.

"As you command," he says. "But you need to come to my place."

"What?" I jump a little, shocked. My hairs are suddenly on end at the thought. I gulp. Going to a boy's house? But not just any boy ... my one and only, handsome and immensely charming crush, his scrawny tanned body sitting expectantly and his annoyingly cute curls dangling into his eyes ...

Girl, stop looking at his eyes for the millionth time! I know they're the most beautiful shade of cinnamon ... but maybe look at his cute, kissable lips.

God, I want to palm my face. Does he know that we could do lots of things at his house ... in his room ... when his parents aren't looking or are gone, or if he asks me to spend the night. Like kissing passionately, or other things that are far more risqué that couples do in beds?

I groan and stare up are the sky, trying not to scream.

Eu asked me to see his parents! Eu asked me to see his parents! I caterwaul in my head.

But only as a friend. I sigh and look frankly back at him, keeping my expression and my voice as neutral and not squealy as possible. "Sure, Eu. I'm delighted." Hopefully that didn't stray into sounding like sarcasm, because I swear, I'd kill myself if it did.

Time to eat some pancakes! Yippee!

And see Eu's family ...

Keep it together, Veiria. Please. For his sake.

Eu leads me out, keeping a friendly distance.

We move across town—people wafting through the spread-out market, the grasses on the sky island rippling in a small breeze.

Yelyaa sits in the sky straight out from us at eye-level and I frown out at it once more, shaking my head to listen to Eu's charming dialogue. It had sizzled out of the water above this morning, forming a brilliantly warm yellow ball.

Eu points to a charming little house in a field surrounded by the most gorgeous golden flowers and white-picketed fences around the back with herds of fluffy, winged creatures, wriggling around like caterpillars, but looking like legless sheep with dragonfly wings and serpentine tails. Are those the Mislerime creatures Eu mentioned herding earlier? "That's it! Home sweet home!"

"The one and only home of Eu," I giggle.

"That it is."

From a distance, it almost looks like a little mushroom.

As I get closer, it looks a little less like a mushroom, but I can't get that image out of my head.

Maybe his family are little mushroom people, and I'd join them as another mushroom person under Eu's roof.

"Watch'ya thinking about, Veiria?" Eu looks back at me inquisitively.

"Mushroom people," I mumble, my forehead still wrinkled from the odd trajectory of my brain.

"Ah-ha," Eu nods.

Eu passes a fence and opens it for me, motioning very gentlemanly and I hop through the door, giggling and spinning back towards him in full ecstasy. "Why thank you, Eu!"

"Pleasure." He grins, but I swear he's red as a tasty tomato.

I stick my tongue out and pretend to lick him, making an 'eh' noise.

Eu crinkles his forehead, perplexed. "You look like you're choking on a furball."

I snort in laughter, shaking my head. "No, it's not that! Anyway—" I turn to hide my embarrassment. "Where were we?"

"Oh, yes. My home!" Eu waves his arm in an extravagant, sweeping motion. "A little unsightly to behold, if I do say so myself." Eu pinches the bridge of his nose. "But I do adore them. You're in for a real treat. It's not often I bring friends."

Friends. I swear, I'd pout if I weren't so nervous to meet them. Does the great Eu-Eu think so lowly of me? He's boyfriend goals, after all. I wonder if he has abs. I mean, I know he's scrawny, but he's active too ...

I shake my head, giggling silently under my hands. *Calm down, Veiria.*

Eu guides me to the door, hands stuffed deep in his pockets, before he reaches up and bangs a metal ring against the door. "Better not just walk in with you in my arms." He smiles. "We want to treat you the good way."

I feel myself blush scarlet at that. Actually, he had better do that ...

I hear scuffling a minute later and a woman with darker skin than Eu's and long, frizzy hair opens the door. She looks at me curiously for a moment, then adopts a motherly smile. "Eu, I see you brought a friend."

I look down and feel my cheeks growing warm. "Veiria, ma'am. You have a very nice son."

She chuckles and it lights up the air. "Yes, I'm his momma. Come in, come in." She motions us in with her hands. "Eu seemed a bit perplexed this morning. Mumbled something about 'apology' and 'guest.'"

I glance at Eu, who's looking in the other direction.

"I believed I was a *little* more forthright." He holds his pointer finger and thumb slightly apart. "Just a little?"

I look back to Eu's mother—Eu mentioned her name was Marjory.

"Well, I don't mind, Veiria. I've worked out the situation enough."

"I promised her pancakes." Eu cracks a grin.

Eu's mom just smiles at me, her eyes seeming to gleam. "And did you say yes?"

I nod repeatedly. "I like whatever it is Eu does. So, yes, I do love pancakes." *But I hope he didn't expect you to make them for me*, I'm about to say.

Before either of us can say much more, a little girl pads into the hallway. She has the same shade of tan skin and cinnamon eyes as Eu and the dark frizz of Eu's mom's hair, that's just a bit bouncier and slightly tighter than Eu's.

"Are you Eu's girlfriend?" the little girl asks innocently.

Eu laughs her off, kneeling and hoisting her up in his arms. "No, Lizzie. This is Veiria, my good friend. Veiria. Lizzie. Lizzie. Veiria." Eu introduces us, motioning with his eyes. "My little sister, the reading prodigy."

Lizzie tucks into the crook of Eu's shoulder and eyes me like I'm something incredibly interested.

I curtsy. "Hi Lizzie."

She gives me a shy smile, hiding in Eu's shoulder a little.

Eu ruffles her hair, bouncing her gently in his arms as he glances at her affectionately. "She's a timid one sometimes."

She clings to Eu, and I want to 'awe.' "Let's go get pancakes." Eu cradles her, still rocking her a little, before 'booping' her on the nose. "I know you like them, Lizzie," he teases.

Lizzie giggles, muted through his shoulder.

Mrs. Ledora—this I'll call her for the sake of politeness—moves into the kitchen, flipping some pancakes on a burner as Eu, Lizzie, and I enter the dining room where Eu's mother had started laying everything out.

"Dine on our exquisite course of pancakes and maple syrup." Eu motions to the table.

"This feels like Wonderland," I say, grinning madly as I see teacups, clutter, and stoppered bottles and tiny labeled jars—that my brain makes out 'drink' from. "Where's the tea, Eu?"

"Alas, there is none."

I punch his shoulder. "You were supposed to get me everything, Eu. I'm disappointed." I pout.

"Sorry, my princess."

Then I blink and Eu's in a tattered top hat with cards poking out at odd angles, dangling a teacup in one hand and a kettle in the other, huge mushrooms appear in the room—red-capped with white spots dotting them sporadically. Eu spins. "Perhaps I was joking. Some tea, miss?"

He pours the kettle into the cup from up high in a stream of hot liquid and in my hallucination, I clap rapidly like a schoolgirl and drown the cup in one gulp, smashing it to the floor. "Why thank you, Hatter!"

Eu twirls his hat before him. "Tea time, tea time, Veiria likes tea time."

Then a mist surrounds him and I'm sitting at a disappointingly ordinary table with Eu beside me. I eye a bottle with a stopper on the table, wondering if it'll make me shrink so I can climb into Eu's pocket ... or his shorts ...

I cover my mouth and glance at him.

Eu's voice comes to me, and the mushrooms reappear—I'm sitting on them, the room misty. "I see you've fallen into Wonderland, my friend."

Then the mushroom topples and I'm falling down a hole, Eu catching me and bounding with a mischievous expression, pressing his hat onto my head and yanking it tightly over my eyes.

"But don't despair! For in Wonderland, all will come true! You'll find a love more precious than that of the true love you seek, a friend will sail off from your dreams with you, two lovers will walk hand-and-hand beyond death's door, you'll even take a piece of your choosing to heaven and save your heart from certain doom."

I lift the brim of the hat and see the eerie grin of teeth in the shape of a half-moon.

"My little Alice, your time is ticking to a halt in your Wonderland. You've fallen too far into madness," the teeth say playfully.

"Whatever do you mean?" I ask quizzically.

"No bother. Not to be bothered."

The moon seals its lips with a zipper and an 'out-of-order' sign drops down.

I hear a giggle and turn around. "Eu, this isn't funny." My brain starts to go fuzzy as I run through a field of mushrooms, bouncing off one onto my behind as I run into it. Then I giggle and take a piece.

"You're greedy, Veiria." The voice is quieter. "You've taken too much."

My eyes go wide, and I fall through the floor, yelping in surprise, and into a chair around Eu's family's dining table, the teacups clattering at my downfall, but no one seeming to notice.

I frown and gaze into my teacup to see a blurry red color and the wrong-colored eyes staring back at me. I frown, perplexed, and drown the cup, leaning back only to realize Eu's family's staring at me like I'm crazy and I hurriedly sit up, rearranging myself and dusting at my lap.

Eu looks like he's silently laughing, and I squint at him, wondering if he's pranking me.

I decide he's not and try to act ordinary again. What was that? It seems so familiar.

I jolt up in my chair, like a light had gone off in my head. *I remember!* It suddenly dawns on me. *Alice and Wonderland! It's a children's fairytale, isn't it?*

I sit there smugly, with a group of people who have no clue as to my insanity and finally huff at the fact that I have no one to share my dream with, pulling myself back to reality and to Eu's family. I guess this is better anyways.

Well ... when I say family ... um, one of his brothers entered to witness my spectacular downfall.

I pull on a nervous smile, wishing I could shrink down into my dress. "Hi there, sir."

He looks at Eu. "Hey, little bro. You never call me that!"

This time Eu makes a face at his cup. "Why I would call anyone 'sir' is beyond anyone's guess."

I think about throwing a teacup at Eu. His brother is *extremely* handsome. Enough to make me silently swoon in my seat. He's decently taller than Eu—also thin, but in a less scrawny, less unique way—aka, more defined, muscled, and 'manly,' whereas Eu is cutely *boyish*. His hair is cropped shorter than Eu's and he wears a crisp suit. A woman walks in shortly after and he holds her waist—his wife, I assume. His highschool sweetheart. I look at them dreamily, my chin resting forward against my palm. They're a beautiful couple.

She has powdery white skin with a beautiful white, airy dress and she shines next to him. They both radiate a mature beauty.

He smiles at me. "Thanks—"

"Veiria," Eu mumbles.

"Thanks, Veiria. You seem a lovely, polite lady. My brother has some maturing to do."

Eu takes a long sip and puts up a finger. "That I do!"

The woman smiles at me. "This is Thorson. I'm Miriam."

"Miriam. You two are lovely," I say with a blush at them both, eyeing them back-and-forth. I couldn't imagine

I'd be in a room with two gorgeous humans. I find my palm drifting to my cheek as I appreciate their beauty.

She presses a hand to his chest. "I *love* hearing that."

He guides her to the table, and they sit across from us. Eu looks at me. "I poured us both peppermint tea."

I eye the glass. "That's an interesting flavor."

"Eu has a very unruly taste ..." Thorson comments. "Margory rolled with it eventually."

"I'm a true prince," Eu mumbles again. "More people like Veiria ought to share it."

"I love my prince of mushroom hill," I giggle as Marjory comes in and pours me more tea, then flips a pancake onto my plate, pink apron caked with dough. I wish I were *his princess*.

It's still bothering me that I can't figure out where the story 'Alice in Wonderland' came from. I obviously remember it fondly enough for it to reappear in my brain with no context.

"Oh, you didn't have to ..." I look down. She's too kind for treating me to so much. As she looks away, I call furtively, turning a little too much. "You should join us, Marjory. I want to know more about Eu's mother."

"Well, well, Veiria. If you insist." She pulls up a chair to my right, Eu on my left.

Suddenly I feel so small at Eu's table. My heart is a flighty mess.

I look over at Eu braiding his sister's hair and smile. Okay, maybe it isn't too stressful. Eu and his sister are too cute.

"So, Eu?" I ask nervously, suddenly too nervous about her to ask about her directly.

She smiles affectionately. "He was the cutest little boy, if you were wondering."

I look back at him. "I bet."

She smiles, kind laugh lines appearing under her eyes. "Want to see him when he was young?"

I cock my head and nearly squeal. "Yes!" My legs flail under the table. "But how?" I pause, thinking that I'd never seen a photograph here.

She smiles and opens her palm. "I have a small gift called 'Record.' It only captures the most precious moments in my life with my loved ones." A cloud of blue mist seeps from her fingers and forms a hazy image in the air around her hand of an adorable little boy running through a field with a stick, trying to tame and ride the Mislerime.

I stare at it in wonder, then back at her. "You're a witch!" I say in awe.

She chuckles. "I wouldn't call myself that."

"He's precious." I grin.

Marjory closes her palm as the boy looks up and runs in slow-motion towards the foreground with his arms outstretched. "He always had a knack for living things and for living in the moment. He captured everyone's hearts who met him."

"I bet," I mumble, glancing back at Eu playing with his sister. "Thank you for showing me."

"Thank you for coming. And may you guide him, Veiria of the Skies."

I whip my head back to her, eyes wide.

She crinkles her lips. "Those with magic recognize a true Goddess when they see her. Be kind to him and guide him. I want my child to grow up happy."

I gulp, not knowing what to say. Instead, I dip my head. "Thank you, ma'am."

"Thank you, Veiria. You're as modest as I'd hoped you'd be—down to Airenant. You have a gentle beauty for a woman your age."

I smile weakly, but before I can be any more awkward, she smiles like a mother and moves on with small talk like I'm just any other normal girl visiting her son, which makes me feel so much better, until I almost forget about it, and she talks about her hobbies of baking and knitting and her craft as a seamstress and artisan, to which I listen, intrigued, intermittently she sprinkles in stories of family—of Eu, but also of her two older sons, daughter, and her husband and I can see loving pride that I see in her eyes as I think dreamily of what being a mother and a seamstress would be like. She's a poised mother, but also a skilled craftswoman, which I respect.

Before I know it, I'm waving Eu's family off as they stand in the doorway, Eu gently prying Lizzie off his shoulder and handing her off to his mother.

"So, whad'ya think?" Eu asks, hands in his pockets as he walks me home.

I smile weakly. "You have a lovely family."

"I think so." Eu smiles affectionately. "Though they still treat me like a little boy."

"I mean, you *are* cute." I shrug casually, before glancing sidelong at the handsome planes of his brown face, his decently broad shoulders, and his slightly taller frame than me. "But you do look very manly too."

Eu rubs the back of his neck, blushing. "Is that so?"

I bite my lip, looking down. "I think so," I murmur quietly and watch sidelong as he hides a self-conscious grin.

For the rest of the way we walk in mostly silence, before he drops me off, waving goodbye with his curls hiding his eyes cutely.

"Goodbye, Eu," I whisper as I watch his back and can't help but grinning a little, standing on my tiptoes and letting out a silent, giddy shriek through my hands. *What am I to you, my lovely, sweet Eu-Eu?*

A Thousand Years in Your Eyes

Veiria

I stay in my room restlessly for the early part of the next day, waiting for Eu. More and more I feel a little useless in Bell and Diel's home—not that I didn't already.

I tell myself it's fine that Eu hasn't shown up at all, but I find myself gazing out the window long past sunrise, like Juliette waiting for her Romeo, sighing when I realize he probably won't be coming today. It's not like anything *really* happened between us at the dance. He said as much.

Bell brings me some food that morning and I finally bring myself to turn away from the window with a sad sort of smile, still yearning for Eu like a love-sick schoolgirl who had her heart broken. "You should go out, Veiria. Make some new friends."

I smile at her. I know I should. I should do something, because Eu isn't everything, far from it. I know that, but I have a hard time convincing myself to want anything else.

What do I do though? I don't have a basis for who I was, but I can't live here forever. All I know is that Eu has given me one thing I'm missing out of the puzzle of my last life—and maybe I've clung to that one aspect a little much.

With a sigh, I head into town, pulling on a cute polka-dot blue-and-white skirt and flowery pink blouse. I stop at a bookshop for a moment, a wooden structure nestled in morning sunlight, with books on little mushroom shelves. It's adorable, like a little tree stump out of a fairytale. I can just imagine a horde of friendly mice inside ready to fix up a dress for a bedraggled princess-to-be. But of course, I frown. She's always tossed aside like she's nothing. I wonder why stories always have to start from such a hopeless place. My heart ached for those princesses who had nothing—but they were still strong and kind.

I'm ... not a princess-to-be like them. I can't be. My shoulders sink—my li'l monster friend from the other day would understand. I wish a little bit that I'd kept it—though I doubt it'd want to be trapped and I don't blame it ...

With the thought of mice and princesses in mind, I search the shelves, my fingers skimming several old-fashioned bindings and dusting off a few cobwebs, until I come to the poetry section. I don't know why I have a thing for poetry. Maybe it's because people poured their hearts and souls into it, seeking some sort of understanding from their loneliness.

Mary Onest, my eyes catch on the name on an emerald green spine. I immediately recognize it from the poetry I read the other day. I scan the author section; *Mary Onest, a famous poet from Denelsi.* A spark seems to light in my head at Denelsi, but nothing else. I read through a few poems out of curiosity, but in the end, I close it, disappointed, or maybe relieved that it didn't get me any leads on my past or why I'm here.

I stand, the chair in the corner creaking in the slightly unkempt place. I wonder how these books all haven't rotted. There's mildew and lichen in here, which is odd. At least there's a nice earthy smell mixed with that of fresh parchment. I don't know why it's fresh, but I always liked that smell—of new books that is.

I walk out with nothing in hand for today. Bell and Diel's small collection will suffice for now.

I walk by several stalls, the grass billowing in the wind and a few tufts of dandelion drifting in the air. The cliff just off in the distance into the fresh open air, while an array of unfamiliar colorful birds circle in the distance and squawk at prey in the rocks and roots drifting above.

Then I turn away, an odd structure catching my eye at the end of a gap in the stalls, the sunlight glints off its smooth surface. I halt abruptly.

There's a strange building of glass, shining glossily like a mirror, standing much taller than the colorful tents and stalls around it and pointing far off into the sky. Was that here a minute ago?

I curl my hand reflexively as if to find comfort, feeling my chest unfurling wildly as I can't find Neihdria in my grip. I jerk my head down and of course it's not there, and so, I hold my hands over my heart, forcing myself to take breaths and calm down.

That thing shouldn't be here.

It's a ... it's a ... *skyscraper*? Is that the right word?

I approach it guardedly and suddenly my heart lightens and skips a beat, for across the glass are the most beautiful wedding dresses.

I stop a few inches from the glass, my eyes trained on the window and a tender smile on my lips.

My eyes catch on one in particular. Gorgeous and slender with a few pure white feathers on the shoulder, the other one bare, and white roses on the hip. The dress has a long white train, a beautiful heart-shaped neck, and the most gorgeous, starry veil ...

I stand there for long minutes, imagining what it would be like to stand at the end of the aisle, my eyes behind the veil, my heart beating like it has a thousand years ahead of it that I've been waiting for, as I stand there waiting for Eu ...

Waiting to see him at the end of the aisle and stare at me like I'm the only woman in the room. The only one that matters. Like I'm his and I've always been, and he'll marry me as the girl in front of him who wanted this moment, but never spoke about it, because she couldn't. Her lips were sealed, and her heart was behind bars like a caged white bird, until Eu set her free, only for her to come back and bed with him.

But she can't remember why she couldn't have that dream. Why she wasn't privy to all the things little girls were told they could have. All the things little girls were told they should want. *Isn't that unfair?* That girl was locked behind a cage, watching this dream play out like a movie she couldn't star in, because she was never offered the role ...

I stand there, gazing at that one dress for a while, until everything disappears except the wedding dress, a brilliant spotlight shining down upon it like it's a shooting star come to earth.

I imagine my wedding—at a sunset beach in my dreams, as I walk barefoot in the sand with my lover. I'd have bridesmaids that I met in high school. We'd have been inseparable, like true sisters, with all the experiences and struggles of womanhood and girlhood tying us together— my chest tightens and my throat bobs. I would have people there that wanted that for me. I'd plan it with my mom and my friends. The chairs would be arranged on the beach, there'd be an adorable flower girl walking a dream, musicians playing the most gorgeous, sweeping love song on lush violins, and at the end, before the sunset like a painting would be an alter under a wedding arch encircled in ivy and roses, like a gateway to heaven set in the golden reflection of the water with a man I can't discern quoting verses I can't make out. We'd give our vows, offering our hands and slipping on rings, then I'd be Eu's forever. I'd devote everything to him happily. I'd give him my life, my heart, and my soul.

I blink and the spotlight is gone, my fingers pressed gently against the glass, my breathing shallow. I can't remember what I was thinking, but the dress is truly breathtaking. I can't take my eyes off it, but I can't get myself to go in either.

Suddenly, I blink, and in an instant, the glass building shatters into stardust, scattering and swirling in the wind like magic. My heart pleads for it to come back, before the building and the dress and the dream of a beach at sunset fade from my mind so achingly quickly. I'm left standing with an empty heart and limbs that won't move in a field of nothing, apart from a gouge in the land before me, once-gorgeous white roses wilting in an oppressive heat.

Silver Melodies

Veiria

"Bell?"

"Yes, dear?"

"Who's Melody?"

Bell pauses for a minute in the doorway, dressed in her morning slippers and bathrobe. She sighs, and for a brief moment she looks so tired and worn in the morning light. Vulnerable.

"I'm sorry." I smile nervously. "I just saw the name on the flute case."

Bell walks over and sits next to me, talking gently. "She lived here a long time ago. She was my daughter ..." Bell looks off distantly.

"Was?" I swallow. I shouldn't ask, because I think I know the answer. But still, I'm curious. I feel desperate to connect with such a kind woman.

"She died." Bell smiles tightly. "She didn't live long enough. She was still a teenager when she got sick. There was nothing we could do."

I look away from her, scrunching my hands together in my lap. "I'm so sorry."

"Don't be. It's been good having you here. You remind me of her a little. You have a bright, gentle spirit."

"Do I really?"

"Yes," she says simply and soft.

I glance back at her. "Did she like the flute? I, um ..." I nervously play with my seafoam blue skirt. "I think it's a beautiful instrument."

Bell smiles and pats my hand, getting up. "Yes, it is, dear."

"Where are you going?" I wrinkle my forehead.

She laughs lightly, walking a few feet to the case. "Showing you something, dear." Bell grabs the flute case off the nightstand and sits back down. "Yes, her name was Melody and she loved the flute and to read and write. We still have her journal." Her lips quirk up sentimentally. "The bunny's name is Erin. You're sleeping in her old bed."

My stomach sinks a little. "You really don't mind?"

"Nonsense, dear. Here." She places the cool metal of the flute into my hand and I admire it longingly. It's such a pretty instrument and I wish I knew how to play. "Try it out."

I shake my head, smiling tightly. "I can't."

"Why not?" She smiles invitingly.

I shrug uncomfortably.

"Nothing says you have to, but the look on your face tells me it's something you want."

I rotate it lightly in my fingers, staring at it and smile. "My favorite composer wrote beautiful music for flute. I'd like to deserve to be able to play for her someday."

"What makes you think you don't deserve it now?"

I glance up at her, wanting to say that I'm not good enough or that I have no reason to live for that. Instead, I take her advice and place the metal to my lips, my fingers clumsily positioning over the holes. When I blow, a sweet, but awkward sound escapes the metallic instrument.

Bell clucks lightly and I blush. "See. A beautiful star."

I bring the flute down, my heart sinking. "I'm not. Music helped me a lot. It meant a lot to me. But what reason do I have to play?" I can feel the melodies, but they would sound just as sad as me if I played them.

"What reason do you need? Play for yourself. Play because it makes you happy. Learn because it gives you a reason to live and to smile."

I hold it to my chest, feeling a warm smile coming to my face. "I'd like that ..." Well, only if things were right ... different like *this*. *Always* like this. My smile drops in an instant and the sky outside darkens. What good is playing for yourself if there's something severely wrong with you? Music usually makes me feel safe, but not when I have this strong feeling the rest of my life was awful. I'm too sad to play now. To do so feels like I would be living a lie.

Suddenly, I feel way too lonely. "Thanks, Bell. Could I have a moment?"

"Sure." Bell gets off the bed, looking back with one last smile. "Veiria. It's good to see you smile. It's been years since I had someone to care for like my daughter. Your parents, wherever they are ... I hope they appreciate how beautiful a young woman you are."

My mouth goes dry and as soon as she closes the door, I start crying into my hands, setting the flute back in its case bitterly when I'm done.

My parents wouldn't recognize me. I know it in my gut.

At least, not like Bell does.

She sees me and I hate that. I don't deserve that.

Golden Hearted

Veiria

Eu knocks on the door the next day and I run to it on bare feet as I finish up breakfast with Bell and Diel, who look at me like they know what's up.

I stop in my tracks, glancing back at them. "Sorry!" I dip my head.

"Go off, Veiria. We understand." Bell smiles.

I nod several times and run the remaining distance to the door.

I put my hands around the doorknob and throw it open. Dear non-Goddess, did I miss him.

He stands there, hands held in the pockets of his leefy green shorts, looking dorky as he slouches there with his messy curls dangling over his eyes.

"Hey, Veiria." He looks up and I breathe in as his eyes lift away from his curls gorgeously. "I hope you didn't miss me yesterday. I was busy." He grins sheepishly.

I feel a nervous laugh in my throat. I've been constantly worrying about whether he had a change of heart at the ball and decided to leave me—that I was too much. It doesn't matter that he took me to see his family. I don't know what to think.

Maybe I didn't mean that much to him, and I was just a little distraction. He does seem to be cheery with everyone after all.

So yeah ... Maybe I did miss him just a tad, but I find I can't be mad. A sly grin creeps across my lips. "It's a pleasure to see you again."

"Aw, mark me glad. So ..." he muses, with a snap of his fingers. "Where are we off to today?"

"Someplace new and exciting." Anywhere really.

Eu looks comically perplexed. "I guess I'm going to have to make someplace up."

I sag my shoulders.

He frowns. "Is something wrong?"

"Take me anywhere, Eu ... I don't care." I smile, though not very convincingly. I'm increasingly aware of how sad a girl I am here. Maybe after a few more days, I'll pluck up some resolve to sort out my plight and the star ...

I grab the pendant that reminds me of it protectively, furrowing my lip.

But I don't really want to. I want Eu to keep distracting me.

"Actually, Eu." My eyes light up a little in curiosity. "I want to heard the Mislerime with you."

He looks startled for a moment, an arm scratching behind his neck and his brow furrows. "Well, okay then ..." Then he grins toothily. "If you insist, though it isn't the most pleasant experience for newcomers."

I stand in the field, giggling as a Mislerime wraps its forked tongue around my wrist, looking up from its buggish eyes to see Eu petting one and looking back at me, a herding stick in his arms.

He walks over to us, looking incredibly happy and my heart stops as the wind ruffles his hair in the sunset. "You like them?" He kneels, getting down and ruffling the fleece around the Mislerime's neck, snorting affectionately as it sticks its forked tongue in his eye and wiping it.

"I love them," I say dreamily, tentatively kneeling beside him and scratching the Mislerime's ear. It hisses, ruffling its dragonfly wings as I do.

"Her name's Nella. She's 9," Eu says, coddling her neck in his arms.

"Cute," I say, entranced.

He curls up in the grass next to Nella and looks up with a peaceful expression. "The one thing I can do is get a sense of their emotions."

"Magic?" I ask tentatively.

He shakes his head. "Not at all. It's just normal, Veiria."

"Oh, okay ..." I almost ask for him to follow up, but as much as he's a friend, I feel like I'll sound stupid to ask my crush that.

He sits there for a moment and starts humming with his eyes closed as the Mislerime starts snoring.

He smiles toothily as it does, patting her flank and getting up, rubbing his back nervously. "I don't normally do that."

I lower my eyes to Nella. "It's a beautiful tune." Ethereal.

He starts walking, the fluffy masses scattered around us seeming so blissful. "It's a bit embarrassing the other day. I pretended not to hear, but there's just something about it here. Being off in the middle of these guys." He motioned, then he sweeps his hand. "At the edge of the sky. I mean, I still want to get out of here. I want to teach, but this isn't all that bad a life." He shrugs.

Eu walks through the field with me, gesturing calmly at them. "Herding can be a bit daunting at first." He turns around and whistles through his fingers. Another larger Mislerime stumbles over to us. "Silly little creatures. This one's name is Amber." He rubs her under the chin, looking up to me and smiling. Then he grabs my hand, bringing it over to her. "Try it. She's a nice girl."

"Eu!" I jump, startled. "She's cute, but ..." Amber looks at me with those big bug eyes and my heart melts as I stroke her flank. "Yeah, she is." I chuckle.

"Here." Eu gives me a stick. "Let's walk and I'll show you how to whistle. They're stubborn creatures, but once you know how to handle them, they're a piece of cake."

An Attack in the Dark

Veiria

Eu spends a while showing me the cruxes of herding. I admit, it's daunting and immensely tiring, but I can bear it with Eu.

Afterwards, I leave him, biting my lip.

If only there were something I could do for him. Subconsciously, I find my way to Marjory.

"I want to make something for Eu ..." I say as I stand in front of her awkwardly.

She smiles at me and accepts my request. I spend the next several hours with her learning how to knit.

Quietly, I promise to repay her for the favor.

I walk out several hours later, my hands clutched behind my back. I wince a little at the Knitted doll. I'm terrible at it of course, but I've been trying to find something to help Eu with ... or do *something*. Anything.

Since he diverted me from his herding to give me a romantic ride, the one thing I could think to do was make something for him.

So, I thought: A Mislerime doll.

He'll have to pardon my absolutely horrendous knitting. I haven't done something like this before ...

I know I'm useless at helping, so hopefully he sees something in this.

I approach him on the cliff, the stars out—him with his legs out over the cliff, singing a hymn of some kind.

I grip the doll, feeling a bit like an eavesdropping intruder.

But I force myself to speak softly, after spending an agonizingly long time half turned away from him, half listening.

"Hey, Eu ..."

He stiffens, turning around with a furrowed brow. "Veiria?"

"Is it okay that I'm here?" I grip the doll, my heart thundering. Maybe this was a bad idea.

"Sure." He turns his head more to face me as I walk closer, glancing up at Neihtyaa's silver glow, reflected where the heavens should be. "What's up? You should sit."

I sit a bit away from him. "Thanks." I tuck my hair behind my ears, feeling a blush. "For being so kind ... and for the other night."

"Huh," he sighs, leaning back on his hands. "I really don't get it at this point, but I mean, I'm here. We need to sort out your problems. I don't care about Goddesses or whatever ..."

I look down. I wonder if he's avoiding the conversation. "That's not what I meant."

"Sorry?" He turns to stare at me, ducking down to look me in the eye. "What's wrong, Veiria?"

I shake my head, feeling myself getting emotional again. "Forget about it."

"Veiria, come on," he encourages. "I don't bite."

My hands slacken and I tuck the doll away. "You'll laugh."

He puts a hand on my shoulders and turns me towards him and as much as I try to look away, I just can't. His eyes are gorgeous. He looks gorgeous illuminated in the moonlight. "No, I won't. We're cool, Veiria." He chuckles, giving me a thumbs up. "Cool as the Pockets of Altrisses."

"Thank you, Eu." I look down at his hand. "But another time ... You're gonna laugh. I'm ridiculous."

He rolls his eyes. "Well, I won't *make* you. But Veiria, you're definitely *not* ridiculous. Stop putting yourself down. Now that's *not* cool."

I smile just slightly as Eu gets up and stretches. "Hey, I know this cool place. Let's explore."

"Okay, Eu." I extend my hand, and he takes it gently, his hand lingering longer than I'd hoped. "Take me there."

He blushes, but pulls me up. "Sure thing."

I peek down over a sheer cliff, seeing a dimly-lit curving path descending along the cliff face below us with several abrupt switch backs.

I glance sidelong at him questioningly, quirking my eyebrow up. "That looks ... safe." I swallow.

"It really is. Great observation." He seems to notice my hesitation. "But are you alright with that?"

I nod. "I wanted you to show me something unique."

"Righty." Eu walks next to me and we descend, Eu gentlemanly walking closer to the cliff edge and periodically checking up on me. "Are you ...?"

"Yes," I say a bit shortly. "Sorry," I laugh nervously.

He steadies my back, and I suck in my breath. Before I know it, we're ducking into a cave with an odd, multicolored glow. I glance around, subconsciously rubbing my skin and feeling my body break out in goosebumps. The air is unnaturally, yet pleasantly thick. I realize why in a moment. A substance, almost like ice, replaces the air around us, acting in a way that seems like it's inconsistently freezing and unfreezing, while luminating in an almost pulsing flow of brilliant whites, lurid blues and purples, and startling reds. It's unnatural, it's eye catching ... and I don't know how I should feel about it. "What is this place?"

"I found it. I wanted to show you something interesting."

"Is it safe?"

"Wait a moment."

The colors mellow, grow softer, then start to flow up towards the cave's ceiling, before dazzling lights of white, violet, and gold descend from their retreat, miniature pinpricks of light, like stars.

"Our world is strange, isn't it?"

"Yes ..." I gaze up in a startled wonder, taking in the otherworldly room.

It all happens in a moment. I blink ... and Eu's not there ... The colors aren't there, and I'm thrown into that very same cave, but filled with an oppressive white. "Eu!" My vision blurs back to life and he's there again.

"Veiria!" Eu rushes to me, concerned. I'd almost collapsed again, but I'd placed my palm against the wall. The fluid air-like substance seems to stiffen around the entrance to the cave, as if blocking something.

My vision pulsates rapidly.

"Let's get you out of here." Eu moves to support me.

I'm stuck there for a moment. For some reason I almost feel safer here. But then I take a trance-like step forward.

Eu doesn't notice, taking it as consent and we move through the ever more restrictive fluid. A dim and ever growing red seems to flash beyond that fluid, and then we're through, no longer being held back.

My mind feels assaulted from a million needles and I constrict onto the ground. Eu attempts to help me, and I can barely see him being thrown back. My mind becomes jumbled and incoherent, and then I'm nowhere, back again ... without realizing anything, I black out.

Mirages of Memory

Veiria

There's a sound of a broken record scratching in the darkness.

I wake from my thoughts, impulsively hitting send on a text hovering on my screen for the past half-hour: *Can we talk?*

I wait a few more minutes before I press the name 'Eu' and then 'call.'

There's exactly four loud drones before he picks up and I hear his muffled breaths on the line.

"Veiria? It's late, what's up?"

"Oh. Hi, Eu. Nothing much." I lie on my stomach.

"Oh, well then?" I can almost see him scratch the back of his head. "You sound weird, you sick or something?"

"What? Oh, er ... Do I sound that bad?" I hold my breath tightly.

"No, no, you sound fine."

Fine. There's nothing wrong with that, right?
"Alright." I'm quiet for a moment.

"Hey, you know I just got done feeding my gerbil. He's the cutest." I hear him perk up in light conversation. "Billy's a fine guy. Took a few laps around the track. I think he's outpacing me."

I grin, trying not to laugh. "No, REALLY?" I exaggerate. "No one beats you." In more ways than one, wink, wink.

"Well, this little guy does."

I cup the phone to my ear, enthralled by his voice and the thought of getting a cute animal pic, though I wouldn't admit it so readily to *?**?-*, holding back my smile. "I want a pic."

I pull my phone back until I get a notification from *******.

It's a cute spotted gerbil. The accompanying text reads 'BILLY WANTS PISTACTIOS. FEED YOUR OVERLORD OR DIE.'

I'm so close to saying cute, but instead I text back: 'lol. Funny, *******.'

"He's a good boy." I say into the phone, barely holding back my amusement. He's an adorable gerbil ... and an adorable owner. I think I have a thing for animal lovers. **/%#?'s caring and funny.

"The goodest. Hold up, ?????? I was just at the gym lifting some weights after practice, sorry, I got chemistry homework I gotta do before bed, so I think I might hit the showers." Showering. Just showering, which he *won't* wear clothes doing.

"No, no it's fine." I feel hot in the face at the thought of him 1) at the gym, 2) showering, 3) sweaty, and 4) on his bed talking to me, also sweaty.

Oh, how I wish he could be on top of me on that bed. His breath heavy in my ear and his hips aching between my legs, inside me. Letting him love me. Or he'd take me in the shower, feeling me and kissing me and loving me and maybe I'd get on my knees for him and do something a bit extra, flipping my wet hair back vainly and tasting his love … Hehe. I think that's a bit too much thinking for tonight.

I cover my mouth, breathing heavily just beyond the phone speaker.

"What's wrong, ?*>?-/"

"It … it's nothing," I giggle, kicking my feet, only to wince a second later at the rough sound of my voice. "I hate this." Without realizing it, I voice the thought aloud.

"Hate what, ******?"

I hold a tight smile. "It's nothing. You'd never get it."

"Come on. You can tell me." I can hear the concern in his voice under his prodding.

I'm quiet for a few moments, running through everything I could say. "Do you ever just feel weird?"

"Weird? Like what?"

I prop myself up on my elbows, holding the phone closer. "Like, I don't know: There's something wrong with you, but you don't know what it is."

"I think everyone has their days."

"No … that's not it." I sigh. "Vincent. It's like … I don't know. You said my voice sounds weird."

I hear a pause. "I don't know why I said that."

"Right. You've never, I don't know ... wanted a lighter voice, felt weird in your clothes, wished to never go to the pool, I don't know, looked at the girls playing soccer and thought, 'I want to be them.' Like, I just feel so, so weird all the time. I wish I looked more ... felt more ... that I could ..." I start mumbling as I progress.

"I haven't the slightest clue, ******. I'm sorry about whatever's bugging you."

"Don't you hate your deep voice, or the shape of your jaw and every time someone calls you h****o**, or the fact you can't play with the girls, or that ..." *you can't wear a bra.* But I stop myself short of the last one realizing just how ridiculous it sounds.

He laughs nervously. "You'll get over them. Come on, I'll help you. They're just insecurities. My dad says every ### has them."

I feel a strange sadness in my chest. I whisper, "That's just what I mean."

"Exactly."

"No, I mean, I can't grow up a #!/."

"Huh? ******, that's just part of growing up. Listen, adulting is a responsibility."

What if I didn't live that long? I think. "Just forget about it. Please, Vincent."

I swear I hear irritation on his end. "Okay, *7***, but you can consult with me whenever, okay?"

I don't answer, instead rolling on my side and covering my forehead with my sleeve. I press the 'end call' button and sigh, staring at the ceiling for … probably an hour, before loud knocking comes at my door, and someone enters before I can say anything about privacy. I roll over, still in all my ugly, worn, mismatched school clothes. I hate how I s431-, and I wish I sw3lled prettier, like a flower. I'm pretending to be asleep, but I know it will be no good, as I hear a deep, commanding voice and I slip off into darkness.

The Ending of a Fairytale

Veiria

I wake to the flaming ball of fire above, heat waves blistering over the land of a new sky island.

Pushing myself up from my splayed position, I notice Eu next to me. A chill passes over me as I gaze from him to the unfamiliar sky above, no semblance of where we came from remaining. And clutched in my hands: the familiar, sharp weight of Neihdria.

"Eu." I crawl over to him and whisper, reaching my hand out to him gently, then draw it back. With my lips pursed, I look up at the sky and my heart sinks.

I don't recognize anything above us. Nothing looks like Eu's home.

And Eu …

I … this isn't right, but I'm glad he's here. Selfish as it is, I need him.

Instead of being near him, like I'd like to be, I sit a fair distance away, feeling awful about bringing him here. And self-consciously, as if to distract myself, I run my fingers lightly over my maroon pendant. It feels like it's throbbing in the presence of the flaming star. The star that I strangely feel immune to, even with the clear heat emanating from it.

I frown, starting to wonder if there's a way to help Eu in that very heat. I long to curl up next to him, to feel him next to me. But I know I don't deserve that.

I sigh, staring at my brooch and ticking the seconds by.

Eu wakes after what seems like forever. I hear him groan and scurry to my feet, kneeling next to him and gazing at him with concern.

"Veiria?" He blinks at me wearily.

"Eu!" I say, choking up.

He frowns and looks up at the sky. "Where are we?"

I swallow and look away, mumbling after a moment, "I'm so sorry, Eu. It's my fault."

"Veiria. What's wrong?" he asks with a voice suddenly strained.

"I don't know ..." I shake my head, my voice cracking with guilt. "I ... We fell and I don't know where we are. I'm sorry, Eu. We're lost and it's because of me."

I turn to Eu. He's staring at me, his voice wavering. "What do you mean?"

"I'll try to get us out. I'm sorry." My voice turns small.

Eu's silent for a moment and when he speaks again, his voice is quivering. "Okay. Let's ... let's move then."

I nod guiltily and follow next to him as he walks silently over the dry ground, just a few paces ahead.

Eu's been clammed up more than I've ever seen him. He won't talk to me even when I try. I feel useless.

I should tell him to go back home, but the problem is, I don't know where that is. And even if I did, I don't want him to leave. I need him here so I'm not completely alone—so I can go on.

Eventually, Eu seems to give out from hunger, or the heat and we make do in a cave for shelter. Eu gazes off at a small fire and grimaces, looking lost and small.

"Eu." I inch a little closer to him along the bare cave wall. "Is there anything I can do?" I pause. "For you? I just ..." I bite my lip. "I don't know how you're feeling ..." I don't particularly think I've been a good friend, either. All I've thought about is how much I want to spend the rest of my life with him. But he's hurting now. What can I even do about that?

Eu finally looks up at me, smiling painfully and his eyes moist. "I'd be with my sister, Lizzie right now ..." Eu swallows. "In the rocking chair by the fire. I'd be reading to her, and she'd be the happiest little angel alive." Eu's throat constricts a little. "She's the best sister, really." Eu makes a fist and looks at the fire longingly. "Mom and pop would be coming home from their work and maybe my brothers would visit and tease me. I'd sit at the table with Lizzie after a day herding the Mislerime. And later I'd help my grandparents remember just a little of life ... maybe I'd get a smile. You know mom and Lizzie. They ..." He swallows. "What are they going to think when I'm gone? Who's going to read to Lizzie and tell her how amazing she is?" Eu pulls his knees in, and my chest sinks as tears start to run down his cheeks and patter onto the dry sand in the following silence.

"Eu ... I'm so sorry." I move closer to him. I want to lean on him in the moment, but I hesitate. Maybe that's too selfish. What would he want? "Hey, Eu?"

"Hmm ..." He looks up, his throat constricting and his eyes red.

"Do you need a hug?" I ask tentatively. I feel a little awkward and I wonder if he'd even be open to something like that, but I ask anyway.

He sniffles, nodding and I scoot closer to him, and I circle my arms around him—platonically this time, trying to find some words of comfort to show him I'm a friend he can trust, not just a girl insanely attracted to him. "You can tell me anything, Eu. I promise I'll help you get back home." Maybe I can be a little more than the head-over-heels lovesick girl I am and be a better friend just this once?

Eu shudders and I pull back, leaning against his shoulder, not sure in what way I mean it, but I try to shut those feelings off for now. He lets me and I close my eyes.

"Thanks, Veiria."

I smile weakly. At least I'm not a total burden. "I'm sorry. I don't understand, Eu. But I'll get you back to them." I think of Lizzie's smiling face. She's a bright child and Eu's a perfect older brother. I sigh.

Eu's chest steadies a little and I close my eyes. Growing just a bit selfish, I ask, "Mind if I call you Eu-Eu? It's your nickname." I feel my cheeks on fire as I ask it.

Eu chuckles a little. "Sure, Veiria."

I smile that I got him to laugh, even as I look down at the space between us in embarrassment. In a sudden realization, I remember the knitted Mislerime doll I'd made with Marjory's help and reach into my pocket tentatively. "Hey, um … Eu … There's also something I wanted you to have." I slip the doll out of my pocket as I glance up at Eu's surprised face.

"What's that, Veiria?" Eu perks up in curiosity.

I slip it awkwardly into his hands. "I made it for you." I adjust my hair shyly. "I made it for a different occasion, but since we're here, I just thought it'd remind you of home." I shrug. "I know it's silly, I just … You've done so much for me. I wanted to do something in return."

Eu grins a little. "Thanks, Veiria. It's wonderful. And I appreciate it."

"You do?"

"Yeah," he says softly. "It's the best." Eu wipes his sleeves over his eyes and comes to his feet.

"Eu …"

Eu tries to hold his grin, but I know he's struggling. "I … I want to try to see where we are again …"

I nod. I lick my lips and glance up at him as a vision of a crystalline city in a dark cavern flashes before my eyes and I gasp, breathing heavily and clutching my pendant.

"Veiria! What is it?" Eu starts, getting to his knees in front of me. "What's wrong?" He looks full of panic and I stare at him heavily as he places his hands on my shoulders.

My eyes focus again and I whisper. "Jespaira. We're going to Jespaira, Eu."

Eu's eyes cloud over, and he looks away darkly. "Right." He grits his teeth and walks towards the cave's exit, sighing, "Jespaira it is then."

I find Eu looking lonely off into the distance.

He looks like he's been crying again, and I tentatively sit a few feet from him.

"Are you okay?" I say after a few minutes of silence of him not acknowledging me.

"Yeah." He stares forward, as if scanning the sky for something familiar, before his body untenses. "Not at all," he sighs with the slightest frustration. "Everything looks the same."

I don't respond to that, because what do I say? It does.

Then I look down at the sky around us. "I envy you, Eu." His life. His family. His bliss. I want to get it back for him.

Eu turns to me, searching my face. "What do you mean, Veiria? Do you remember something?"

"Not really." I tuck away the blurry, punctured memory. I don't remember enough to clearly communicate it. But I know I want to be part of Eu's beautiful world—to be with him in this place. I want to get him back to it. "It's not important. But Eu … I'm sure if we find a settlement, we can get some information on finding Anvi again. Then you can …" I twist my fingers close to my chest. I want to say 'you can leave me then,' but I find I can't. My mouth is too dry. "Then we can get you back home."

"I guess you're right, Veiria. But, you mentioned Jespaira?"

"Something came over me." I look distantly away. "I don't know why. But there's a presence there—someone or something. I'm sorry. I shouldn't have mentioned it."

I turn back to Eu, who's looking at me oddly. "I'll go with you. But let's be careful."

I nod. I wonder if he trusts me, but I know he's just being rightfully cautious.

Interlude III ~ Telvin

The attack comes out of nowhere.

Meren manages to dodge, largely unscathed.

I'm not fast enough … Before realizing it, I feel an unbearable impact on my body. I convulse on the ground, in pure agony. The silver dust bores holes through my body, ripping at my innards.

Meren stays frozen in shock for just a moment, staring wide-eyed at my wounds. "No," her shaking voice cracks in fury. She whips back, blasting the dust around her, lashing out to protect me.

I reach for her weakly, blood running from my mouth and pooling around my body. "Run," I mouth.

Abruptly, the dust retreats.

Meren stumbles towards me, holding her arm.

My eyes are watering. "Meren ..."

She falls to her knees beside me.

"You need to save Veiria," I say weakly.

She's crying too. "Telvin you idiot. Don't you know, I'm not leaving you. The three of us are getting out of this together."

"But what about Veiria?" I try frowning, but only wince from the pain lancing across my entire body.

"I'll choose to believe in you. She may have broken my trust, but if there's any chance ..." She chokes, shaking her head in bitterness, her eyes not leaving mine as she emphasizes: "I'm *not* leaving you. If you think there's still hope for her, then we haven't failed." Meren clasps my hand tightly. "Now breath. Stay with me. Please ..." She closes her eyes, blinking through her tears like she's sending out a prayer. I know Meren's grown disillusioned with Veiria and the other deities, so this strikes me as desperation for her—like an old, forgotten memory.

My consciousness rapidly fades as I try to keep the image of my sister clear in my head. Despite my pain, my lips waver in a nostalgic smile. "We'll all be together again. You'll see. I promise I won't leave you," I say as Meren chokes on her tears, placing her hand behind my head and hazily calling my name as my vision fades to black.

The Curtain of Mourning

Veiria

In my dream, there's a city black as shadow, yet filled with this ethereal light. It's not quite a gloomy place, but I wouldn't call it warm either.

I observe it from a distance in the musty, dank air of the place—a crystalline city of violet, crimson, and black stonework built high-and-low, encased in a stitch-work of interwoven rock in a gaping cavern. And across the land and set into the inky smoky, towering structures are glowing, scattered veins of crystal in brilliant, neon shades of pink, purple, red, and orange.

Jespaira—the name comes to me on instinct—the sacred home and domain of Mallorn, a gentle goddess of life. I swear that name should ring a bell. For a moment, there's a flash of memory through my mind of a woman with a gentle, kind face and umber skin tending a garden in the center of one of those stone structures. She's not an ordinary woman—there's an aura around her that commands respect and a calm admiration—one of a healer of a higher power.

She smiles. "Welcome to the domain of life, my fellow traveler."

The memory grows blurry, and I purse my lips.

My heart trembles.

Something from my past. That woman has a power like Noctine ... and like mine. I swallow.

She could kill me or Eu in an instant, but something makes me think she wouldn't ... Perhaps I know she wouldn't.

I won't see her on this trip. She has no interest in this form of mine.

The dream shifts and I'm winding my way through the dust and cool damp of Jespaira in the forever night, my breathing calm and collected.

As I descend the windy, rock-strewn path, I step into a veil of water, feeling a ripple of energy up my spine. Neihdria seems to solidify slightly, its weight becoming more perceptible. I cast my gaze up. Fleeting through a gap in the rock rests the moon and stars, though heavily concealed by the cave's dimness.

In the distance, I see the central spire of Jespaira illuminated in a soft glow. It's beautiful—glowing silvery-white veins etch and wind around it like roots. My eyes soften and I stop and take it in for a moment, before I feel a shiver in my spine. I adjust my grip on Neihdria, before ducking into the shadows, the dust dancing along the air around me.

I find myself outside the tower and cast my gaze up. There's something up there that makes me feel cold, makes me shiver—a presence I don't understand, but it's here in this city, like a sleeping horror. I don't know why, but there's something about this place. Something trapped and wrong.

Neihdria breaks into shards, settling my unease as it reforms into a thin stair that I ascend, eventually exiting onto a balcony of lavish black.

I stand there, bracing myself as a chill creeps from within and the curtains part before me like a whisper.

Within is a decadent room, candles and chandeliers burning with a blue flame, ornate vases and embroidered rugs, and to my left, a veiled bed.

My knuckles tighten.

I take a step forward towards the bed. On it is a young man.

He's not supposed to be here. I know it. I've been here before and this isn't his bed. This should be a bed for a sister or maiden of Mallorn.

This I know is wrong. An illusion.

I squint, a chill in my heart. *Who are you really?*

My vision flashes and I'm in a different room—it's smaller with a simpler bed, a dresser, and windows that look out on a different night sky—one from a different lifetime and a world away. Familiar somehow. My vision flickers between the two rooms, like different realities.

The boy on the bed has red curly hair and a pained, pale face. Something recoils in my stomach at the familiar sight, and I clutch my dress, my knuckles white and shaking as I walk around the bed to stand next to him, looking down at the deceptively peaceful face—a face that looks awfully like mine. I know deep down, this person is a tortured soul—a ghost of a person.

Neihdria flows in through the window, reforming in my outstretched palm and I hold it, poised, over the young man sleeping in the bed. The veils go, the rug goes, and I'm back in that much plainer room, like a distant memory that I want to make disappear.

My mind clears of everything except the hatred I feel for the puppet, the ghost before me—someone dead and lifeless, and I bring my blade down.

Neihdria shatters and I'm left screaming. There's no man there, just me, another me.

We're in a dark room, and she's screaming, clawing at the edges.

And I'm crying … not her. I bring up my wrist to wipe at my eyes. I'm crying and I don't know why.

All I know is there's a loud beating noise like a heart, thumping in time to the other Veiria's anguished screams.

I can only watch her because I can't seem to find my voice.

Then she collapses and starts sobbing, and I feel a jolt of pain as blood scorches the ceiling and sizzles at my feet.

I feel primal in my fear, but stationary, like I know all too well that the other Veiria is trapped.

The sludge of blood starts pouring into the room, slowly reaching my chest, crushing it.

"Hey, Veiria."

I wake up gasping.

Eu shakes me, frowning and drawing his hand back. "You alright?"

I sit up, rubbing my eyes and cringing a little. I glance away. "Yeah. It's nothing ..." I sigh.

Eu shrugs, sitting in a field of glowing orange flowers. "I guess it wasn't worth it."

I sit next to him, glancing next to me. "What wasn't worth it?" I raise my eyebrows defensively.

"Why am I even here?"

"Eu ... I ..." I breathe out quietly. "I don't know." I close my eyes. "Look, it was just a weird dream." I pull my knees in. "It's not ... something I want to remember. You should be worrying about you."

His lips twitch and he looks down. "I can't worry about it anymore."

"Eu, I'm sorry ..." I squeeze my eyes shut. "I don't know for sure what these visions are. I don't want to remember them. I know this may seem weird." I fiddle with my fingers. "But I like your family. They love you."

I glance up and see Eu purse his lips.

I continue. "In my dream ... just now, there was a monster. Well, not quite. I don't ... I don't know exactly. But he made me angry. I don't like that feeling ... And you were in another dream, after we fell. You were ... different. I didn't like it." I feel a familiar emptiness in me. "I was ..." I shake my head.

"Veiria ... what are you trying to say?"

"I don't know," I croak. "I felt numb in the dreams, especially the first." I pause and switch the conversation. "Marjory showed me your younger self with her magic. You were cute."

"Thanks." Eu rubs the back of his head. "I didn't want her to show you that, though." He chuckles.

"But I'm glad she did." I elbow him with a playful smile. Then I scrunch my brows. "Did you have friends?" I swallow. "I can't be the only one."

He shrugs again. "I get along with everyone. The town's a rave."

"Oh. Yeah." I nod uncertainly.

"But yeah. I had a childhood friend named Travis. He was nice and kind and a bit reckless." He laughs lightly. "We had a blast." Then his voice turns a little dour and he gazes off. "We'd play every few days. I showed him the Mislerime and the microscope my pop bought me. He'd show me his swing set and his toy sword. My best friends now are Jason and Veronica." He blushes a little on the name Veronica and I feel my gut roil.

"Did you like her?"

I think Eu won't answer, but strangely he does. "I guess, but it doesn't matter now."

I bite my lip and stuff down my jealousy.

"Travis moved away."

There's a long silence following that. "Oh. I'm sorry."

"Yeah." He nods and I hear the slightest strain in his voice. "We were close."

"Thanks for telling me about that, Eu. And ... I get that. I ... I've had friends leave too." But Eu, he's so jovial despite that. Surrounded by so much. "I ... Could I tell you something?"

"Sure, Veiria."

"I ... I don't have a lot of people to talk to, but you have everyone." I glance at him in need, feeling an increasing sense of unease about why he's stuck around ... whether we're really friends. "Why did you befriend me? Answer me honestly."

"I don't ..." He grasps his forehead. "I just like you. I felt like I *had* to."

"Had to, huh?"

"Something like that. But I think you need someone there for you. I don't take friends for granted anymore. And just because I had to, doesn't mean I didn't want to," he adds as if to reassure me.

I purse my lips, reaching down between the twining flower stems to grab Neihdria for comfort or reassurance.

Eu tilts his head at it. "Why do you have that thing?"

I wince. "I don't want to. It came to me. I hate things like this."

"Why so?"

I shrug. "Violence, I guess."

"Makes sense. You're not the confrontational sort." Eu's eyes light up teasingly.

But even as I try to smile back, I feel so troubled. So exposed and alone without the safety of Bell and Diel or Eu's home. "I'm scared, Eu. I thought I'd leave things like this behind here." I grip Neihdria tightly. "But I like holding it. Your friend would probably be a better fit. Tell him I said 'hi' if you see him."

Eu nods. "Will do."

"You like adventure, Eu. I don't." I want to be safe. I want to shrink. "You're the only reason I haven't given up here."

Eu grins. "I'll have to make you adventurous, then."

I poke Eu's handsome chest and laugh. "I'd like that, Eu-Eu. Very much."

"You should find more friends."

My smile drops a little, but I just put on a larger one. "You're all I need." Everyone else would think I'm disgusting and weird right now, I think, though I still can't figure out why I know that. The weird memory of Eu in the dream … the little that's making sense … he didn't talk to me this softly, he didn't look at me with this much need, he didn't want me like this Eu in front of me seems to …

That scares me, but I stuff it away.

A different feeling has been making me scared. Horrified.

That shadow.

The presence coming into the room makes me want to hide in a dark corner and never come out.

My heart pounds and I clutch it until I stuff the memory away and it vanishes like smoke.

He can't find me here, can he?

I glance up at Eu with a need.

Eu would protect me, wouldn't he?

From whatever these flashes are. He's so bright and merry and full of life and I love him for that. He's my sun and I like that he makes me forget those kernels of another world. Like a salve. Like something healing. He looks at me in a way no one else has.

In a way I think I wished he would have back then ...

Meeting of Past Lives

Veiria

"You know, Jespaira: I've never been here. It's rather … mmm, how should I put this?"

"Dark?"

"Musty is what I was looking for."

"But at least it's pretty."

"Just the stones. We get a lot at the market."

I look around, still holding his hand, mind you. My heart's still fluttering, of course.

We're on a dusty trail with a bunch of dimly glowing crystal.

As we pass through a narrow chasm of rock, squeezing a little too close for comfort, Eu plucks one and it snaps right off with a brittle sound.

"Right … brilliant, Eu. You've just broken down a whole rock."

"It's a special rock." He snaps it in half. "One for me, one for you."

I accept it graciously, eyeing it in the faint light. It matches his, like half a heart. "Why thank you, Eu-Eu." I pocket it to look at later.

It's honestly stuffy here with all the dust, but it's cold. I look up, barely making out the ceiling by the dim crystal between all the patches of darkness, light from the outside world occasionally shining through the crevices.

"I don't like this place, Eu."

He looks back at me with a frown and holds my hand tighter. "It's okay," he says as we climb over a ridge. "See, we're here." He points to a dull city interspersed through the rock. There's a market with canvas tents, spires, and what looks like homes set in the sides of cliffs and rock formations.

I recognize the glowing crystal and black stone from my dream. It's eerily beautiful.

"Home sweet home. Don't get me wrong, it's still dark as hell, but you can't deny it's a little bit charming."

"I guess you could say that." I creese my brow, wondering at what the word 'hell' means. It's an oddly familiar phrase.

"So, what's the deal?" He says as we get closer. "Where're we going?"

"I don't actually know."

He clutches his forehead dramatically. "The irony."

"Well, I'd like to know what I want too. We're equal players in this game."

The two of us leave the patchwork trails of glowing crystal and barren dirt and approach the city's entrance—a black stone arch with the words 'Jespaira—city of sacred life' along with flowers and trees engraved on its surface.

Eu takes my arm and pulls me close. "Stay by me, so I don't lose you," he whispers. I feel my chest skip a nervous beat at his closeness as we pass through a throng of people from all walks of life and skin tones from across this world—Jespaira seems to be a prosperous city of commerce and trade. I stick by Eu as we make our way, gazing at the black stone above and beside us, laced with violet and crimson crystal glowing faintly like veins, stretching up the cavern wall high to the ceiling and the drip of water from cracks far above, small cracks and the occasional fleeting sun the only light besides the glowing crystals that are the same color as the trees.

As we pass into the city, there's a lot of sharp noises, clanking, and echoes. I cover my ears reflexively.

"Quite the welcome."

I smile, finding reassurance in Eu. "Immensely."

Eu and I wind our way through the streets and while I hold his hand, I feel the slightest drop of shame.

He's here with me as a friend. And what am I doing?

I let go of a hardly audible sigh.

You're hopeless. Romance isn't what he needs right now. And I guess, I know I can change ...

Would have changed, had it not been for someone else ...

The two of us pass through the city and I occasionally make eye contact with a few women who I recognize as dignified followers of the Goddess, Mellorn—dark skinned women with ornate clothes and jewelry.

I purse my lips, somehow feeling very familiar and very disconnected from this place. Have I ever met the Goddess, Mallorn? It feels so strange that I would have, but I can't help thinking I've been here before. It's a nagging feeling that I just can't shake, as much as I try to dismiss it.

A stray image fleets through my brain of a courtyard of lush, glowing flowers, the walls of a dark, but surprisingly warm and familiar palace stretching up above us.

I'm kneeling in reverence, looking up to that woman, Mallorn, who smiles down at me and when I turn to my left, there's an oddly familiar face of a young woman I swear I've seen before standing expectantly off to the side and simply observing with an almost proud look. Much more comforting and familiar than even Mallorn's kind gestures.

Mallorn beckons to me and I glance back at that young woman—her face still indistinct and ever-shifting, like a distorted memory.

She smiles assuredly at me, rolling her eyes. "Go. It's perfectly fine."

I find strength in her smile and offer one back. I know I'd ask her to come too.

The vision falters and I shake my head to clear it, feeling utterly lost in this damp, surprisingly crowded city.

I try peering over the crowd of dusty faces of various shades, until I spot a glass making shop that catches my eye.

I point it out to Eu. "Look, Eu."

He squints in the direction of my finger. "Finally, a destination. You and your penchant for jewelry."

I clutch my maroon pendant reflexively, feeling a bit defensive. "I just like it. It feels like, I don't know, I didn't have it before, or wasn't allowed or something."

"Mysterious ... Was someone controlling what you could buy? That sounds a bit sad."

I shake my head. "I don't know, Eu. Not exactly, I don't know. I'm probably just imagining things."

"Don't do that to yourself, Veiria. You're not delusional. You're quite smart actually."

"Thanks Eu, but I sort of doubt it."

"Hey Veiria, don't bring yourself so low all the time, okay? Let's just go look. Sorry if you thought I was deriding your interests earlier."

I smile coyly. "It's okay, Eu, you can deride me any time."

He looks at me sidelong, raising his eyebrows confusedly.

I look away and feel heat in my cheeks at my embarrassing thoughts.

Hold it together, Veiria. Friendship and mystery time first, flirting last. Okay, mission friendship, go! I hold in my internal cringe and pick up my step to the jewelry store, weaving through the throngs of people and trying to remind myself of just a little while ago.

Just ... remember what you said when you hugged him and what you thought. It's not about you, so calm down until we figure something out. Eu's still in shock and neither of us even know why we're here.

Interlude IV ~ Meren

Telvin leans on me. He's weak and losing blood and I hate Veiria for it.

Goddess of this world be damned, I want to kill her. For what seems like the thousandth time, I'm close to tears.

Damn my emotions.

I grunt from exhaustion. Telvin may be light, small, and not the strongest person, but it's still a pain to walk with him half-alive. We're short on time, though, and we came to this stupid agreement.

It's not what I wanted, but if Telvin is truly right, the Veiria we both know can be saved. Saved from bringing about our end like the crazed Goddess I witnessed.

In the distance is Jespaira, twinkling in its crystalline caverns and crevasses.

Telvin moans lightly and I try to be lighter on him. "It's okay, Telvin, we're almost there."

He gasps in a breath. "I'm sorry I'm so weak."

"Don't do this now, Telvin. I thought you liked being fragile boy."

He laughs. "I do like being fragile boy."

"Twink," I mutter. "Do you need a rest?"

175

He looks up groggily. "I don't know, maybe. I think I can do it."

"Are you sure, Telvin? We need to succeed." *And I can't lose you*, I add quietly in my head.

He stares ahead, the wind starting to ripple past us in waves. "You should go on, Meren. You're much stronger than me. You know what you're doing."

"Don't give me that confidence! I AM NOT—I repeat: am not leaving you."

Telvin starts coughing.

"Oh for—was that for real?"

He nods between coughs.

"Okay, Telvin." I soothe my voice and when he's done coughing, we start limping toward Jespaira once more, the wind getting awfully violent. "But if things get too serious, I'm finding you a safe space ... from Veiria and from this damn storm."

He winces, saying, "I hope you don't have to."

"Fuck." I look to the skies—well, the dark impenetrable ceiling—and sigh. "I hope I don't have to either."

Veiria

We weave our way through the shop, and I suddenly get a prickle of familiarity that I can't pin down.

Frowning, I glance absently at the displays of beautiful glass carvings blown into otherworldly shapes.

But as we get further, that feeling doesn't subside.

Neihdria starts to rattle in my bag, and I look up. There's a young woman there and our eyes connect.

Her hair is dark, cascading down her back, her face a tanned mahogany brown, and her travel clothes are worn and dirty. Her face is sharp and full of harsh lines, but her eyes ... they're glossy and full of pain.

She stops, her eyes wide open.

Behind her, a boy limps in with his clothes caked in old blood and clearly labored in breathing. His face shows his anguish, but it's a kind face. His hair is a tattered black over his soft-looking, chestnut skin and he looks at me pleadingly.

The girl opens her mouth then. "Veiria?"

I look to Eu, who shrugs. "I've never seen them."

She's speechless for several more moments, and I stand there, unsure.

Then ... BANG!

Eu and I are thrown back against a glass display as my bag explodes and Neihdria's dust shards escape and coalesce into a wave form, shooting at the two.

The girl pushes the boy into a corner and dives away, skidding across the floor.

I shake my head. "Eu!" I scream, rushing over to him. His forehead's bleeding.

"What the hell is that?" He grits out in pain.

I turn around, trying to make sense of the situation.

The young woman snaps her fingers and there's a loud bang as a display shatters and Neihdria's shards backfire across the room.

The young woman pushes herself up, dashing across the room and snapping her fingers again as the glass shards of Neihdria snake towards her.

BOOM!

The closest shards scatter to dust and ricochet off a chandelier.

I see the young man clutching his side, looking at Meren helplessly. Miraculously, the shards seem to ignore him for now.

I swallow at the destruction as Meren jumps over a display and ducks as Neihdria pinces at the air above her.

She covers her ears and sets off another blast with her fingers that shatters the display behind her and sprints to us.

"Run!" She reaches us, motioning us to move.

"Who are you?" I say in confusion.

Pain flashes across her face and she grits her teeth, looking around. "Doesn't matter right now. Come on! Go! Go!"

I look at Eu and he nods.

We both get up as the girl spreads her arms wide, squeezing her eyes shut as her breathing gets labored.

A stream of glass shards slams into the space just in front of her and we're sent flying backward.

Disoriented, we get up and she pushes us to run.

"Telvin! Telvin!" She looks to the boy—Telvin. "Shit," she mutters. "We'll meet you there!" She calls across the room.

I see him nod meekly and we stumble-run forward, the glass sculptures fading into pinpricks of light and the room warping into a pitch-black void.

It looks like ... a miniature universe.

I grab Eu's hand reflexively, my heartbeat settling as we come to a walk and look around.

The girl turns around, panting.

She sits, leaning back her head and sighs.

"Who—"

She puts up her hand, breathing unsteadily for a minute, then looks at me with a strange amount of familiarity.

"I'm Meren. Trust me, Veiria, we've met," she says, seeming surprisingly collected after what just transpired.

I swallow. "When? I don't know who you are."

She looks from me to Eu, biting her lip. "Of course, you don't. Let's just say we're old friends."

"Old friends, my ass." Eu gets oddly defensive. "Look, you stay away from Veiria, okay?"

Meren raises her eyebrow at Eu but doesn't comment.

"Leave it alone, Eu," I say quietly, feeling oddly defensive of Meren.

"No, Veiria. We need to know who she is." Eu crosses his arms and stares her down.

I take a deep breath. "Eu. My sword attacked her. I owe her something." I don't know what Eu's doing, but we don't need this right now. I don't *need* defending from her. Something about her *does* seem familiar and not in a bad way.

"This isn't about owing anyone anything. Those two showed up looking for *you*." He motions to me, and I swear his voice cracks just a bit.

I turn to Meren, my resolve wavering as I try to genuinely take in Eu's apparent concern or anger or whatever he's feeling.

"I'd hoped Telvin would be here for this part," she goes back to muttering. "Can we just find him? I'm worried and his protection won't last forever. I'm not exactly doing too great here." She snaps her fingers to demonstrate, and nothing happens.

Eu stares at her incredulously. "You did something like that?"

"Yes, he's like my brother. The sooner we get back to him, the less likely we die."

"What?" I ask, turning to Eu in confusion.

He runs his hand through his hair. "It's complicated, Veiria. I don't know much about magic like this, but she just handed him part of her life force—her magic. If we don't get back, she dies."

She smiles tiredly. "I'm used to it." She looks at me. "You know the way out. You've heard the rumors: You're THE *Goddess*. This world's yours." She stares at me accusingly, lifting her chin. "That sword's yours."

My skin crawls with my discomfort and Eu comes to stand in front of me.

"Will you stop it with your 'knight in shining armor' tirade? Who is *he*, Veiria?" She points at Eu as if to call him out.

"He's a friend," I say, stepping next to Eu.

Eu stiffens, then seems to loosen up a little. "That I am. We've been friends for several long days, and I intend to not die, if you don't kill us." He extends his hand.

Meren pouts her lip and sticks out her hand to shake Eu's. "To Telvin, okay? Please, I promise I'm worried sick. We'll explain." Her voice is soft but high, as if to reassure us while betraying a slight bit of panic.

I look around at the pinpricks of light. "But how do we get there?"

She smiles. "You've lost your touch."

I look to her, uncertain. "My touch?"

"You've shrunk yourself, lost your essence. I wonder what you're trying to protect yourself from. Just ... close your eyes and imagine somewhere safe, preferably someplace near Telvin. Um ... transporting him too far won't help his well, current state ..."

I look to Eu for what's probably the millionth time and lose myself in his cinnamon eyes.

"You can do it, Veiria." His pretty voice immediately soothes my spirit to no one's surprise.

With that, I feel some weight lift off my chest and I close my eyes, feeling Meren's sarcastic stare bore into me.

"What?" I murmur.

"*Why do you need a man for your confidence?*" I hear her in my head.

"*Because he's all I have. I'm not me without something ... to compare myself to.*"

"Veiria." Her voice is full of derision. "*Who were you?*"

"*What do you mean?*"

"*I mean, ever since I've seen you again, you've been propping yourself up with this boy, to what? Seem pretty? Innocent? Girlie? Cute? You cling to him. Need his approval for every little thing. Your very femininity leaches off of him? What's with you? Who are you?*"

"I'm me!" I cover my non-existent ears. "*I need him,*" I whisper. "*I need him to feel whole.*"

"*Because there's something you never had. You won't find it in him ...*"

My eyes fly open. We're in a cave. The three of us are there, plus Telvin has appeared, slumped against the wall.

I stare at Meren, unblinking. How much of that was really her in my mind, or was I just imagining it?

"What?" she says as she notices.

I look away. "Nothing."

I look out of the corner of my eye to find her assessing me closely and I want to crawl away.

Telvin slowly opens his eyes and Meren is finally distracted enough to turn away.

I realize I'm buried in Eu's side, clutching his arm tightly.

"Veiria, we're here now." He holds me close, and I hide my smile.

I look back at Meren again. I'm not using Eu. I would *never* use Eu. She's wrong about that and I know it, even if it wasn't her speaking in my head.

"Something's troubling you."

I make sure to avoid his eyes. "I don't think it was real. You didn't hear Meren talking when I closed my eyes, did you?"

"Did you hear something?"

"No ..." I lie quickly.

"Well, I didn't either. So, no one talked in that minuscule millisecond of time that either of us are aware of. But ... say that they did. I believe you."

"Eu, do you feel like ... I'm mistreating you?" I say, looking down a bit.

He looks at me with concern, trying to duck his head down a little to meet my gaze. "What makes you say that? Did someone tell you that?"

"Not exactly, I just wanted to know." I smile with a strange tiredness.

"Well, besides dragging me to the depths of this glorious cave, well ..." He grows serious. "I'll tell you again and again, Veiria, but I came of my own will."

"Are you just telling me that?"

"What? No!" He throws his hands up quickly. "Sorry." He apologizes as I fall out of his grip and rub my head. "Want me to treat that?"

"Not right now." I force a smile. "Thanks, Eu-Eu." I poke his cheek, admiring his jawbone and the planes of his tan face for a second too long, before shaking my head.

He smiles with cute dimples, and I giggle, tripping into his arms, before pushing myself up abruptly and slamming into his chin. "Eu! Eu, I'm sorry! Oh, I'm so sorry!" I nearly cry out.

I hear a snorted laugh from behind me and ignore it as I reach for Eu's chin.

"It's okay, Veiria, really." He gives me a decently gratuitous, fake pained smile.

"No, it's not okay!" My voice sounds screechy, and I feel on the end of freaking out completely. "It's not okay!" I choke on the last words, the sudden events of the past hour catching up with me and I feel tears on my cheek as Eu-Eu holds me back to his chest tightly.

"It's all right, Veiria. I'm here."

I feel safe and cared for in his arms and embrace that feeling until I remember who else is in the room with me and my skin crawls with embarrassment.

I close my eyes and wince at Meren's obvious ire, as if she's silently saying 'I told you so' into the crevices of my brain.

Yet, I open my eyes as I push back to sit alone, watching Telvin smile at me kindly.

I brush my hair out of my eyes sheepishly. "Hi."

"Hi." He looks pleasant, with no intensity or hostility in his eyes, only warmth, kindness, and an oddly comforting docile quality. He just looks soft and huggable ... Is that a weird thought? Because that's all I can think of looking at him. "I'm Telvin."

"I'm Eu," Eu says first, oddly fast, and I look up at him, but he's masked his expression.

Whatever, I think. "Veiria."

He nods. "Nice to meet you."

"Don't you and Meren know me?"

"It's hard enough not knowing who you are. I wasn't sure if you and Meren got to that part."

Meren crosses her arms. "I wanted to wait for you."

Telvin closes his eyes and breathes in steadily again.

"Sorry I pushed you, Telvin. I was desperate."

"You protected me, Meren. I wouldn't be here if you hadn't."

Meren looks about to cry again and the two hug.

"I hate it when you scare me, Telvin," she says, like she's talking to an annoying, but beloved little brother.

"I know." He looks up at me. "We want to help you, Veiria."

Unlike with Meren, Eu doesn't argue.

Meren props herself up on her elbow and rolls her eyes, muttering something about "double-standards." Meren sighs impatiently. "We weren't trying to merely 'help them.'"

Eu bristles and Telvin is quick to reassure him, smiling with that sweet docility that seems to stop Eu in his tracks. "Meren's scared, is all. You won't remember, Veiria, but we lost you once. Meren's afraid we'll lose you again. You remember what just happened?"

I nod. "Is everyone all right in the shop?"

"Everyone." He nods. "Though there's nothing we can do for damages."

I look down at the dirty floor.

"There's nothing you could've done. Your sword, Neihdria is an extension of you."

I feel a pit of dread form in my stomach. "Why would I want to hurt you?"

Meren huffs and stomps out of the room.

We look after her for a moment, before Telvin talks softly. "She's been through a lot and lost a lot. She's still too hurt to talk to you. That's why she's leaving it to me. She ... doesn't let things go. It's saved us enough ... She'll open up again. Your sword, Veiria. It's trying to protect you. We're a threat to you. Not by choice, but you have to understand that things didn't go so well between us in the end. This world"—he opens his palm—"is fragile." Then he closes it and looks at me. "You made this world, Veiria. Our job is to save you from yourself. You're this world's Goddess, whether you like it or not." His voice is deathly sober, but soft, in a way meant to console.

"She's not a Goddess," Eu grits out through his teeth. He's saying what I want to hear, that I'm a normal girl, yet it's as if he's not acting entirely on his own. It's as if there's something secretly guiding his reaction. But I want to believe him more than anything.

Telvin shrugs. "Think what you want, we're past reasoning with that possibility. Think: Isn't everything you've done or felt since you've come back to us a reflection of this world? You've altered the very fabric of it simply through your existence, Veiria."

I shake my head impulsively. "I couldn't have."

He sighs and smiles. "Veiria, I get it. You're not the person to think you're capable of *anything*—to think you're worthy of a world of your own. But you do have a world." He starts drawing in the dirt—a girl like me with wings. "I can't change how you think or how you see yourself. That's up to you." He meets my eyes. "You're a sad sight trapped in there."

"I don't know what you mean."

His expression is sad. "It's just—you could be so much happier if you weren't …"

"Shut up, pretty boy."

I look at Eu, who's awfully red. "Eu?"

"I'm sorry …" He eyes Telvin. "I'm sorry, um … Telvin."

Telvin laughs. "Meren would get a kick out of that." But he starts drawing in self-consciously. "Thanks."

"I didn't do …"

Telvin keeps looking down. "I said I took what you said to heart." He swivels a bit.

An awkward silence falls between the two as Telvin awkwardly scratches at the dirt and Eu looks down.

"Um, guys? What's going on?" I feel unsure of myself, like I'm intruding on something, but I don't know what that is or what I should do.

"Just perplexed is all. Wondering is all." Telvin looks up and smiles broadly, like he's trying to hide something for

Eu's sake. "You two should rest up. We have a long way to go yet."

Eu gets up abruptly and mumbles something about having to go to the bathroom. I don't think I've seen him quite so ... weird.

I lean over to look at Telvin's sketch. He's rolled over onto his belly, looking cute in a different way than Eu. The sketch is a heart with a smile on it.

"It's cute."

"You think so? Meren sometimes gets annoyed. She calls me docile or a goody-two-shoes or just infuriatingly kind. But she likes it. She tells me when she's being genuine."

"You're really close, aren't you?"

"All our lives!" He smiles brightly, like a little, adorable lamb. "We grew up together. We sort of gravitated to one another and we've been inseparable since. We were both only children, so we made our own little family, sticking together through all our troubles." He looks at me quizzically. "Meren desperately wishes you'd remember our time together. For me, I'll embrace and treasure the time I have. I don't even know what's real."

"What's real?" I pick at the last word.

"We aren't real in your memories, so the only real us you know is in the present. It can't be helped."

I peer closer to him. "You seem wise."

"Not really. We've been on a wild goose chase the past year uncovering clues and preparing for your return."

"What's the deal with my return?"

He demonstrates the fist closing again, raising his eyebrows askance.

"Oh, right. You really think I'll destroy the world?"

"No, I don't. Meren thought you were long gone until I convinced her otherwise. Again, her pain runs deep and it's not mine to tell. One snap and her faith in you may just collapse."

"Brilliant." I sit cross-legged across from him. "So, magic?"

"Magic," he repeats sing-song.

"Why can she do it, but you can't?"

"Ah ... because Meren's gifted and I'm not." He shrugs. "Well, not in the same way. I can do a little, start a cute little campfire. Simple stuff. Meren's isn't the most complex either, it just blasts things."

"Into oblivion," I state with ire.

"Right, but see, she requires a great deal of concentration for it to work. One slip-up and it all falls apart. She's had to hone it all her life. As you saw, her shield took a lot out of her. She just barely had enough to transfer to me."

"Right, and the void?"

"Can you guess? It was of your own creation."

My chest is once again unsettled, and I get up. "I need some air."

Telvin waves me off with a smile and I smile and wave back tiredly as he continues to draw his cute heart friends. Such an interesting boy. I frown. He's nice though.

What's Eu's problem with people all of a sudden? Maybe he's just stressed, or his homesickness is getting to his basic treatment of others.

The Crush of a Schoolboy

Eu

I put my hands in my pockets as I trudge back to the cave, feeling a bit terrible for snapping at Telvin. I don't know why, but something just overcame me.

I feel that same embarrassment from earlier as I think of him.

My mouth gets dry as I get closer, and I lean against the opening to steady myself.

I smile good-naturedly, but then I remember how unbelievably well … cute he is, as he lies there drawing his adorable pictures. "Hey, Telvin." It's stupid, I know.

I wonder how Veiria would feel about this. I'm not too dense that I haven't figured out she's been crushing on me. Don't get me wrong, she's pretty, beautiful even, but …

Telvin smiles and it lights up the room. "Hi. Something up?"

"Umm …" I laugh nervously. "I came to apologize."

He just smiles unwaveringly. Even though I don't feel great about everything, I'm finding that his hopefulness takes some of the weight off my shoulders. "None needed."

Okay, that again. Humor mode engaged. "You know, I think you're nice beyond belief."

He sits up on his knees, squinting at me. "Why are you here?"

"I don't know, Telvin. Reasons that defy expectations?" I say, grasping at words.

He pats his side and I move over to him, though my legs feel like lead. "You're the odd one out in this equation, you know. Neither Meren nor I expected you."

"Encouraging. And what's that supposed to mean?"

"I don't know yet. But I accept anomalies."

I take a moment to look down at his drawings. "They're cute." *You're cute* is what's in my head.

"Thanks. You didn't come here to say I have cute drawings, did you?"

He looks so ... so ...

"Could you please stop staring at me? It makes me nervous."

"Sure." I look away. My mind seems to clear up enough to think rational questions. "So, what's the deal with Veiria? That wasn't everything, was it?"

He frowns. "I tried to get what was reasonable out. It's not my job to tell her who she is. It's hers."

"You really believe she tried to destroy the world?"

"I saw it." He smiles grimly. "Noctine sealed her."

"They sealed her?"

"That's what I said. I take it you've met. When worse comes to worse, Noctine is Veiria's only match. If things get out of hand, Noctine may be forced to end Veiria before it's too late."

My hair bristles. "You mean kill."

"I told you we don't want that. Neither does Noctine. That's why they sealed her. For Veiria's temporary safety."

"You're a real joy sometimes, you know?"

His smile remains grim. Suddenly, I'm feeling much heavier than a moment ago. "I can't decide when it's time for practicality and when it's time for levity. Meren and I have been through enough."

"You keep saying that. What's your deal?"

"It's not your business. Just Meren's, Veiria's, and mine." He goes back to thoroughly sketching. "I like you, but I won't pretend like I trust you with everything. As I said, you're unexpected. Meren already suspects you. It's probably just annoyance. I think you're good for Veiria."

I blush. "It's not like that."

He grins sheepishly. "I didn't say it was like that, did I?"

"No," I say, tongue-tied.

"I take it you don't really want to be here."

"Stop prying into my business," I say, a bit agitated.

"You're not the only one." He sighs. "My time has passed. I'm ready to move on and I wish Meren was too, but she needs closure. It's not like I don't want to see Veiria with her good memories, but if it weren't for Meren or the threat Veiria poses, I'd want Meren and I to take some time and slow our lives down. I'm ready to settle."

"I have a family to get back to, okay."

His eyes turn sympathetic. "Want to talk about it?"

"No. Stop looking at me with those gosh damn cute eyes."

He recoils a little in puzzlement and then covers his mouth.

"Sorry." I get up, feeling unsteady. "Shouldn't have said something so stupid."

He gives a tentative smile. "You seem a bit out of your element. But Eu, I wish that you find something of your own from all this." I hesitate at his expression and then stalk back out to find Veiria.

I Promise to Run Away with You, My Love

Veiria

I smile fondly at Eu, trying to get over my apprehension at his treatment of Meren and Telvin.

We're out facing the city. It's dark, like it always is, but there's a sliver of the moon squinting through a rock crevice and the crystals below it shine silver-white.

Eu seems a bit disgruntled and it makes me uneasy.

"So, what's the plan, Veiria?" There's a slight snap to his voice.

I hesitate. "You don't mean to follow Meren and Telvin?"

He scoffs. "Veiria, pardon me, but they were looking for you. We're not going with them."

I open my mouth, feeling some intrinsic need to defend them, but to still appease Eu. I'm not good at this. My mouth feels dry, and it takes all my instinct not to latch onto every word of his, but curiosity gets the better of me. Isn't Eu a bit, well ... "I thought you asked what I wanted?"

"I did!" He braces his shoulders defensively, then calms himself. "I did ask that. It's just that ..." He sighs, pressing his fist to his forehead. "I'm just confused, Veiria. I'm sorry, I'll support you. I want you to get your memories back."

I look directly at him and smile, feeling my heart race as I get over my hesitation and slip my fingers through his. "If you ask me to go, I'll go."

He draws back reflexively, and I feel a bitter pain in my heart. "I'm not, I don't ..." Then he takes a step back and another. "Sorry, Veiria, I just can't do this right now." I see him swallow and I do my best to hold in my hurt at his rejection. He's his own person, I know, but him turning his back on me feels so wrong to me. Even he looks conflicted while he speaks. "I'm going to go, Veiria. I promise we'll figure this out. We'll go with them if that's what you *really* want, but you are not a Goddess. And ..." He looks down. "I don't trust them. I'm keeping you safe and if that means we run, then I'm ..." He looks at me sadly. "Then I'm taking you with me."

Part of me thinks, maybe we could just abandon what I want, take him home. If I embraced who I was, leave Telvin and Meren behind, but then ... What would I be?

I don't want to know the truth, do I? I can't settle down with Eu and even if I did, the truth would still chase me. I just think that maybe I can face it with Eu.

I don't want him to leave me. If he makes me run, makes me leave, won't I do what he wants? That's what I want, isn't it?

But at the back of my mind, there's some ache of longing to trust these two people who say they've loved me dearly.

But all I say is: "I promise I'll run with you, Eu. I'll always run with you." Because at this moment, I still believe I will. That I need to.

Straight to the Heart

Veiria

I walk back in to find Meren and she gives me a reluctant nod.

She looks at Telvin. "How was talking to the 'goody-two shoes?'"

Then I look back and witness Meren groaning and leaning her head back.

"Telvin, can't you do anything about this?"

Telvin just smiles. "I told you she wasn't a threat, Meren."

"Fine. I admit that maybe ... maybe I was just a little wrong."

Telvin smiles with what I think is relief.

Meren crosses her arms, looking between us again. "Do you really want him tagging along?" She's staring at Eu. "Just so you know, you'll be kind to Telvin. If you try anything to get to him, you'll have me to answer to."

Eu shudders. "I would never hurt him."

Telvin chuckles. "That's just Meren being a big sis'." He looks at Eu for a moment. "Now that that's settled, I think we're finally in agreement."

"Goodie," Eu scoffs.

I look to him. "Eu?"

"I'll do what you want, Veiria. Just for a little while."

I frown. "So, what do we do?"

Meren and Telvin look at each other, Meren tapping her finger impatiently.

Telvin winces a little. "That's ... up to you, Veiria. Noctine is an option, but I'm afraid they might lock you up again if they perceive you as a threat."

Meren braces herself on the wall, getting up. "They let you off the hook."

Telvin nods, again doing his curious drawings. This time, a realistic heart. "Or we could go to the heart of this world: 'Goddesses Heart.' We don't know what we'll find there. The only thing we know is that you're the solution. If you can't remember anything ..."

"Then we'll fucking snap some sense into this damn world." Meren smirks.

"She means, you need to remember. The world's heart may be a solution."

"If you could control your suicidal glass, this would be easy."

I look down. "So—"

"Ugh, are you for real, Veiria? You've become a difficult, pitiful people pleaser."

I stare blankly at her.

"Don't have me believe you're doing that as anything other than deflection."

Eu steps closer to me again on instinct as I look down and Meren leans her head back and groans. "I'm tired of this shit. I feel like I'm babysitting toddlers."

"I don't mind being a toddler," Telvin interjects.

"Yeah, because you're a friggin' softy." But her expression gets tender at that.

Telvin claps. "Wonderful. And I think now we've dealt with a few petty squabbles."

"Oh yeah," Eu mutters.

Telvin smiles broadly. "Should I tell them about a few minutes ago?"

Eu goes tomato red. "Sorry." He rubs the back of his neck. "Something's wrong with me today."

I honestly feel a bit useless and disoriented. And if I had a bit more confidence in myself, I'd almost consider shaking Eu. But I couldn't do that because he's so good to me ...

He's still gorgeous, confusingly angry or not.

The Journey Ahead

Veiria

The four of us pack up once Telvin's healed enough to travel. Meren acquired some ointment from a small trading outpost.

I stare off at the brightly glowing crystals and the dust-strewn paths of the cavern as Eu stands by my side.

Meren and Telvin are inside discussing and I'm not even sure I want to know what they're talking about.

Telvin walks up beside me. He still has a slight limp in his leg.

"Are you okay to travel?" I feel concern welling in my chest, even if it feels like a lie to say I know him.

"I'll be alright," he smiles. "I'm in pain, but you have a much greater ordeal ahead of you."

"Will you always talk like that?" Eu says.

"Yes, indeed, I will. You don't like it?"

Eu looks away. "I don't mind. I'm just ..." He closes his eyes long and hard. "I just don't know what's going on."

I turn to him. "Eu, we don't have to."

"I promise, Veiria. You have things to find. I'm just here for the ride." He turns his back. "Just give me a few days to unwind, then I'll be your perfect Eu-Eu." He rubs his eyes, then abruptly takes my hand and smiles tight-lipped, looking at Telvin. "Are you ready?"

"Eu?" My heartbeat quickens and I forget that Eu's angry. "I guess." I glance at Telvin, who's gone back into the cave to find Meren again. "I think you scared him off."

"I'm sorry. I'm not feeling myself. I could be with my sister, Lizzie, right now. At least I'm with you, sorting out your problems." Then he walks down the trail, pulling my hand along. "Come on. Let's go. Favorite flower? Mine would be Marillay. I love the purple glow."

I tug him back and he stops. "When we were at the dance, what did you feel?"

He turns his head around, as if looking for an escape.

"Because I felt happy. Too happy. It was the best night of my life."

"Veiria." He cups my hand in his. "I can't do this right now. I'm really happy I could make you feel that way, but I'm just confused. You ever have a feeling for one person, and you feel that same way for someone else, but you're not sure if you should, or you're doubting yourself?"

I make a face, in thought. "I don't know what you're talking about, Eu." I look down at our hands, feeling the warmth of his body heat. "If you could just tell me, I might understand."

He pulls his hair a little with one of his hands. "It's just a feeling. I don't even know if it's real."

"Okay," I say, trying to meet his eyes as he looks away. "I'll give you some space until you're ready."

"Thanks, Veiria." He grins, more relaxed now. "I promise I'll get along; they're just throwing me for a loop. I can deal with problems, just not problems of this scale."

"Yes," I say. "Well, you'll be dealing with my severe, world-ending problems, I'm afraid. I didn't mean to pull you along."

"But you need me." He finally meets my eyes, looking into them deeply.

I swallow. "Yes. I do."

The four of us arrive at a port, outside the caves and along the coast of the cloudy sea—rising, falling, and twisting with the air currents.

We board a sleek wooden ship with silver sails and a dozen oars sticking out from the side.

I run my hand along it before we board, feeling the coarse hull that would take us away to some place unknown.

I look to Eu as he walks up the boarding plank and he gives me a reassuring smile. "I'm sure this thing is plenty stable."

That's not what I'm worried about, but I smile back, something loosening in my heart as I board after Eu, Meren and Telvin waiting on the planks, preparing to unmoor the ship and set sail.

I look back, the trees of orange and pink in the caves entrance scattering glowing leaves in farewell, and I wave back at them as if to give myself some sense of closure on my time with just Eu. There's a new journey ahead, filled with three people who long to save me, to care for me, to love me. I don't know how I feel about that, but I do know something aches in me and I send a heartfelt farewell back to Bell and Diel. "Thank you," I say on the winds to Bell. Neither of them I knew for long, but Bell especially gave me a home and a comforting hand to help me with things I didn't have in life. They were both sweet to take me in and I will be forever grateful.

Somehow, I know I may never see them again ... and I might never look back.

To Fly on Starry Skies

Veiria

The ship skims over the starry sea and I reach my hand out, the oars a gentle lullaby.

The water sparkles in stardust and there's an odd melody on the wind, as I look around for its source, before I turn my head and I'm lost again in that sea of infinite stars.

I hear the creak of wood and turn to see Meren, the slivers of moonlight revealing her reluctant smile. "Beautiful, I bet. You were encased for so long."

I smile at her nervously.

"Your brooch. It's mesmerizing."

I bring my hand up, running my fingers over the smooth stone. "Thank you. I ... really wanted it. I don't know why, but I think it's been making me feel okay."

"Veiria." She comes up beside me, leaning on the railing and gazing at the stars. "When all this is over ..." She shakes her head. "It never will be." She seems lost in thought. "When I was a girl, I wanted a lot of things." She reaches her hand down and skims the stars. "I wanted to chase the stars and see the world. But one thing I could never explain was that you were always in my dreams ... I wanted to meet you, our creator. Maybe it was some twisted fate that made us sisters when I had nothing but Telvin."

"I didn't ask to ruin your lives," I whisper.

She laughs long and hollow. "You aren't making things easy, Veiria. You sure are dense and a little infuriating. I don't care how cute he is or how enamored you are with him. But like … I'm tired of walking in circles around you, so I just want to put it behind us."

I look more closely at her—the hard lines of her face, smoothed by the tranquil night, her softer white nightclothes, her eyes that are somewhere between tentative joy and tragedy. Then I stare off. "Before this, I think I had nothing … But there were times … times I almost had something worth it." I take a deep breath and frown at her with a pained concentration. "I think you were those times."

She looks at me, tight lipped, then away.

"But I don't think I can give them back to you. I don't know what I want, and I'm scared, but …"

"You sound like Telvin, reciting some sort of riddle," she says, far off, her eyes reflecting the stars.

"Oh … well, I suppose I am a little mysterious," I say with a nervous haughtiness.

"Gods, you are," she taunts playfully, looking back at me, her lips crooked. "I may have called you a freak when you attacked my brother."

"I didn't—I mean, I didn't mean to." My words blend together in agitation.

She rolls her eyes, then she reaches out. "Wouldn't you like to fly … Away from here … Away from all your problems ... Away from the world ..." Her voice is strange, unlike her—like a recitation of a spell.

Her voice fades out and I'm the one saying it, as I take a step and then another into the infinite starlight. I spread my arms, my white nightdress rippling in the cool breeze ... and I step into the eternal light. My arms stretch and ruffle into beautiful white feathers and my gaze sharpens.

I float, glide through the air, reaching and soaring between flecks of stars, all thoughts fading into a pure joy and a childish amazement at the beauty and loveliness of the stars, until ...

"Veiria, Veiria." She shakes me lightly and I come back to reality on the ship. Meren shakes her head. "I believe you're harmless now, but I also believe you're clueless. I know you're fighting in there and for some reason, you gave up. You're 'a trapped bird wanting to be free,' as Telvin says. Some brother, but I think his big brain is onto something."

"Can I be a swan?" I say, still a bit scattered. "I'll be a swan of war, if you'd like."

She shakes her head. "That's not quite you."

"I guess not," I frown, looking back at the stars.

"Hey, Veiria," Meren says in a quiet voice, tugging on my nightdress in an out-of-character shyness.

I turn, my eyes on the troubled lines of her face, confused.

"Thanks for bringing me to Telvin and to you. You, Telvin, and Eu … You're real in a way I'm not. I'm just living in your memories, like … like there's no tomorrow …"

"What? Meren?" I look down at her hand as she draws it back and smiles.

She perks up. "I'll fight back defiantly, though. I'll make this world hell on earth. So remember me, okay?"

"I don't … I don't know what you mean."

"I mean, don't let us die without a fight. Make it count." Her grin wavers. "I want to see your fire before the end."

Then she crosses her arms, walking back inside.

"Meren!" I call.

She turns. "Hmm?" She raises her eyebrow.

"I'll fight with you. I'll make sure you live!" My voice cracks. "I don't understand, but I'd burn the world for all of you!"

Meren's lips quirk up at the edges. "That's the Veiria I know. You have a fire. Just don't let it die for the wrong reasons. Don't throw yourself away for a boy or conformity or to hide. You're a fighter, not a coward. And I will personally kill you and drag you to hell if you die a coward."

"I wouldn't blame you," I feel a laugh deep in my throat.

She smiles at me. "Go see your boys and tell them I said hi."

"Will do," I say, something cracking in my heart. Because I'm starting to realize that maybe Meren won't be there when I … If I went back.

I can't let her memory die. I promise her, she'll be there with me, whatever happens in my future.

The Cards of Friendship

Telvin

I eye the anomaly as he's strangely brightened up since our short time on the ship. I'd invited him to cards— something I'm not sure if I'll regret or not, but I'm starting to get into it. He's charming and funny when he's not sulking, and apparently a little teasing. Maybe he's *too* charming, I decide.

"Let me see your cards." Eu tries leaning over me and I boop him on the nose playfully.

"There, you saw them." I hide my face in my cards to hide the blush creeping onto my cheeks. "Cheater."

"Hey, you gave me access!" Eu throws his hands up and plops down beside me, looking closer. "Now we can both do it."

I eye him suspiciously, my eyes narrowed. "You have evil motivations, Eu."

"Sure, sure." He waves his hand in the air, snagging a card from my deck as I open my mouth in protest. "Let's play."

I pull on a neutral expression and pull a card.

"Not bad," Eu nods.

"Do you even know how to play?"

"Why of course." Eu nods emphatically, picking a card to counter mine.

I try not to frown.

"What? Is it bad?"

"Not quite." I start to smile. It sort of is.

I lay mine down and Eu winces.

"Defeated." He winks at me.

I laugh a little, feeling my gaze lower. "I wouldn't say that. Don't give up, Eu," I encourage him.

"Wise words." He stares harder at his cards. "If I weren't playing against you, I'd bet with all my hands in your favor."

I smile. "I'm blessed with Veiria's favor."

Eu points to himself. "As am I."

I can't help myself and I keel over. "No, you're not. Not like we are. We're granted the ..."

"Hey, special," Eu snickers. "All I hear is Goddess this, Goddess that, we're the chosen ones."

I shiver self-consciously. "That's not what I ..."

"Chillax, starry-boy."

"Hey, I have foresight." I cover my eye.

Eu frowns, stroking his cards. "And I have eyes. You don't need any powers to look so cute. Or maybe you're enchanted."

I purse my lips as my blush deepens. "It's just foresight. Thanks."

Eu throws down another card. "Take that!"

"It's not your turn," I resist the urge to laugh.

Eu rubs his cheek furiously. "Right. Heat of the moment."

He looks at my eyes and I swallow. "You're looking at me."

"I am, apologies." Eu taps the table. "I think I surrender."

"You can't do that!" I smile broadly with indignation. "We haven't even started."

Eu frowns. "I can see that, and I'm not liking my chances. I claim that there's no great prophecy for you and your friend and I claim your defeat."

"I don't think so," I mutter, preparing my cards as I stack them meticulously, listening to Eu's rambling with a small smile. *Don't get too carried away, Eu. Your presence is strange as it is, but not unwelcome.*

Veiria

I make my way back into the interior of the ship, ducking under the low wooden beam to the lower decks, and making my way through the murky hallway, rocking calmly with the waves. I stumble a bit and yelp, catching the wall.

It may be beautiful out, but I'm still a little seasick. I would think drifting on stars would be calm, but the second I stepped inside, the calmness vanished, replaced with the feeling of a ship at sea and my stomach roiling unpleasantly.

I hear Telvin's musical laughter from an open doorway with a wavering candlelight spilling out and peek my head around the corner.

"Veiria!" Telvin waves childishly from Eu and his card game. "Come join us."

I point at myself uncertainly and move around the doorframe into view.

"Meren!" Telvin scampers up to the doorway, peaking around the corner, then he looks at me innocently. "She'll want to play too."

Eu looks at me and squirms in his seat. *What? I* mouth.

He gives me a death glare, but smiles again when Telvin turns around and his eyes alight on Eu.

There's something infinitely soft in Eu's eyes that strikes a cord of jealousy in me.

Before I can dwell on that, I hear Meren's footfalls rushing towards us down the hallway.

"What?" She says breathlessly, still in her nightgown, but barefoot now. "Telvin, I was getting ready for bed." She pouts. "This better be worth it."

"It's a card game." Telvin spreads out the cards in front of him, staring up eagerly. "Bonding."

"He's demonstrating to me how to pick cards," Eu says and snatches one, with a gentle look at Telvin, before hiding it in his trousers.

Meren lifts an eyebrow. "You boys are having fun. Maybe later."

Telvin gets up again and tugs Meren towards the table with both hands. "Meren!" he pleads. "Pleeeeeassssssse?" He gives her puppy dog eyes.

"Fine, fine," she sighs, a hand on one hip as she lets Telvin pull her. "But I'm not going easy on my little brother, or that sorry excuse for a man." She points at Eu accusingly. "You better have Telvin in good hands, or else you'll be hearing about it." She smashes her fist into her palm.

Eu spreads his hands up. "Not doing anything. Just minding my own business." He whistles.

"Meren? It's fine. Eu's fine," I say, my voice high, as I look at Meren's threatening posture.

"Right." One side of her lips twitches up in what I believe to be a look of disgust. "Did you remember nothing of our conversation from FIVE minutes ago?"

"Sorry, Meren."

She huffs and walks over. "It's fine." She waves her hand behind her. "I can't expect all the change in the world in one night. Just loosen up a little."

"I forgot, Meren." I pull on a smile and follow her.

I sit next to Meren who seems to relax for a moment and smiles more calmly at me. "Sorry. Let's be partners. I have a feud with those two." She jerks her thumb.

"Perfect." I grin. "I mean, as do I. Eu, at least …" Not Telvin, of course. Telvin's too cute in an adorable, harmless way to be mad at in any sense of the word.

"Fair. But trust me, Telvin will get on your nerves, but he's a good cook."

"I am," Telvin beams, shuffling and then passing out cards before us. "Two kings, versus two queens," he chortles off. "Who will win is a perilous guess," he says in riddle. "I confess I find the odds perplexing …"

"Hey, I thrive in peril." Eu tilts his head.

"Well …" Telvin looks to his side at Eu. "I wouldn't want that to come to you, but that does sound like an advantage."

Eu scooches closer to Telvin all too obviously and takes his stack, brushing his hand against Telvin's, as he leans over to glance between him and Telvin.

"Are you ladies familiar with take the Queen?" Eu says.

"Are you two dimwits ready to lose?" Meren retorts.

"Alas, the scourge of humanity. My sister, Meren," Telvin says, his face behind his cards.

Meren throws her cards at Telvin, and they spill onto his shirt.

He picks them up from his lap with a sigh. "Good luck, my sister," Telvin says. "I wish you had worse aim." He rubs his eyes.

"And may best woman win," says Meren, as if daring him.

"I think you mean Veiria," Eu says.

"I think you should decide who to root for, Eu. False signals make me want to vomit." Meren makes a sour face at Eu.

Eu turns his face up to the beams of the ceiling. "Goddess, is it cramped in here."

I wince.

"But not Veiria. She's just a regular old ... I mean young, Veiria. No goddess here."

"Done prattling. Let's take your ass." Meren throws down the cards, then whispers to me, "Don't worry, I got this."

"Erm, I don't know the rules," I say uncertainly.

"Don't worry." She cracks a grin. "Just follow my lead and watch them burn in agony."

Telvin smiles crudely, and Meren directs two fingers from her eyes to his and mouths something ominously.

"Okay. I'll follow my sister, then you'll follow me, Veiria, then Eu is last."

"I see who you're sparing." Meren sits cross-legged, thumbing her eyes.

Telvin ignores her and places his cards.

Meren whispers to me. "That's a lowly bunny rabbit. Telvin thinks they're cute, but I think they're lowly vermin. He sends them out in spades."

"I think they're cute too."

"Oh my Goddess." Meren palms her forehead. "Take my side, Veiria."

"Sorry, I'm being honest."

"Okay." She shuffles through my cards. "So, bunny beats tortoise."

"I thought the tortoise won."

Meren glares at me. "You're in my rules."

I shut up.

"The hare has to beat the tortoise, silly. Then dove beats bunny, then it's knight, suitor, lord, prince, king, queen, princess, deity. Save the deity and the princess. Princesses rule. At least badass ones. Telvin threw away the Goddess card at Eu's request. Thank him with your fist."

"Um ..."

"Pick the dove." She guides my hand.

I do like doves. I put it on the table.

Telvin sighs and Eu confers with Telvin, before placing a suitor.

We pass another round, before getting to me.

"Hit him with your fly!"

"What?"

"It's a decoy, Veiria. Lowest of the low. They don't matter, so just do it."

I eye the cards, then her.

We run through rounds, Meren increasingly giving me free rein. She's a better teacher than I expected. Until we near the final rounds.

Eu seems to be doing some deeply introspective work, staring between me and Telvin, to the point I wonder if he's sick. When I try and get his attention, he looks away and says something that makes Telvin laugh, which just makes my heart drop more in my chest.

"Pick Queens or Princes," Meren whispers to me. "Last resort. Save your princess for the finishing move. They need to lose their deity. Don't sweat it, we'll make them sacrifice it all for you to make your move, so don't screw it, you got this." She gives me a thumbs up under the table. "Deal?"

"Deal."

"Alright. Those boys won't know what hit them," Meren exclaims when we get back from a short break.

As the cards whittle down, Meren whispers encouragingly, "I've set you up. Wait for it, and you got them."

I eye their cards, trying to think of something. Meren nudges me with her leg, and I frown at Telvin's card as an unsightly glee springs into my mind at the sign of victory. Meren said Eu failed him last round, but now I know what that means. I grin as a thrill runs through me, eager to place my next card.

"Haha! The loser has to fall!" I throw my card in the heat of the moment, and it lands face up. "Whoops. Sorry." I feel my cheeks flush with embarrassment. "I still won, though. Take that, Eu," I say quietly, glancing at his face in victory.

Eu laughs, his cheeks flushed. "Victory to Veiria!"

I bury my head in my hands and as he reaches his hand over, I pull my head up and shake it with a broad grin. Then I shake Telvin's hand, then Meren's. "Thanks, Meren."

"No problem, friend."

Some tension creeps off my shoulders and I feel something lift my spirits. "You didn't mind me being your partner?"

"No, Veiria. As I said, I've always missed you. Now shut up and eat your cake."

"My what?" I ask, looking around in confusion.

A cake pops into existence in the center of the table.

I jump, startled.

Meren raises her eyebrow and cackles, shaking her head. "It's from Telvin."

"I think you two rigged it," Eu says.

"Eu! She's fair!" I laugh. "She may not like you, but she's not like that."

"I wouldn't be too sure, Veiria." Then she nudges me forward. "Let's enjoy this. It's for your happy return. Don't mind it being a century old."

"Is it really?" I say, shocked.

"No," Meren covers her mouth, laughing. "But your expression is priceless.

I swallow, knowing I'm probably red in the face and I move to sit down with the others. I never exactly liked celebrations of myself. I think they made me uncomfortable for some reason. But this ... this is okay.

Conversations in the Night

Telvin

Eu and I share a room. I look up at the ceiling contemplatively as I hear him shift every few moments on the lower bunk, before he pops his head over.

"Hi, Telvin." He clears his throat, smiling. "Listen. I never really apologized too well for the other day. Sorry." He looks at me hopefully.

I hold a smile to my lips. "I don't mind."

He leans on my bunk. "I enjoyed playing cards with you."

I smile at him. "Me too."

"You're a real ace." He grins.

I search the lines of his face, remembering his heartfelt laugh as we played before Meren and Veiria walked in.

"You seemed distraught when Veiria got there," I observe.

Eu chuckles. "Maybe a little. What makes you so good anyway?"

I touch my forehead and smile deceptively. "My foresight."

"Ah, so it lets you crush your foes?"

I lean closer to him, and Eu looks startled. "It would have if you hadn't played your Queen."

"Ah, my bad." Eu blinks, staring long into my eyes.

"It's fine. I was setting up Veiria anyway—Meren and I, that is."

"Were you?" Eu creases his brow.

"Yes. We have a special connection that we don't share with you yet. I can't say I wouldn't welcome you too, but it's just ..."

"Complicated," Eu finishes.

I nod, turning and leaning back as I feel the gentle rock of the ship. "Have you ever been on a ship like this, Eu?"

"I suppose not," he says. "The closest I got was farming equipment and some small boats transporting goods and people from island to island. I visited the Velsh Hills once. They were spectacular—summer and winter meeting as one. But otherwise, no. I am out of my depth."

I close my eyes. "Out of your depth, huh? Eu, you ever heard of the cat who jumped in the lake?"

"No." I can hear confusion in his voice. "Should I have?"

I shake my head. "He nearly drowned, but he got out with his momma and went back home." I frown. "You have a physical home to go to. I have Meren. You'll get there," I say softly. "You'll find your home. The place you really exist."

I hear him turn under me. "The place I really exist? I exist here."

I turn on my side, silent for a moment. I think it wise not to answer further. It'd destroy him. "Your memories are precious, aren't they?"

"What?" Eu hesitates, then breathes out. "Yes, they are."

"Good. I'm glad you found something you love in this ephemeral place. I'm sorry fate can't be kinder now."

I hear Eu clamor up and then feel him shake me.

I turn to face him, and he looks scared. "What do you mean?"

I search his eyes with pity and something like fondness growing. "You're scared like you were just born, aren't you?"

Eu opens his mouth, then nods, his knuckles white on the bed post.

"Don't worry, Eu. All will be revealed in time, and you'll find a different peace before the end. Get some sleep. Meren and I have the world to show you tomorrow."

Eu hesitates like he's going to say something, then the ladder creaks as he moves down the rungs, the ghost of clouds and stars and water sending his shadow, wavering and indistinct, onto the walls.

"One day, Eu, you'll leave this place," I whisper. "I'm sorry that your family isn't real. That your life isn't real." Then I close my eyes, thinking of sleep. "One day, you'll find a new dawn."

The Wealth of a Woman

Veiria

"Acellia." Telvin points in the direction of the gulls, as the clouds part to reveal a towering city of pristine white spires. "Noctine's domain. They may channel darkness, but they thrive in the light."

The ship banks in water, cascading off the edges of a glass bowl—the transition from clouds to crystal-clear water, seamless, apart from a few bumps.

"We need to be careful," Telvin says wisely, his eyes trained thoughtfully on the city. "Noctine is dangerous, but they're also a potential ally. We don't know how they'll react to Veiria in their city. This could be a terrible idea, but Noctine's blocked off the heart of the world to Veiria and only her. She can't pass."

"How do you know?" Eu comes up to Telvin's other side on the railing.

"Foresight." Telvin turns to him and taps Eu's forehead. "It doesn't always work well, but it's useful in a hazy, far-in-the-future sense."

"Ah." Eu rubs his forehead. "Tricky."

"Yes." Telvin turns back to the city.

Meren clears her throat. "I think it's entirely useless."

Telvin smiles broadly. "Only because you don't have it. Veiria would be done if we didn't go this way. Though I admit, it hasn't ever saved us in the short-term, or given us clarity. It's more like"—Telvin closes his eyes and concentrates—"a feeling. It comes and it goes like the tide of the sea or the phases of the moon."

"It sounds amazing," I compliment.

"Thanks. When it comes to me, I do my best with the feelings."

I look to see Eu gazing at him against the railing, cheek lazily on his hand. "I agree with Veiria. Astounding."

Telvin ducks his head as we sail closer to shore, the gulls flying off to circle the distant spires. "We better prepare."

I look at Eu and he shrugs. "Maybe Noctine will be generous."

I look at him doubtfully.

"I won't let anyone hurt you, Veiria. Plus, we have those two. I ... changed my mind. I was being too paranoid earlier, but I'm fine now."

"I'm glad, Eu-Eu." I look at Telvin, feeling an odd dejection in my heart. "You should go follow them."

"What's this about, Veiria?" Eu steps closer to me.

"I just—I want to see you enjoy yourself. I know you want to. Go on, I'm okay." I give a forced smile. "I'll catch up."

"Alright," Eu nods slowly. "But scream like your head's cut off if you're it trouble."

I laugh raucously. "Will do." Without thinking, I scream on the ship deck at the top of my lungs and laugh at Eu's wide eyes and the way he jumps a foot."

"Not here!" Eu lowers his hands in a 'quiet down' motion. "You'll scare Noctine out of their socks."

"Sorry." I wipe my eyes. "I've been holding that in. There's too much going on, Eu. Too many emotions. Suddenly I have three friends, and that makes me really happy. You all treat me in a way that makes me feel really … affirmed? I don't know how it's different than before. But I … There's still something off. I can feel it. Nothing feels truly mine."

Eu gives me a brief hug. "Thanks for telling me. Trust me, this is all still crazy. I want you to figure out what you really need. I'll be here to the end."

"Thanks, Eu-Eu." I push him away lightly. "But I really do just need a moment alone. I'll catch up, okay?"

"Got it." He shoots me finger guns again, and I giggle, sticking out my tongue at his back.

The moment he's out of sight and on the docks, I sink down onto the planks, the railing against my back, and hold my head in my hands, feeling infinitely lonely for some reason. I press my backhand to my mouth and rock in the silence as I feel like crying or maybe screaming. I watch the seagulls circle in the sky above, feeling a few tears welling in my eyes as I let the sight of the gulls calm me down.

I'm not sure if it's just me, but I feel a jolt on the ship that makes me jump, yelping and covering my mouth as I look around, before running after Eu, even though I want to stay there for who knows how long, with the gentle lapping of the waves to quiet my anxiety.

I catch up to them, Eu pointing out a pair of seagulls to Telvin that are gliding together.

Telvin watches enamored as Eu comments something that makes Telvin laugh.

Meren turns, looking at me questioningly, before slowing her pace. "I know you miss him. Trust me, Eu's being a little unfair to you, but he'll figure it out soon enough. He's a good boy."

"You think?"

"*Sure,*" she says, drawn out. "I mean, he isn't my type or my cup of tea, or whatever you want to call it, but he seems fine enough. It's just some internal drama. I wish I could strangle him for you."

I smile. "Thanks. I want to do that a little too."

"I never thought the current Veiria had it in you, but good for you." She grins, looking around to take in the city—the white towers rising infinitely high above us, clothes and white banners draped on close lines and string from window-to-window, bridges connecting the spires, also in seashore white, and open air venues with well-dressed chefs and servers in fine black. Musicians fill the air from every corner and customers sit outside in the sun under the gulls nesting and gliding through the corners and air of the city, and everywhere is the smell of the open ocean. I look around, just as enraptured, until Meren catches my eye. "I think I know who you were in your world, or something like that."

I stop, searching her face as my breath slows.

"Come on. Let's walk and talk and leave the boys." She motions to me. "I guess you could say I'm worried about you. It's more a feeling than anything concrete."

"What do you think of me?"

"I think—" Her brow creases. "I think that you're wonderful and you're intelligent when you want to be. You're very afraid. As I said: You've gotten so much more frightened of the world since last we met. It made me wonder, the way you looked at things, the way you looked at women with longing and gratitude and hope. The way you looked at men with something like longing and something like disgust. The way you just want to belong. It makes me think—" Meren approaches a lovely opera singer, draped in velvet black with pearls around her neck—she's plump and light skinned, her brunette, curled hair up in an elegant bun, and with a gorgeous, deep resounding, rich voice that carries. She has expensive, beautiful black heels, a huge angled hat with a feather and several men and women are gathered around her, their bows gliding over violins with grace as she sings an aria on a small dais, enrapturing me for a moment. "You like this?"

I nod. "Yes, I think I do."

"Good." She nods and smiles at a server, who whips us out a white-clothed table, pouring us a glass of champagne with a gloved hand and pulling back my chair for me to sit.

I look at Meren, the sounds of gulls in the distance and the sound of the waves and sight of the sun on the beach behind the singer and the vibrant color of her voice and stunning look. "But I'm not dressed for it."

"Close your eyes," she says affectionately. "You know the drill by now. Believe in yourself."

I do, and when I open them, Meren's slipped into a graceful dress of scarlet red and I'm in a dress of iridescent silver-gray. I gasp, turning in my gold heels. I feel the ocean breeze on my leg through the slit of my long dress. I reach up to feel my hair done up with a silver clip. Meren's hair is held by a red headband, her heels a brilliant blood-red. I feel my face and pull out a mirror, seeing my lipstick and makeup done like a model.

"Better now?"

"Yes," I say almost wordlessly. "And you look"—I eye her up-and-down—"stunning."

"Thank you, Veiria." She nods her head at me. "As do you." She extends her hand back, taking two menus from a passing server and sits smugly, as I feel my heart pound with nerves and joy. I notice a slit in my chest area and want to laugh with embarrassment or more joy.

Meren gazes at her menu. "You look like a child given her first real treat. I think you have an event called Christmas. It must be that." She eyes me again, grinning and bringing her hand forward to place on my arm. "Remember that you deserve it. You can be a queen if you want. Don't let anyone tell you you aren't worthy."

I have a hard time thinking I am, but I don't say that, because I almost feel confident enough to put that all behind me.

Meren purses her lips. "I think you were told you couldn't be a girl in some way."

I swallow, my mouth dry.

"It's just a guess. It's like you long for womanhood with all your heart and when it falls into your grasp, you don't know what to do with it. I think you weren't born a girl, like me."

"You're wrong." I stand abruptly and Meren pulls me gently back down.

"Veiria, listen to me. That doesn't change how I think about you. I know you're a woman. You don't need to prove anything to me. I just wanted to check in and make sure you were alright, before you spiraled too much. I could see it in your eyes. I know my old friend to not make the same mistake twice. I—" Her voice cracks. "I couldn't stop you from hurting yourself the first time."

"I won't hurt myself."

"That's good. But Veiria ..." She takes a sip of her champagne. "You can't let yourself stay in dreams and waste away where it matters. I don't want to see you go, but Telvin and I can both see this place isn't good for you. It'll ruin you again."

I look down at the flawless silverware, crossing my legs under me protectively. "This is the only place where I'm happy. I can't leave it."

She lifts my chin. "Look at me, Veiria. You aren't happy here. I know you tell yourself that, but you're not."

My face contorts and I hide my tears in a napkin, as Meren gets up from her seat and leans down with her arms around me. "There-there. See, Veiria? I don't know what you're going through or how hard it must be. I just think you can be brave."

"I can't. You don't get it."

"I know." She hands me a tissue from a purse that appeared by her side, then she bends down. "I may be stubborn and angry, but I know when my friend needs a hand. Telvin and I will help you. I'll help you get out of here and make your dreams come true. I know it'll cost me, but we were family."

I blow my nose, looking up as the aria comes to a close, my outburst strangely having no effect on or reaction from the audience as the woman places a hand to her heart, the other extended gracefully, and sings the final notes.

"I don't know how you listen to this, Veiria." Meren dabs at my drying tears and re-applies my make-up for me.

"Thank you." I close my eyes as the singer fades out, replaced with tragic, graceful strings playing a gently nostalgic melody that cracks at my heartstrings. "Everyone says that. People hate opera or orchestral or whatever else I like. Sometimes I try out some pop or country to be like the other girls. I like it sometimes, but I just can't listen to it the same. Live the music—have it capture my heart with emotion."

"You suit you, Veiria. But it fits." She shrugs. "This string-opera stuff probably wouldn't be bad once I got used to how depressing it sounds. I think I'd go for pop or EDM or something."

I make a face. "EDM makes me go insane."

"All the more reason." She offers me her hand to get up. "When you get up, we're partying. I have no clue in any hell what those words mean, but I'm finding out and I'm enjoying it. I guess you know what I should like ..."

"But I thought you knew?"

She looks to the horizon, clapping at the singer and the musicians and I join her as they bow. "Those two things don't exist here. It's just your presence and the feeling of my existence. I'm not much more than that. Anyway, I'll take you around—offer to do things you missed all those years."

"Thanks. I—I wanted a sister to do everything with that was girly."

"There's no right way to be a girl, Veiria. Look at me." She gestures to herself. "I'm dressed all fem now, but am I really the spitting image of a lady?"

"Not really, but I still admire you like one."

Meren gives me a sulking expression. "I'll pass that onto our friends. I'm sure they'd get a kick out of it. Let's walk around and enjoy ourselves. Catch the sunset, buy you a dress or something, talk a bit more." She shrugs. "Whatever you want."

We end up at the shore and I pose at the water, like I'm in a photoshoot.

Meren scoffs from a distance, as I take off my shoes, running barefoot in my dress and spinning with my back to the sun, my hands forming a heart and my eyes closing. "What are you doing?"

I open my eyes. "Posing. All the girls I knew took these beautiful pictures by the water or under flowers or at a manor. They wore these beautiful dresses and owned the room with their beauty." My voice goes off and I turn to face the setting sun, my hands behind my back. "They always looked so happy ..."

Meren walks up behind me, throwing her heels in the sand. "Hated those things anyway. Don't give me that look," she says at my probably aghast expression. "When you're expected to wear those things, the novelty wears off."

"Well, I don't think so." I smile into the sun. "I'd wear them forever."

"Figured." She looks at me, crossing her arms. "Veiria? I don't know what a picture is."

"Oh." I turn back to her, spinning with my arms stretched out. I stop myself, dizzy as I feel my dress whoosh around my legs. "You take it from these things called either a phone or a camera. Like this box that captures a moment. It like ... prints light onto a page, or something."

"Interesting."

"Here." I grab her hands nervously and form the rough image of a rectangle. "Just, um ... press your right pointer finger down when I've hit a good pose."

"Okay?" She looks from me to the inside of her box. "I guess that makes a little sense. I wish I could see it, though."

"I don't care." I wave, hopping on my feet. "Just one imaginary picture and make it perfect." I spread my arms and Meren snaps an imaginary picture, then I transition back to forming a heart. "Say, 'Meren's the best.'"

"I'm not saying that, Veiria. Veiria's the best."

I pout my lips.

Meren rolls her eyes and holds her hands up in front of her eyes. "Fine. 'Meren's the best,' if that'll make you happy."

"It did." I jump, then I turn longingly towards the ocean and brush my hair back and Meren snaps an imaginary picture. "Let's take one of us."

"Umm ... Veiria ..."

"Just, hey look." I wave as Eu and Telvin walk towards us. Eu says something to Telvin, then he waves at me and runs across the sand, skidding to a halt in front of me.

"'Sup!"

Meren palms her face. "Could you please say something less embarrassing?"

Telvin walks up to us a minute later. "I don't mind," he says softly.

"Hey, Eu-Eu!" I interject. "Take a picture of me and Meren!" I jump excitedly.

"I see something has you riled up, but I have no clue as to the meaning of your words!"

"I know," I laugh, taking his hands gently and feeling that spark between us that's overshadowed for a moment by my day with Meren. I form his hands into a rectangle and then demonstrate the click.

He shifts his lips back-and-forth, perplexed and thoughtful. "Well, here goes."

I get alongside Meren before the sun can fade, her hand on my hip and I do the same, giggling a little.

"Are you drunk?" she asks in my ear.

"No, just excited."

"Well, mark me not surprised."

She looks forward and smiles. Eu makes a click sound.

I run forward and look at his hands. "Yay!" I exclaim at the nothingness between them.

"Yes, it's a swell photo-thingy. You better keep it." Eu places the nonexistent camera in my hands and I hold it to my chest.

"I will cherish it for the rest of my days."

"You're so sentimental," Meren looks at me with some new sort of closeness. "And I don't mind that."

I breathe out, standing there for a few more moments with Meren and enjoying the silence, before I follow Eu and Telvin back into the city.

Silent Nights & Days Passing By

Veiria

I gaze out the open window, the starry sky hanging over the calm city with whispers of music and lights below. The breeze gusts in warmly, the waves lapping quietly in the distance. To all the world, it's calm, serene. And some of my loneliness from earlier has vanished, replaced with something new.

I rest my head on the windowsill. Maybe Eu wasn't all I wanted. I still long for him, but my time with Meren was nice. She's more perceptive, and although she puts on an 'angry face,' she's caring in a way Eu's not.

I mean, Eu is. He's good for me. But I think I always longed to just 'be' with a girl as just an everyday friend. To just exist and enjoy moments with another girl as one and the same. Do things I thought girls always did, of course, but more than that. I guess I'm just glad she hung back with me. I'm glad we got a chance to talk.

I feel my head loll, counting sheep as I listen to the waves.

Then I sing to myself. It's one thing I never felt I could do because I hated my voice, but here I'm free. Here it sounds wonderful. Here my voice, my body, my mind feels wonderful, more settled, more at home, but still discordant even so, like there's still something wrong but it's so far off that I wouldn't even realize it until I went back to my world. Except it never was my world.

My voice comes out in a soft lullaby.

There's a girl who sleeps

On the starry skies

She dreamed a dream

Of a thousand lies

She stretched her hand out

Cuddled a star

And she wished

And she wished

And she wished

For more

And more

Deep in her heart

She held a door

Kept it locked

And chained

From the world

She kept

A million lies

Cuddled in dreams

She held a sigh

In her dreams

She wished to be free

So that no one could hurt her

Or trap her

To be

In a world

Not hers

Anymore

Forever

Entrapped

In chains of hers

In her dreams

She soared through the sky

She could be anything

If she just closed her eyes

    I open my eyes, and blink back the glossy sheen that had formed on them. There's something so beautiful about singing. I could never do it. Now I can. I loved music. I wanted to play the violin or viola or piano or harp or flute or oboe or something soft. Music felt like escape.

I just didn't have the confidence, and I think my passion was dead.

I hold my chest. "I can't lose this," I whisper into the night. It's beautiful, and I don't want to let it go. So, I sing a little more, long into the night, the stars shining down like a wish granted as I listen to the sound of my voice in peace, without the agony or the panic or the dysphoria.

I call on that freedom to last forever—for the stars to hear my plea and let me stay here forever.

Perched on Heaven's Staircase

Telvin

Eu had finished pointing out several birds to me, admiring their wingspan, their anatomy, their scientific names.

He smiled the whole time, taking me to get gelato, we admired the flavors. I picked chocolate and mint, he picked strawberry and mango.

The two of us sat that afternoon on a bright alley corner, feeling the warm white steps underneath us.

I work up my courage and pull out my sketch book when Eu asks about my stick drawings.

"I liked them," he says.

I flip through, past pages of people and places and objects and animals and plants from Meren and I's journey. "Sometimes I'd just find a quiet spot while Meren and I rested. We had the world ahead of us. Sometimes we just stopped and enjoyed the sights." I flip past drawings of the clouds drifting in the sky over the moon, a flower sitting in the foreground, of little kids playing at a fountain, of even these towers in this city, and of spots Meren and I sat, and people watched or watched the horizon or the birds.

"They're gorgeous," Eu says. "I mean, your heart figures were cute, but these ... You're an artist."

"Thank you. I do my best." I cover an image of Eu I'd started to draw, flipping past it in haste before he can see. He's been perplexing me, twisting my heart in knots.

I flip back to one where I imagined us from a distance, camping out on an island as we looked after each other, I made Meren her favorite stew, and we sat out under the stars in a conversation that makes me nostalgic. It was a time before Veiria, where things were so much simpler. Where Meren and I didn't have the knowledge of the world ending. Of the friend we'd meet and lose—the friend who'd become a sister to Meren and tore her heart apart when Veiria tried to end things and take her own life, leaving me to watch my sister tear herself apart in her grief and helplessness from the sidelines.

I know we both felt useless to help our friend, but it hit Meren harder. She took it personally. Blamed herself and Veiria for leaving and going somewhere she couldn't follow. And for letting Noctine take Veiria's soul into eternal sleep to save her from herself, instead of doing what she regrets not doing then—talking to Veiria before it was too late. Not seeing the signs that I couldn't see either.

I sigh, looking to the past before those days. Not that I dislike Veiria. I loved her almost as much. But there's a difference. I had just Meren for so long. I didn't feel like I needed anyone else. Meren did and she got her wish.

"Meren and I took each other in at a very young age. She was young and desperate for family, though she couldn't even remember her own. I was from an orphanage. She came to me through the window one night and everything else is the history between us. Struggling together, sharing secrets, sneaking out for Meren's fun, eventually uniting with Veiria and making new memories— giving Meren all the family she wanted: a brother and a sister, before Veiria was taken by her own hand and Meren was left without someone she'd grown to love." I trail off wistfully at those bygone days.

"That must have been hard on her ... and you." Eu's unnaturally quiet, listening to me intently. His gaze has drifted up from the sketch to me, my thumb still on it in reminiscence.

"It was, but we made it, and we just waited patiently, because we both believed she'd come back. She hurt herself severely that day to save us and to punish herself. Meren was heartbroken. And I was lost. But it's done now and Veiria's back. We have a purpose again. We're self-made protectors of Veiria and of the world."

"An honorable title," Eu says, tilting his head.

"True. Or a burden," I say bitterly, gazing long at the image, before Eu turns it over and back to the picture of him.

My heart pounds.

"This is good." Eu grins, admiring the details. "Even more handsome than I thought I was."

I laugh and try to flip it and Eu puts his hand on mine.

I swallow and he flips the page with me.

My mouth is dry. I close my eyes and he lets go.

Eu laughs and runs his hand through his hair as I look at him, swallowing. I draw my hand back into my lap, wondering what I want to do with it.

"Sorry. Momentary judgment reflex." Eu turns back to flipping through the sketchbook and I relax after a moment, starting to describe several scenes as Eu sits back and listens, occasionally commenting on a place or animal.

"You've gone so far," he says distantly. "Unlike me. You've lived a very different life. A prospective, adventurous one."

"I wouldn't call it that," I say. "But I guess I could call it a good one."

Eu smiles, slurping his nearly melted gelato and I give him a face.

"What? Where's your soup supreme?"

I laugh and ask him shyly, "Can I try some?"

"Sure. Only if I can try some too."

He takes a spoon and brings it to my lips, and I close my eyes in embarrassment, ignoring Eu's adoring gaze. He brushes a finger under my lips to capture a trail of gelato and I stiffen, my heart racing at his touch, like that of a painter delicate not to ruin his painting—his eyes just on my lips.

"Uh, thanks," I say awkwardly shifting on the step. I hand mine over to him—the whole cup and Eu laughs and turns his head away, looking at the gelato stand a few paces away, beyond the alley entrance in the bright sunshine.

"Don't mention it."

The sun flickers down from above, bathing us in light and the area at our feet in long shadows as Eu finishes slurping the rest of my gelato, licking his lips greedily, and in the end, casting the briefest of glances at me that sends my heart into loops.

Later we find the girls on the beach and I'm not sure if I'm sad to no longer be alone with Eu or grateful for someone else to fill the awkwardness or save me from the tension and my feelings as I'm all too aware that Eu's pursuing me. Meren told me to stay away from men like him, even queer men. I don't know if I want to.

Veiria

I go to bed late after my night singing—of feeling free in my voice and somewhat at home in this body, even though I still know it isn't quite mine. I feel way too groggy, and I know it's my fault, as I yawn softly, my eyes bleary as I walk to the window, the translucent white curtains billowing inwards with the salty morning breeze, and I look at the ships in the distance, sailing with white sails in the hazy morning.

Meren stretches behind me and yawns much louder in a way that's almost obnoxious. "Morning, Veiria."

"Good morning," I say, turning with a smile.

"Jeeze, you look exhausted. You have bags under your eyes."

I rub them. "Just singing."

"Hmmm. Well, I must have been out stone cold." She eyes me with a smile. "Want help with your makeup and hair?"

My smile blossoms. "Yes, please."

Meren finishes helping me prepare and I feel some sort of glee. We dine on breakfast with Eu and Telvin in the lower levels, open to the city and the currents of wind in wide arches, then make our way into the cool breeze of the city, gulls shrieking in the morning air.

I pull Meren into a clothes shop at one point. "Just one thing," I say, and she doesn't resist.

My gaze travels over the racks along three corners, a display of sea-worthy elegance displayed on mannequins in the window. Airy dresses to blow on beaches with beautiful sundresses, pretty sandals, and wide sunhats.

That's all fine and dandy and nice and it draws my eyes and makes my heart skip a beat just as much as every other day I got to wear a dress, but my heart is captured by another dress, and I hurry towards it as Meren gapes in my shadow.

"You are not wearing that," Meren says, somewhere between amusement and embarrassment.

That said, she reluctantly waits for me outside. "Let me see this dress."

"Almost ready," I say theatrically. "There. Last touch," I say, stepping out.

Meren eyes me with an upturned eyebrow, looking like she's trying to hold in her amusement. "Honestly, I can't stand your fashion sense," Meren mutters, arms crossed.

"That's what makes it so fun to wear." I twirl. "I always loved to look at the night sky."

I look down at my dress with a girlish, delighted smile. There're a few globes stuck to the side like galaxies and stitching on the side of constellations. The belt sparkles like the milky way and the top hugs my chest in a transparent illusion top, some puffy, bespeckled shoulders glittering like stars and cute silver heels, plus some silver moon earrings newly clipped to my ear—they aren't pierced yet.

"No offense, Veiria, but it's a bit much." Her judgy expression fades away to a smile. "But I do like it a little. It's very you. You are a bit silly sometimes."

"I am," I giggle, looking down and spinning as I stick my tongue out. "Thanks, Meren. I'll add it to my collection with my jellyfish dress."

"You have a jellyfish dress?" Meren snort-laughs. "Why am I not surprised. Alright, though I feel like I'm parading around my little sister, but why does it matter?" She shoos me to the counter. "Go, go, I'll treat you with my non-existent funds."

"Don't worry, Meren." I tuck my hands behind my back and step awkwardly to the counter, still growing used to heels.

A young woman sits behind the counter and she's striking in a simple way—her light brown-blonde hair is tucked behind her ears in a ponytail, her expression is bored but so pretty, and she just sits there, a little dressy in a short black skirt and pale green polo top.

I stare at her behind the register a little too long, as she sits there and smiles.

She's pretty.

I realize I'm starstruck by her.

I shake my head. No, Veiria. You only like boys. You're a girl. Girls like boys. Please. *I can't.*

Because in my heart, I know I'm tired of that. I'm scared of liking girls. I've had too much assuming I liked them from others—of liking them when I didn't want to—when I wanted to be one of them, laugh with them, cry with them. I want to gossip about boys with them. I want to fit in and not be seen as a threat. I just want friendship and platonic feelings. I want all my attraction to go to boys. All the affection directed towards me to come from boys. I just want platonic love with girls—the love of friendship and sisterhood. I want them to see me as one of them, and attraction will make them leave me, even if I don't ask for anything else, don't want anything else. They won't want me as a friend. They'll think me a creep.

And somehow, in this place, I forgot I liked girls too. I don't want to remember.

She smiles at me. "I'm Miranda. Are you alright?" she asks, concern in her eyes.

"Yes," I say, a bit tongue-tied as she rings up my purchase and I get away before I remember this feeling of dejection too well. I want to fit in.

She hands me back my purchase with another smile. "You have good tastes."

"Thank you," I say gratefully, my heart still beating as I look in any direction but her vermilion eyes.

I turn away as I clutch my head and the feeling stops, forgetting what I'd just thought, and I look at Meren and smile, holding up my purchase in a cute little gift bag as she rolls her eyes.

And now that Meren's in front of me again, I feel more at ease, more grounded in the things I want and that I have here with me.

I have a sister in front of me and she sees me as just that—another girl, another young woman. Someone that she just wants to spend a little time with that's uniquely ours. And my heart cherishes that.

My eyes go wide in the center of the city, and I freeze, a flock of birds lifting up from the white square filled with families and children laughing and fountains into the blue heavens above.

"Eu, it's an astronomy tower," I whisper to Eu beside me.

"That's what you wanted to be, right?" he looks at me, then to the tower.

"Yes." I nod. "It's ... awe inspiring."

Eu sweeps his hand forward but doesn't take mine. "Then off we go."

I look back at Meren and Telvin, who are catching up behind us, beside one of the fountains.

Meren smiles at me. "Now it makes sense. Telvin, my sister has a place she wants to sightsee."

Telvin sits up, padding back to Eu, who shifts on his feet between us and Meren laughs, reaching over to pinch her brother's cheek.

"Ow." He swats her hand away.

"You have your hands full, Veiria." Meren looks at me, and I look at Eu's awkwardness in confusion.

"You all are making my ears red," Eu says quietly, grinding his toe against the white stone of the square. "I think it's time we go do some sightseeing."

The four of us enter the astronomy tower, winding up the spiral steps to the top and passing window after window, the city getting further and further away and the air getting thinner as we approach the top.

"I think I'm getting height sick," I say, my feet getting wobbly.

Eu catches my back. "You've been in plenty of high places with me."

I laugh nervously, feeling my heart falling away as we pass another window. "I think this is a little different."

Meren comes up next to me and offers me her shoulder.

"Thanks," I say.

"No problem."

Eu shrugs behind us and Telvin trails just behind Eu, marveling out the windows as the seagulls soar past.

Then we pass through the opening to the top and I gasp, turning in circles at the numerous scientific instruments used for astronomy, a huge telescope in its center.

I touch it tentatively, as the other three leave me to do their own thing—Meren looking off to one side, Eu and Telvin off to the opposite one.

Eventually, I approach Meren, casting a glance back at Eu and Telvin as my heart sinks a little. It almost seems like I can never catch Eu alone anymore.

Telvin

I marvel at the city below me, the outside of the bowl and cascading water far in the distance and the sky beyond, seagulls screeching in the wind far below as the wind buffets us at our high vantage point.

Eu walks up next to me, and I watch the wind ruffle his curly black hair. "Hey," he says.

"Hi." I close my eyes and feel the wind. "It's wonderful up here. Humans could be anything, you know, so why can't we fly?" I stick my arms out and open them as Eu steps incredibly close.

I turn, my heart racing. "Eu? Umm ... What are you thinking?"

"Just that I like listening to you."

I swallow and meet his eyes. "Do you like me, Eu?" It leaves the tip of my tongue, as I don't know what to feel.

"I think I do. I need you." He says it like it's something cathartic and strangled over the wind—something he's still getting used to and is still figuring out if he should say it.

Then Eu abruptly grabs my face and presses his lips to mine, closing his eyes.

I'm startled for a moment and step back as my heart races, but then I kiss him back, gasping for breath at the desperate press of his lips.

Eu pulls away. "You're cute."

I can feel my cheeks flush. "I know I am." That was a little unexpected. I feel a strange feeling burning my soul.

"It came over me. I've been wanting to. Was that okay?"

I press my fingers to my lips, delicately feeling the lingering touch of his lips. "I suppose so. I liked it." I swing my leg a little and stumble starstruck towards the railing.

Eu catches me in his arms, and I look up at him.

"Just ask me next time," I breathe quietly, his face still so close and concerned.

"Understood," Eu says, stroking my cheek.

I laugh nervously and then place my hand over his, closing my eyes as I listen to the sea. "We should be getting back to them."

"Okay." Eu takes his arms off me and steps back, his eyes still on me and I smile tentatively, my heart still racing with a strange exhilaration. "I'll meet you by the girls. Later." He points a finger gun at me and shoots in a gesture I thought was reserved for his dorky friendship with Veiria, but I don't mind. It makes me smile and my heart hammer.

I stand on my tiptoes and look off over the railing at the gulls gliding through the towers and buildings below— the city is like a white, crowded maze.

And I think about our kiss and what it means to me. Whether I have a place in my heart for Eu beside Meren and Veiria and my duty to this world, knowing it could all end in a moment if Veiria so chose.

"I think that's a possibility." I crane myself over the edge, looking at the shore.

Then I sigh, bracing myself against the railing and closing my eyes to the wind. So much for my foresight and the anomaly of Eu.

In my thoughts I even fail to notice the growing black cloud on the horizon.

The Irony of Tortured Souls

Telvin

The day after, Eu and I found ourselves on the corner again. I decided to be brave for Eu and ask for a moment apart from the group.

Which seems all fine, thanks to Meren's newly established bond with Veiria again. I wouldn't let that bother me, except that I worry about Meren torturing herself again if it went awry. I can only hope that it doesn't happen this time. I can only hope that Meren's wounds don't spread and that Veiria breaks free from her cycle and mends her inner world before it's too late and Meren's resolve crumbles again.

"I wondered if I'd be kissing Veiria at this point," Eu admits. "I didn't think it would be you. I didn't think it'd be a boy." He looks at the space between us. "I just couldn't help myself."

"Fate moves in strange ways. Consider me a blessing." I uncurl my hand in my lap, as if it'll send me a sign.

"Is that your way of saying not to worry?"

"I'm just saying I liked it. What's your dilemma, if you like me?"

Eu sighs. "I just ..." He leans his head back. "These feelings make me scared. I know I like you. I just didn't know I *could* like you. It's complicated ..."

"You can like men and women at once. That doesn't compromise any of who you are."

"Says the boy who has everything figured out."

"I don't," I say a little defensively. "Look. If you like me, just feel it. Enjoy it. I know you probably have some things built up, but what's the difference?"

"The difference is that my family expected a girl. My classmates. My friends. My female crushes." A silence follows that. "It should have been Veiria, but I can't get past seeing her as a friend and just another girl."

"Then accept it. Bring back a boy. Bring back me ... and Meren for defense purposes. She'll straighten everything out. Fix things up."

Eu laughs and something clears up in his gaze as I lean over, and he pulls me against his shoulder.

"I like you when you're cheery. You worry me when you're not. Make me nervous."

"Is that so? Well, I am deeply sorry. Ashamed, really."

I close my eyes as we lean into each other, feeling the up-and-down of his sturdy chest, our legs touching and forget all about that. "It's fine. I'm just going to enjoy this. Meren's known for a while who I like and she's okay with it. She's a good older sis' who'd stick up for me."

Eu kisses me on the forehead. "She's a piece of work."

I laugh as we sit there for a while, Eu pulling away just enough for us to talk a little. He makes me laugh and I like the sound of his. I don't know if I really want forever with him or anything like that, but I'd date him, at least for a while and see what happens.

Eu seems more desperate and confused than I am. I've lived for millennia. I'm something out of time—Meren and I are cursed by Veiria's love to live in her cycle of a dream until she ends it and us with that dream. I can be patient. He can't.

But I can't tell him that. I hope he'll understand that we're all just puppets here, as if it's a cruel irony.

Murmurs Under the Stars

Veiria

We meet under string lights and streetlamps—music and dancing in the wind.

I wear my galaxy dress and Meren wears a deep sapphire one—like that of the deepest ocean.

The boys wear boring tuxes of black-and-white.

My stomach wants to revolt at the sight of them, no matter how handsome they are. Can't they wear something a bit more interesting to match their personalities? Add some emerald or something.

Something seemed to convince Meren and Telvin to spend one more night in the city. I wonder if that something was me or Eu.

I shrug. I don't care. I'm enjoying myself.

Telvin looks a little furtive, looking from the sky to the crowd to the sea. "We should really leave tomorrow."

Meren nudges him. "Shut up. You wanted to stay too. Admit it."

"I did admit it, I just have a feeling we should leave now."

Eu stands exceptionally close to Telvin. "I'm sure everything will be alright."

They look at each other for a long moment and Telvin goes quiet.

Meren whispers to me. "I'm betting they kiss tonight."

Something wells in my eyes. "I think you're looking into things. Eu ..."

"Veiria, rest assured he sees you as a girl clear as day. He's just as distraught as you are. Telvin gave me the deets."

"What do you mean?" I turn to her, scrunching my lip.

"I dunno." She shrugs. "You tell me. I knew you forever."

"I guess I don't want to know." I glance around the line as we move up, a waiter in crisp white with deep russet black skin and brown eyes greeting us with a smile.

Meren holds up four fingers. "Four, please."

He nods. "Right this way." I watch the waiter's tailcoat, trying to distract myself from Eu and Telvin. Telvin and Eu. I must be imagining things.

We're seated under the stars, an assortment of lights around us and chatter in the air of couples and groups, a heated box above us as the cool night air makes me shiver.

Meren pulls out two coats and hands me one. "Better to be warm than stylish, though I know you want to look perfect."

I accept with a tight smile, watching Eu and Telvin almost touching and trying to control the rising bile in my throat—the jealousy that Telvin had taken my Eu-Eu away from me.

Eu was all I wanted, after all. I swear I'd snap and tear this world down in fire right now and cry a river if Meren wasn't next to me to keep me company.

She flips through her menu. "I think I'll choose the calamari."

I make a face, my tongue out in a silent gag.

"I'm sorry, would you choose differently?" Meren squints at my improper expression.

"Squiddies are cute," I mumble. "Who would eat them?"

"*Squiddies*? Seriously?" She sighs. "Well, this carnivore would." She points to herself. "Fine, should I get seaweed or something?"

"No, it's fine. I didn't mean it."

Meren looks at my menu critically. "We need to broaden your pallet. You can't be sparing the squiddies. They're made to be eaten."

"They're born for my joy," I mumble again. "Don't you remember, I have a jellyfish dress? I love sea creatures!" I perk up a little and turn to her eagerly.

"Whoa there, Veiria." Meren puts her hands up. "I like hearing about what you like, but let's tone down the enthusiasm a bit. How about I get duck?"

"No, it's okay." I slouch. "Murder the squiddies if you want."

"I'll get duck," Meren says passively.

I peek at her, trying not to smile. I try not to comment that I like duckies too, but I can't avoid every cute animal.

Meren orders for herself and me and hands in our menus and Eu orders something for both him and Telvin.

"You won't share with us?" I slouch forward.

"Should I have, Veiria? Sorry."

"It's fine." I slouch forward, Eu's genuine dejection rejuvenating my soul. "As punishment, I won't share my food."

"Well, I'll take that pain to my grave."

"Ugh ..." I sigh, my cheek pushed up on my palm.

"You okay, Veiria?" Eu asks, searching my face.

"Just thinking about squiddies," I say in monotone, feeling a bit out of it.

As I do, Meren takes her mixed tropical grapefruit-guava-passion drink from the waiter and passes it between us with two straws. "I thought you'd like it."

"Thanks." I pick my head up, perking up a little and ignoring the strain on my heart as I sip from it, not commenting on the fizziness that burns the inside of my mouth like lava.

"I thought you'd like it."

I don't mention that I don't. For having known me for years, Meren's either pranking me or genuinely never offered me sparkling drinks, but I do love fruit.

The order comes later, and I try to enjoy it under my shifting emotions, glancing at the stars and taking sips of our drink.

Meren honestly looks stunning tonight—she stands out like a gem, unlike Eu and Telvin's boring attire.

I breathe out into the night, staring at the stars. The more I'm here, the more I realize these people might not be with me for much longer.

I wish I had Meren as a friend in real life, I wish I had Eu as a lover, I wish I had more time to get to know Telvin and all his pensive, child-like mystery.

I turn the dial of the telescope that night under the stars, gazing at the brilliant infinite lights covering the night sky. I feel a yearning in my chest.

I focus on each star, deciphering them, studying their beauty.

Until my eye aches, and I realize how hard I pushed it against the eye piece. I rub my eye, the infinity of the stars still filling my mind. They look so peaceful up there. I really wish I could glide up there between them.

I think back to my 'prom' dance with Eu.

That might be the closest I get.

I step away, giving the others a chance to marvel at the stars that I wish I could keep as my own, spinning in the night breeze, the orbs of my dress making me feel a little connected to the stars.

I know that tomorrow we'll leave this place.

Telvin's ominous feeling sits in my head as I think about tomorrow—what could be and what I could possibly lose. Do I really want to go to the end of this journey? What is it that I really do even want? Is it really just Eu or just Meren or the stars or the feel of the wind and of freedom? Was it an experience or a person? Or was it something more?

Meren's words haunt me, and I don't let myself dwell on them. I won't let myself comprehend the idea that she's right—that I'm different. After all, there's too much sweetness here, even if some things are eating away at my chest, this place can't just be a feeling. This body and these people can't just be an illusion of my heart. That would be ridiculous.

I hold my heart and look at them, turning away and feeling building tears, instead forcing myself to look to the horizon.

"Hey, are you alright?" I hear the soft voice of Meren.

I nod, but I don't think I've ever been good at holding it together.

"Your stars are really beautiful. You know, I really appreciate you. All of this. You built a beautiful place."

I sniffle, letting my tears fall off the balcony. "I'm afraid of tomorrow—of what you and Telvin aren't telling me about myself."

Meren silently looks out at the sky. "Trust me, we want to, but even we don't know everything." She holds me close. "You just have to face tomorrow like it's just another day. You have to *live*—live like there's no tomorrow. I'm rooting for you, whatever you choose."

"I don't know if you're even real."

Meren shakes her head. "Does that matter?" She touches my chest. "You're real, so don't think about that. There's more than just us. I know that there's something for you beyond this boundless sky. One day"—her voice quiets, and she looks at me like a tender friend who wishes me the best—"you'll be free as a bird. Free to soar your own skies. And I'll be happy for you. I'll wait for that day, and I'll smile when I see that you found something worth living for ... a self that you could proudly walk another day with. *I'll love you then.*"

Meren looks to the horizon, and my eyes linger on her hopeful face.

I'll disappoint you.

But still, I can't help feeling a shred of her hope. "I'll try."

"I knew you would," Meren says, her eyes in the stars, as she looks ahead to a horizon I still can't believe in.

The Glow of the End

Veiria

I head out with Meren, restless dreams wracking my brain in the night of the world splitting open, consuming Eu, Meren, and Telvin as I reach out, my lungs screaming for the void to close before it's too late. But it doesn't, and they vanish into darkness, leaving me crying as I collapse to the ground, blood pooling as I lift my hand from a gash at my chest, not knowing whether to laugh at the cruel fate or cry that I died before I really got to *live*.

Meren closes the bathroom door and comes out in rough travel wear, tossing me a bag.

I look down at it.

"Wear that. It's a rough road ahead."

My heart drops. "I don't want to." I don't want to go back to pants and all the things that trapped me.

Meren comes forward and hugs me. "Then don't. I'll understand. I'm not your mother."

I sigh and hug her back, appreciating the gesture, but this is just something that I refuse to do. If I'm going to be in this world much longer, I'm going to live in it.

We arrive at the edge of the city, and I glance up at a statue I can almost recognize.

"Is that ...?"

Meren nods. "Noctine."

Recognition dawns on me as I remember: This is their domain. Though they look a little different in the towering statue. Left behind in the square are tiny marbles of light.

Telvin explains, "This is the city's deity. At nightfall, once a month, they thank Noctine with their blessings of light from Noctine's realm. Noctine isn't the most predictable deity, but they've never let this world or their people down. This city prospers because of them."

We pass the statue, and I admire it. This version of Noctine has the wings and feet of a crow, their chest ruffled with pitch-black feathers, as if in mid-transformation. They hold a dark staff, their arms spread wide, fountains around them.

We leave the city and the statue behind, stepping onto bridges of earth. As we walk, golden orbs of light flow up around us dreamily, stretching off in the direction of the faintly beating heart on the horizon.

I hang back a little, my mind feeling awfully heavy with each step, until a tremor passes through the world, and I drop to my knees, clutching my heart and kneeling on the ground, screaming as the breath is crushed from my chest.

At my outburst, the others look back in distress and run to me. Cracks form on the ground beneath me, the shards of Neihdria arching to us in deadly shards as the world flickers.

Neihdria's found us and as I start to dread, the world flashes erratically before my eyes. Neihdria appears and Meren throws up a shield to block the wave of what I know now to be my emotions. It was an impulse to let my despair out all at once—an impulse I'm not sure was a good decision.

"I'm sorry, I didn't mean to," I whine, shrieking as the earth groans and shatters.

Eu kneels by my side and meets my panicked eyes. "It wasn't your fault, Veiria. We'll get through this." He grabs my shoulders and mimics breathing deeply. "I just need you to calm down, okay?"

I try to, but I shudder with every breath, holding my ears as I see Telvin looking around on alert as he talks urgently to Meren. She throws out her hands to keep us and the ground below us intact.

"It's no use, Eu-Eu. It's over, and it's all because of me. You three would be better without me. I should go away with Noctine and sleep, so you all will be okay."

Eu shakes me desperately. "Veiria. Look at me. We will *not* be okay without you. I won't be okay without you. Don't do that." His voice is thick with emotion, enough to where it cracks.

"I'm sorry, Eu-Eu. You mean a lot to me, but you don't need me. Let Noctine come. I've ruined it."

Eu stops abruptly, his eyes wide. "You did this? You *wanted* it?"

"I'm sorry I put you in danger, but I need to talk to Noctine," I say resolutely as the world stabilizes just a bit. "That was all real, though. I don't know what to do, or when you'll all disappear. I don't know when I'll go back to 'my world' and I can't bear that. I want Noctine to fix it for me, so I'll listen."

"Veiria, you can't."

"Sorry," I whisper, blinking my cloudy eyes at him as I feel a presence in the air that tugs at my soul.

Sacrificing the Things You Love

Veiria

The world comes to a halt, Eu, Telvin, and Meren slowing as Meren blocks a last attack.

Then the air shifts, the world stops shaking and splitting, the oppressive red star shivers and flickers, and the shards of Neihdria shudder in mid-air, flickering before abruptly changing direction and speeding to the source of the disruption.

A portal opens up and a shroud of darkness fills the sky in a towering wall.

Noctine glides out, their robes billowing out behind them in purples and blacks and the portal closes with a swipe of their hand, the darkness vanishing with it. Then Noctine trains their eyes on the arc of deadly glass, slowly casting their hand across the air in front of them and the shards, too, vanish into darkness—every last one.

Then they raise their arms up high, and their castle of light appears around us, the walls encroaching Eu and I and blocking Meren and Telvin from sight.

In a flicker of time, the entire landscape around us changes, the threat of my destruction gone in its wake and a new threat in front of me.

"Noctine," Eu breathes just behind me.

Noctine raises one arm from a pedestal and a translucent barrier goes up between Eu and I before either of us can blink, leaving me alone in a room with Noctine for Eu to watch helplessly.

Noctine walks down slowly from a low altar, every step of theirs chilling my spine and the air around me, as the full force of Noctine's power permeates and chokes out the air in the room with its potency.

Noctine stops at the bottom of the short flight of stairs, still a good distance from me, but not far enough for comfort. "Veiria, it's time to sleep." Noctine opens their arms, robe billowing like a sail and suddenly I don't want to do this anymore. Suddenly I'm scared. "You know in your heart that it's the right thing." Their eyes soften. "Don't struggle; it'll make things so much easier."

"I don't want to," I whisper, backing into the barrier as Eu knocks on it soundlessly behind me. The shards of glass poise in the air beside me like knives, as I remember Noctine's threat of sealing me away. *I didn't mean it.*

"Veiria, I'm giving you the chance to let this all end. Just let it all go."

"I told you I don't want to!" I cower, covering my ears and screaming as the glass knives extend into deadly spears and shoot out at Noctine at lightning speed. "Just give me more time."

I look up, terrified that I willingly attacked Noctine, consciously or not. My heart plummets in my chest. But Noctine merely waves their hand, and the spears vanish from reality into a wave of darkness. "I care about you, Veiria. I want to help you, to make it all a little more bearable, before you snap."

I quiver, sinking into a corner on the ground and backing away every inch I possibly can as a dozen more knives appear.

Noctine slowly walks towards me, and I put my fists over my eyes. "Get away from me!" My words trigger a whiplash of sparks and pops of glass as a hundred tiny needles appear and zoom for Noctine, bouncing off each other erratically. Again, Noctine waves their hand in a circle, a shroud of darkness covering them and again the glass disappears before it can lay an inch of harm to their pale skin. I start leaking tears as they stand before me. "Eu-Eu's all I have. He's my heart. I can't leave him," I say in a broken voice.

"Nothing will get better if you stay this way, in this garden of your dreams." Noctine talks with a parental voice. "You'll go in circles chasing that boy forever. You're only hurting yourself." Noctine leans forward.

I raise my arm up instinctively and fire a shard of glass.

They swipe it away and extend their hand to me with a comforting smile. "You're just a child, Veiria. You have the world ahead of you, but you're stuck here torturing yourself. Come with me. Sleep. You'll tear yourself apart in dreams. You must confront them." They stare straight at me with wise, depthless amethyst eyes. "Come with me and I'll steal you. Not to trap you, but so you can face yourself."

I look into the black sky of their robe. "Will it hurt?"

Their eyes are filled with pity. "Only if you let it. But if you want to save yourself, then it's necessary."

I glance back at Eu. He has tears in his eyes for once, slamming himself against the barrier desperately.

"You'll see him again. This isn't goodbye," they reassure me. "Come with me."

I reach up slowly and take their cold hand.

They place their other on top of mine and smile like a guardian. "Everything will be alright. Eu will be safe, along with everyone else. I'll make sure of it, until you're ready to come back."

I look at Eu, blinking back tears as I force a smile and start walking beside Noctine.

I make out my name on his lips as he bangs on the barrier with both his fists, still sobbing.

I feel the smallest spark of joy born from his show of care and grief. I don't want to leave Eu, don't want to face myself, whatever that means, but I want to be gone. I want to sleep. And if Noctine gives me a way out, even if it's not one I wanted, then maybe I should just take it. Because deep down, I know this is all fake and the place I came from isn't somewhere I want to go back to.

Even if I don't see Eu again, I know he never needed me.

I wipe my thumb over my eyes and turn away before looking at him anymore becomes unbearable.

Then I approach the altar with Noctine and they let go of my hand so that I can walk alone up the short flight of stairs.

"Stay still," Noctine commands.

As they close their eyes and spread their hands by their sides, palms forward, the barrier disappears and Eu sprints across the room towards me as time slows and he stumbles in his desperation.

"Eu!" His name bursts from my lips and I reach for him, glass needles unintentionally forming on the tips of my fingers. My blood freezes. "Eu! Stop!" My aim misses and he stumbles up the steps as a hazy sheen of amber starts to form around me.

Noctine hasn't opened their eyes, in complete concentration.

"Eu! Stop it!"

The amber starts to solidify around me in a hard crystal as Eu bangs on it, his eyes wide and terrified and his tears streaming.

"Eu. Eu, it's no good," I whisper. "I can't do this."

He stops, his panicked eyes searching every corner of my face. "Don't do this, Veiria. You don't have to do this. We'll get you out."

"No, Eu. I'm so sorry." I start panting and suddenly feel alone. I gasp, as if for air and my fingers press up against his, trembling when I can't touch him. I try to calm myself as my heart races and I hyperventilate in the confined space. "I'm scared, Eu." My voice is muffled, the amber encasing my body in a vice. "Don't forget me. Even if you find better. I—" I struggle to move my lips. "I—" *love you.* Yet, I can't say it because my body is petrified.

Eu screams, pressing his forehead against the amber as his lower lip trembles.

Leave me, Eu, and never look back. I'm not worth it. I was never worth Eu or this world that brought me something special and fleeting.

I watch Eu's tear tracks on his cheeks, his lowered lashes that are pretty and glossy with his tears, the delicacy of his slightly coarse, but pretty and delicate tan hands clutching the glass just beyond mine and I feel something break deep in my heart.

I mean this much to him, and I just threw it all away. I threw Eu's feelings away and my own, and suddenly I crave the release I hope I'll find.

The amber hardens and creaks far too slowly, until it's finally solidified, and it darkens, leaving my eyes frozen open and panicked at the isolation and the deafening silence.

Then there's a snap through my spine, and my awareness ceases from this plane of existence …

Chills in the Night

Veiria

I wake up on a clammy surface, my breathing still heavy and fast. I push up, my hands sticking to the ground as I feel the ground vibrate, a threatening presence ahead of me.

I back up, the room throbbing around me.

It's nearly pitch black, apart from snaking veins that glow at my feet, threatening to envelop me.

I push my back against the mucousy hallway, holding my breath as the crystal shards of Neihdria snake towards me from the pale-red darkness.

Veiria. Veiria! A booming voice chides me. Then it softens to a purr. *Where are you now? You can't hide from your demons forever, my lovely darling ...*

I inch around the corner, letting my breath go as the shards pass me by.

Then the room blasts white. Images of a man and woman ... husband and wife, holding a child ...

My parents.

Such a disappointment.

I stumble backwards.

Don't you feel their wrath? Don't you feel their heartbreak? Their anger? Their scorn? That they birthed an abomination.

An image of a teen boy with his face scratched out flashes before my eyes. The area where his mouth would be pulls apart in a grin and starts laughing. "HA-HA-HA!"

He's hideous: unkempt face, greasy curls, distinct jawline, rough wide shoulders, and a hideous suit.

My father would have several things to say to you. You're in fantasy land, my little duplicate. I look like him. I breathe by him. I am at his mercy. The horrific face frowns. *You won't let him hurt me, will you?*

My heart stops as he grows viscous teeth and bites at my chest.

I yelp and desperately push him away. "No! Stop! Please!" A deeper pain fills my lungs as I claw at the mouth. "Don't take them from me!"

In a puff of smoke, it's gone and there's a little girl there, her hair braided, standing next to a mother. *You could have been like me.* She holds out her hand with a flower and when I reach to take it, she crushes her hand with a malicious grin, a heart—gushing blood replaces that flower. *But you didn't get that.*

DIDN'T YOU? A chorus of voices scream.

I cower into a ball. "Eu! Eu!" I feel panicked, clutching at my heart. Blood pools at my chest.

The girl vanishes and I see a coffin.

What did you do? A woman's voice screams, and my eyes fly wide.

Nothing, I want to say. *I didn't mean it.*

Didn't you love me?

Then I run. Somehow, I run.

He'll kill you. They scream. *He'll humiliate you.* They'll hate you. *You'll be fighting a world that will never believe you. Then you'll kill yourself and they'll laugh, calling you your nightmare. But they're right.*

I stumble into the hallway and my shadow rips apart to my right, sputtering blood. I stare in horror as I feel thousands of ruptures on my body and scream in pain.

End it! End it! End it now! The voices are gleeful. *All of you are worthless. You'd be no happier, even if the world cherished you.*

"Stop it! Eu, please help me!"

Why would he come? You know he's not real.

My heart freezes. I try to move my lips, but I can't.

You're jealous. An image of Eu and Telvin flashes in my mind. *Don't you want revenge? Don't you want him gone so you can live with your sweet little delusion?*

Telvin's head lops off and I rock back-and-forth, forehead to the ground and scream until I'm hoarse at the sweet boy who deserved a happy ending more than I did.

You're just lying to yourself, and you know it. The world shows you the truth every day. Don't you know what biology is? Don't you know what a predator is? A groomer? A creep?

Images of newscasters spewing hate and twisted stories of mutilated children and a shadowy figure preying in the corners of bathrooms, caricatures on television of a man in a dress, gossip in the hallway, a father's invalidation, scorn, and force on his child to comply, a parent's grief over a living child, a young girl's heart ignored and humiliated by teachers, students, parents until her joy fades, a girl like me murdered by her boyfriend when his peers find out about their relationship, the glossy eyes of a dead girl disrespected in death even after losing her life to that same hate ... flash in my eyes.

Then it all vanishes and there's a hand on my shoulder, but I'm still moaning, my hands over my eyes as I twitch.

His voice gradually comes into focus, as he shakes my shoulder lightly.

"Veiria, I'm here. Veiria, please tell me you're alright."

I stare up at his pleading eyes, then behind him at Telvin, alive and well, and I'm flooded with relief. My shaking stops after a few moments, and I nod, looking between them. "Yeah."

He lets out a heavy breath. "You scared me half to death. Here." He starts dabbing at my face and I feel shame in my chest at the elation I feel. "You're white as a ghost."

"Well, I bet it's a good thing for you I didn't become one. You'd be lonely." My smile is weak. "Right?"

"Don't say things like that, Veiria. But yes, I'd be immensely sad." I look at his eyes and they're exhausted and red.

I look away. "I caused you so much pain running into you all those days ago. I'm sorry."

Eu puts his hands on my shoulders, and looks at me squarely, his lower lip trembling. "Don't do that, Veiria. Don't leave me like that. You know you're wrong."

I look at him quietly. *I know I'm a liar*, I think.

He lowers his hands and Telvin approaches.

I try to keep my face from showing my fear as I look at him.

He cups my hands. "I'm so glad you're alright. I ... we ..."

"I ... Yes, I am." Suddenly becoming aware of my posture, I relax my shoulders.

And just like that, the room pops from existence. And I stare frozen at the white room, realizing I just imagined them there. I try to move my mouth, to scream some more, but my chest is hollow, still aching like it'd been torn out and I shiver on my knees, waiting for the next nightmare ...

The Silence of a Departed Friend

Eu

There's nothing but silence.

I sniffle, my tears rapidly drying in the still-hot air.

In a second, Telvin's in front of me, speechless. I look up.

There's nothing but silence and falling ash—thick hot ash falling so peacefully and Telvin's beautiful, cute, panicked face right there. I'd want him, but …

But Veiria's gone …

I search the spot where she left—where she gave herself up willingly for nothing. Both her and Noctine are gone.

"She's gone," I say with absolute desolation.

Telvin seems to shake, his eyes wide as he turns to Meren walking towards us. "It's not over," she states plainly. She looks like a mess, and I wonder how she's holding it together with the knowledge I have from Telvin.

"Meren, don't," Telvin says pleadingly, before looking back at me. "I'm so sorry. You look so sad." Telvin reaches out his hand but stops short of touching me. "You were closer to her than either of us this time. And we weren't there."

I close my eyes and reach out my hand, cradling his against my cheek and I breathe deeply.

Telvin squirms a little, but he smiles at me. "There's still hope."

I smile, winking at him. "I knew you'd say that."

"It's true," he mumbles timidly.

My shoulders sink. "I want her to see that it's worth it. I want to be there, even if it's not the way she wanted it. Will you two help me?" I sniffle again. "I want to see her again."

Telvin nods quickly. "Of course. Um ... Eu? I'm your boyfriend, right?"

"Sure, sure," I fire off casually, watching Telvin blush.

"Idiot," Meren mutters, crossing her arms. "We're her friend too." She jerks her thumb. "So, let's high tail it out of here before we're cooked meat."

Telvin squints up and I follow his gaze back up to the rapidly re-growing maroon star.

"That is a problem ... I think I'm unwilling to die to this one." I hold Telvin's hand as he helps pull me up. "Just a kiss?" I suggest, clearing my throat.

Telvin's eyes look a bit startled, but he nods, his eyes falling in a way that's rather cute. "A kiss will do."

Then I cup his cheek, softer this time and bring my lips to his as Telvin closes his eyes and breathes in peacefully.

He clasps his hands in front of him and gives me innocent heart eyes as I let go. "I'm beginning to like you better."

With that I grin and turn towards the heart beating in the distance, my worry mounting again for whatever my friend is facing in there. Whatever Veiria's facing. I know I want to be the friend who can save her from whatever demons she holds, whether she wants me there or not. That's the type of friend I'll be, especially after ignoring her feelings.

A Garden of Pleasures

Veiria

I open my eyes to a sunlit courtyard, shaded with fronds and cultivated with brilliantly alluring flowers in an exotic rainbow of colors. The courtyard is framed with marble columns, and glass runs along the ceiling, the sun shining brightly—a greenhouse. It's sweltering and I start to sweat. There's fountains, nude statues, and mini garden aqueducts.

I catch my breath as Eu approaches me, but not as a simple boy, but a young man. My God ...

My mouth feels dry. He's shirtless, his golden-brown skin showing—still a bit scrawny, but muscled from days working with his family. A bit of dark, closely curled hair on his chest and droplets of sweat from the greenhouse.

I stare dry-mouthed. He has nothing on but tight leather pants with a bulge around the groin. *Oh God,* I swallow.

He grins at me playfully, kneeling on the steps below my ornate gold throne and raises my foot reverently to kiss it.

My chest rises and falls unevenly below my thinly-strapped, close-fitting v-neck dress—it's a shimmering royal gold with a slit at the leg—far too fine for anything I've ever known.

I hold my breath, but he doesn't let go. Instead, he continues, gliding his lips up my leg slowly and feeling its length with that same reverent touch. "Eu, what are you—"

He plants a few tender kisses on my inner thigh, and I suck in breath.

"God ..." I close my eyes, tilting my head back for a minute.

He treats me like a Goddess—worships me like one.

He then rises, doing the same to my fingers—kissing each one, my arms. Then he brushes my dress aside from my shoulder, bringing his mouth around my breast, sucking long and sweet. I tilt my head back further. He does the same with my other, caressing my nipple with his lips.

He slowly shrugs the rest of my dress off and it slithers to the ground in ribbons. I stop him before it can fall off my legs.

"Veiria." He eyes me hungrily.

He brushes my hair aside delicately. "You're my goddess," he whispers as he kisses me tenderly behind the ear.

Then he lowers himself again, drawing aside the slit of my dress.

He moves his mouth up further and I feel a tremor of fear. "Not down there."

"I don't mind, Veiria. You're still my Queen," he says ever so achingly sweet. Consoling, even.

It doesn't relax my heartbeat at all. I can look anywhere but his eyes, but I feel just a little pleased.

"You're blushing. It's cute."

I have nowhere to hide my face, so I cover it with my arm.

"You don't care?" I ask tentatively, a knot of fear in my voice.

"I don't care. You're a beautiful woman."

I take a few deep breaths and then smile like a schoolgirl. "Be gentle."

He nods, then puts his mouth between my legs and I moan.

In-between his kisses and the work of his mouth and tongue, he murmurs to me, "You're my Queen. My Goddess. My darling, Veiria." I swoon at his words and at the pleasure of his mouth and hands.

I squeal a bit at his stubble brushing me down there too and take a peek at how stiff he is for me under his pants. He makes me want to faint, but this pleasure feels too good for belief—so sweet and passionate, and nothing like I've ever known. For once, my body feels true pleasure without screaming at me.

Then he takes my hand, leading me to the water. I smile.

He takes off his trousers and I shyly cover my eyes. Then his hands are there, and he's walking backwards, my hands in his.

I don't take my eyes from his.

Once we're both chest height and obscure, he kisses me long, deep, and sweet.

I try not to pay too much attention to below the water and what's down there between his legs waiting for me.

My chest hammers. "I want you, Eu. I want you inside of me."

He smiles and brushes my hair aside. "All too soon, my love."

I swallow. "Am I not good enough for you now?"

"It's not that." Finally, he lowers his eyes and becomes more the Eu I know—a teenager again. "I want you to be with me fully in flesh and with all your heart when you can love yourself fully—when you can love yourself without me loving you and become who you really are." His smile grows bitter. "You must know this isn't real."

I nod, a bitter taste in my mouth. My vision blurs with tears.

His thumb caresses my cheek more clumsily now. "I didn't want to choose, but I'm sorry. I've made my choice." He cups my hand in his, his smile tight, then he awkwardly hugs me. "I want you as a friend. I chose Telvin. I'm sorry." And he's crying like a boy just out of his mother's arms, before he vanishes in a gust of soft wind, along with the courtyard and the fountains—the water, the flowers, the throne—and I want to scream for the miserable feeling in my chest—that this all couldn't be real.

To Travel to Your Loved One

Eu

I walk next to Telvin. We're inches apart, but besides that closeness, there's a tension in the air.

Meren's stiff in front of us, tapping her finger on her thigh.

She turns and looks at Telvin, who shrugs.

"What is it?" I ask.

She looks like she's about to glare at me, but instead purses her lips thoughtfully. "It's just taking forever and I'm tired."

Telvin leaves my side. "I know, Meren. I understand."

Meren's shoulders droop as she looks back over her shoulder. We've gone through a shroud of darkness. Telvin says it's a remnant of Noctine's abilities keeping the world from completely imploding—keeping us safe.

Telvin

"She was finally here ..." Meren says quietly.

I grasp her hand lightly and motion her back. "Let's rest. Just one more night. We've been traveling long enough, and we need our rest. It may be our last night." I glance at Eu, then back at Meren. A last night in this bittersweet memory. I refuse to acknowledge my sister's fate. I can't. I'll imagine a future with both of them, granted with Veiria's love.

Meren's gaze darkens with the edges of grief. "Veiria won't last that long."

"She will," I say softly. "Because we'll trust her this time."

Meren glances back at my hand and squeezes her eyes tightly shut. "Okay, Telvin. Just one night."

Several minutes later, I start a fire in the darkness with a handful of wooden blocks from Meren's pack and a bit of my magic—more a tiny magic trick than anything. It can't do much more than an everyday match. That and my weak foresight is all I have—not enough to be considered a gifted magic user, just a normal being adrift in the world. Well, apart from the gift of Veiria's favor, so not at all a regular being in any sense. Because we're blessed.

Meren pokes at the fire as the three of us sit around it, seeming completely dejected by her eyes and slumped posture, but I don't blame her.

She looks up, glancing between Eu and me with a weak smile.

My eyes fall in embarrassment as Meren sits up and pops out a smore, hurling it between us.

It hits Eu's forehead, and I grab it before it hits the ground.

Eu starts to sigh as he dabs at his head.

"It's for luck, friend." She tosses another, a bit gentler this time.

This time he catches it. "Thanks," he says. He picks at it, but he just doesn't look himself. "But I'm not hungry."

"Oh, come off it. We have a friend to save," Meren says.

I watch his face in the tiny patch of firelight. "I know."

"Eu, we'll save her," I plead softly to him.

"You don't know that."

I get up on my knees and shift around to face him. "My foresight tells me we will. It tells me she'll be happy." It doesn't really. That's a lie and I think I can see in Meren's face that she knows—she's probably overjoyed I'm breaking a sacred rule.

Eu looks up at me and I place my hand on the grass next to him.

"Really?"

I nod, tight-lipped. "Whatever the case, her will is stronger than all of us."

Eu reaches out tentatively, and our hands overlap in the grass.

He looks deep into my eyes, and I gulp. "You cheer me up." He attempts a smile. "I'll try not to mope anymore."

"There's nothing wrong with airing your feelings, Eu."

I sit back and he pulls me against him to lean on his shoulder.

I eye Meren, who's watching us with a smile and her palm on her cheek. "That's my brother." *Go get him,* it's like she's saying.

"He's mine," Eu says, still looking at me adoringly as he traces circles on my hand.

Meren gets up. "I'll leave you two alone. Happy for you, Telvin." She says it with a warm love and approval that brings me some comfort—more than the meaning of this world. There's no better love or approval than that of my sister.

'Sorry,' I mouth.

'Don't be,' she seems to say.

Eu doesn't seem to notice, instead intent on holding me close to him and I really don't mind at all. The only thing I do mind is leaving Meren alone on her possibly final night, a fact Eu is still likely blissfully unaware of.

I turn away from Meren and back to Eu, nestling in his arms, while not failing to catch Meren sitting alone at the edge of the cliff, looking at the stars—something she knows her other chosen sibling adores. Because for a moment, Noctine's shroud of darkness parts a little, as if to remind Meren and us of Veiria. Of the things she loves and the things we all still have to dream of.

Meren

I sit alone, the campfire behind me and Eu and Telvin in each other's arms.

I'm truly happy for them, but I can't even think about that through the chaos in my mind.

I close my eyes and replay the memory of Veiria attempting to take her own life—of me failing miserably to be there for her and then failing her again by giving into my despair.

I can't do that again.

I hug my knees, watching the sparks fly into the nothingness, then stick my feet out over the edge, stretching my hand out and feeling my connection to Telvin just as strong as always. My connection to Veiria is faint and trembling.

The only two people who have ever meant enough to me to keep so close. To worry about and tie my very life force to.

I just ...

I hope Veiria finds something more. I hope Telvin finds something more.

But I'm still worried about Veiria. About that timid girl she became—worried that she won't grow beyond this.

I meant it when I said she'd find her own sky and I've made peace with being a memory, but to be taken away from her so soon ... feels like nothing's really changed.

And every time I get her back, she's gone.

I close my fist, then practice concentrating on my force-field, shielding Telvin and Eu while they're unaware.

Tomorrow. I can't lose them tomorrow. And I'm burning to dispel that anger from the years chasing a friend who was all but lost to us.

Burning at the anger that despite the millennia curse, I was happy to live it, if only for the greater curse of waiting.

But tomorrow will be different. I promise you, Veiria. I can't save you, I might not even be able to properly say goodbye, but I'll root for you till my last breath. I swear it.

I cross my heart and smile, pulling my knees up from the ledge and standing so that I can maybe force myself to get some sleep before the darkness passes.

Bejeweled in Love & Belittled in Spite

Veiria

I stand dazed, covering my eyes at a blinding light. It takes a second for my eyes to adjust and I step back out of the spotlight.

I turn. I'm in a circular room on a dais, a stand around me crowded with shadowy, laughing figures and a red-and-white striped tent material above.

I run to the edge, banging on the metal bars of a cage. The shadowy figures jeer at me and it echoes eerily in the packed room.

A circus. I'm in a circus.

I stumble back, wanting to hide or cower, my heart sinking at all the eyes.

I'm dressed in the most hideous spotted leathers, caged at the neck and ankles.

Threatening strings, a lazy accordion, and a discordant music boxes play a fractured melody that slows as I cower.

Then a young woman steps through the bars.

She's ... me—the me I want to be—beautiful and everything I can't be, brushing her hair aside with a vain grace I can't fathom possessing.

She grins and it lights up the room in gold, but her shine stops just short of my feet.

The music stops and a single piano note resounds eerily.

"You're not good enough to be me, are you? Not pretty enough. Not born enough."

I wince at her words, stepping backwards out of the spotlight, away from the unattainable dream, and into the dark ...

The next second, the room lights in an inky blue, rhythmic waltz music swelling in the air.

A shadowy man approaches me, and though I can't see his face, I can tell he's handsome.

My blood rushes to my face as he bends forward graciously in a bow, taking my hand in his and kissing it oh-so-gentlemanly.

As he holds out his arms, I place my hands gently on his.

One of his hands moves down to my waist to lead me, and I hold my breath, smiling nervously.

Then he leads me, guiding me through the steps as we shift through a crowd of dancers—pairs of men and women.

As if to ease me further into the dance, he spins me, and although he's a shadow of a man, my smile is radiant.

He passes me off and I'm escorted from man-to-man, courted and smiled at and looked at with the longing offered to a beautiful woman—lustful, but respectful gazes and to each one I feel more of a thrill, until I'm spinning in their midst.

Then silence again and a spotlight.

I freeze as my body goes unnaturally tense. It's as if my body is suddenly taken and I'm yanked away.

I want to scream as my beautiful ball gown fades to a pitch black tux and dress slacks. The clips fall from my hair, my features become rougher, and I'm dragged screaming across the dance floor, my limbs torn to-and-fro like a marionette as I yank in vain at my strings.

But I can't scream because my mouth is gagged, and I stare in horror at images of a past played in faded clips and a woman approaches me.

I bow and take her hand, forced to watch, my eyes glued open as the part of a man is pressed upon me—ingrained in my very mind—to be tough and gentlemanly and emotionless and to lead. To become a boy and a man and a husband and father. The very person I swore I would never grow up to be.

The music starts and I lead her, my wrists bleeding in my chains.

She treats me as an unequal partner, and I want to scream at her that I'm just like her, that I don't want this life that isn't mine, in a body that isn't mine. That maybe I wouldn't mind dancing with her if I wasn't stuffed in an awful cage, forced to break every shred of the person I've had to lock inside.

I'm jerked again and again.

You were always in the wrong part, a voice whispers in my head.

I'm transported to a wedding, wishing I could claw at something, anything, until I'm gazing at the bride in envy.

How I wish I was in a different role—maybe she feels the same.

I yank harder at my chains at the awful words from the mouth of the pastor.

"Do you take this man to be your—"

My strings seem to snap, before they're pulled tighter until they rub my wrists raw and blood seeps down my arm.

"Sir—"

"Protect her—"

"Be strong—"

"You're so handsome—"

The voices in the audience laugh raucously and I'm back in the cage. The strings vanish and I collapse, unmoving, until I hear light footfalls and a woman, my desired self, lifts my chin.

"You look awful. Pitiful." Her eyes would be mocking, if there weren't a shred of sympathy. "Do you really deserve this? You know there are other choices."

There isn't, I think.

She kneels beside me and offers her hand.

I feel broken—like I have nothing left but humiliation, but I take it, and a softer melody fades in, a harp strumming gently as she starts speaking.

"You could still be beautiful."

My heart stops for a moment, and I gaze at her with hope, before realizing it's all in vain and drop my gaze. "I can't be."

Then she takes my hand, twirling me gently until I'm in her arms and a breadth away.

Then she places her lips softly on mine. "I think you could reconsider that. You may be ugly, but there's something in the real you." Her voice is still soft as she grazes my heart. "Or you can stay pitiful."

She pulls me closer and as I have nothing left, I let her. A small piece of me stirs at the tenderness of her lips.

Suddenly, I feel strange and as she pulls back a little, her eyes alight, I gasp.

My skin becomes softer, my hair longer and beautiful, my complexion and my eyes brighter, my breasts are there again, pointed and small, but there, enough that I breathe in relief. I'm not blonde or perfectly curved, but I'm me. She holds up a mirror. I nearly burst into tears there— the fat on my face is more feminine, my eyes less tired, and I smile more genuinely.

I touch my face, my hair—a gentle, curly red, now down to my chin and held behind my ears with a butterfly bobby pin. Even my freckles seem to look pretty for once, almost.

She smiles gently at me, holding the mirror closer to us and we both gaze at it. "See," she murmurs gently, but my awe of her is waning—the pedestal I set her on that I thought I had to become. "That's you and you're beautiful."

I touch my face again and feel hot tears.

Then she rushes the few inches to me and encircles me in a graceful embrace. "I'm sorry for being so cruel to you. I'm what you want to be; even girls who weren't lied to, who were raised to be women, feel this way. Womanhood isn't just an aesthetic to you."

I feel a drop of shame at the implication.

"I know that. You love womanhood far deeper." She extends her hands straight outwards. "Shall we dance? As yourself."

I grin sheepishly. "I'd like that."

I accept her hands and a tender music box plays. We lead each other as equals—as two women in a dance. "You feel right. You feel happy." She pulls me closer and then we move out again, stepping in sync as the music grows into an energetic, lovely rhythm of a flute. "I like you this way."

And I twirl, my tux scattering until I'm left naked in a body I can maybe feel okay with and then a dress of a deep maroon, frayed lace around the chest and elegant to my ankles, melds to my body in a way that makes me feel sexual and pretty and confident and at-ease in a 'me' way. She takes a few steps to me, laughing and clapping our hands, as we dance our hearts out to an energetic, lovely tune on flute and cello and my laughter, long and free, mixes with hers. It sounds light now that maybe I can cast my fear of not being her aside.

The music fades to romantic strings and she closes the distance, embracing me like a friend. "I don't know what you want. I'm not you and I'm sorry. I wanted to get to your head. Forgive me."

"It's okay. I might ... like you too. As a friend or something more ... it doesn't really matter." Because I've had enough of women thinking I only want sexual things to last a lifetime, because I'm not who they think I am and deep in my heart, I only wanted a deeper connection—I can't look past friendship right now; I know that's why I won't look at women that way again, why I try to only desire men—guilt and the desperation to belong.

She tucks her hair back, her eyes starlight. "Well then ..." Her smile is radiantly hopeful. "Be happy for me. You can do this."

She holds me one last time, and turning to flecks of light, what remains of her joins with me. *Never give up. I* hear her voice in my head. *For I'm with you always.*

I hold my hands gently over my breast. "Thank you."

I feel her presence smiling, but by now, her words are but a ghost. I can't pretend I was born like any other woman. Can I still be one? Is that okay for me to wish?

Under Tears of Time

Telvin

Eu holds me long into the morning under that shadow of darkness, caressing me as my eyes wonder at the tear of stars in the void, like an endless slit of beauty that still exists in this darkness.

The world may be crumbling, but there's something about being held in Eu's arms.

Veiria is out of our hands, and that I can't change …

I close my eyes, thinking again that I really do like Eu.

I find my eyes wandering to Meren again, but I know she'd want me to be happy rather than worry about her, so instead I turn into Eu's sleeping form—barely at all so as not to wake him.

The sky clears of Noctine's darkness in the morning, the heat rapidly climbing again. They can't hold back the tide forever. And I am grateful for their effort. Noctine alone is what's keeping the three of us alive in this ephemeral place. What's keeping the world from crumbling and allowing Veiria the time to make her choice.

Meren is already alert, packed, and dressed, looking to the horizon with narrowed eyes.

I come up beside her. "We're almost there. You okay?"

She smiles tightly. "I couldn't sleep. Could you?"

I look guiltily at Eu.

"Of course you could, dummy. No stress. I don't blame you. My softy brother deserves all the love." She hands me her water.

"And you do too. I don't believe your fate will come tomorrow," I say, taking it thankfully.

"Telvin." She pinches my cheek affectionately. "It's okay, let's go. I'll be absolutely fine. You know I'm only holding out for Veiria and you. All I ask for is you two"—she rolls her eyes—"*three* to be happy."

Eu comes up to us as I open my mouth.

Meren mouths again, *I'm alright. Promise.*

Well, I'm worried. For the first time, I'm doubting my hope will win out. I do my best to take that thought back as quickly as possible. My faith in Veiria and a brighter destiny will prevail. I must believe that.

And as we start walking, me between the two of them, I pray to Veiria to calm myself, my eyes closed.

Before I know it, the heartbeat is close, a phantom, translucent heart floating in the air. Its vibrations reverberate across my skin and in the hollows of my skull.

"She's in there, isn't she?" Eu asks.

I nod.

Eu runs his hand through his curls and turns to me, giving me finger guns. "Okay, I'm going in."

My brow furrows. "You can't go alone."

Meren strides forward and crosses her arms. "He's right, you'd be an idiot. Not that you aren't already, but I can't have someone my brother cares about throwing away his life for nothing."

"Look," Eu says, hands still in his hair, "I was utterly useless before. It's my fault she's in there."

"And you'd be useless now." Meren's voice isn't scornful, just matter-of-fact, even with a note of worry. "Not only would you be throwing yourself away for Veiria, but my brother too."

Eu sighs. "Great cheerleading, Meren. Now, if you don't mind, I'd love to talk to your lovely brother."

Meren shoos him. "He's all yours, if he wants you."

I approach him, my head down. "Eu, I know you want to save her, but this is Veiria's affair. You must realize that?"

Eu tilts my chin up with his gentle fingers and I feel goosebumps as my throat clogs up. "I know. I guess I'm trying. Just ... I'm trying to figure out how to be there for her."

I lean into his touch and close my eyes. "For now, we wait. Until—"

A voice sounds low and ominous behind us. "Eu ... EU! I'VE BEEN WAITING FOR YOU."

"I guess that's my cue." He puts his forehead against mine and brushes his thumb against a few strands of hair on my forehead. "I won't do anything stupid."

"I don't believe that," I whisper. "Don't go."

He nods and as I hear the wretched voice again, I try to ignore it and take in Eu.

Eu turns, his back shielding me from the force of the voice as he silently motions to Meren who pulls me away from him, despite my protests.

She whispers in my ear. "If he's in any danger, I'll back him up."

I look back helplessly as he faces the heart and the voice with a self-assured smile. "Piece of cake," he mutters. "Now, what would you like with the one and only Eu?"

I smile nervously. Maybe I'm scared for him, but, um … that is my boyfriend, I think with a blush …

And I pray for his well-being.

Specters of Darkness ~ Tears of Love

Veiria

My body is once again a doll, dragged by a cruel destiny, but this time I have something to save me.

I cut my bounds—a kitchen knife and with only the briefest hesitation, it goes through my chest, over-and-over as blood spurts and I feel like I'm born anew a thousand times, until I stand, breathing lighter air and a sigh of relief, as I look down at a doll with glossy eyes and an eternal frown.

I don't look at the ugliness, because it's done—a doll in a play discarded like a costume.

But it's raining—pouring until I'm drenched and my hair plasters to my forehead.

I laugh for a moment, before all that euphoria seeps away.

A woman weeps over the doll and a man stares lifelessly, before he turns and curses loudly as if to pretend he's not in pain and doesn't understand—will never understand.

I get down beside the woman, shaking her shoulder, again-and-again. I face her and plead, "I'm right here. Please see me. Please …" I lower my head and when she doesn't listen, I run away in my grief that no one will understand.

I didn't leave. I'm right here.

The only one who follows me is a dog, spotted and with white fur, its mouth open and its eyes following me imploringly.

As I crouch and weep, he licks my face through my tears, and I laugh.

I reach up, ruffling his ears and feeling consoled in the eyes of one who doesn't care that I may have changed to others—to humans.

I pull my arms around his neck. "I miss you, Scottie. I missed you so much." I choke on those words. "I want you back. I wish you were here."

My vision glitches and I'm in a grave, a name replaced with "censored" and tearing, glitchy faces standing out in the pouring rain.

I bang on the coffin—kick it as I stare at the name, and it slips into the crevices of my mind.

I wish I could forget about you and for what seems the thousandth time, I close my eyes with a heavy heart and wish for sleep.

I can't be remembered as an awful thing.

There's a shadow above me—a mocking God or a terrible monster, I don't know, but he yells at me, commands me, grips my wrists and my mind until I'm warped to be like him—putting a leash around my neck like his duplicate plaything.

He screams at me his disdain, his disappointment, his disapproval, his hatred, his anger at the world. It comes crashing down and I cower and whimper, making him all the more terrifying. He calls me things, says it's my fault—an onslaught of pain forcing me to draw close for the fear of his wrath—to fear what's different like he does and to not embarrass him.

You are an obedient tool to be taken over, and every time you cry, it makes his anger worse, your pain wears and wears and wears, until he's more an oppressive idea to you than a person, and you wish the person you used to know would hold you close and let you cry in his arms, instead of beating your unique heart into silence.

So, you just scream in your corner and hate that man who makes you cry and makes you hurt and makes you feel pain and makes you lose yourself.

You're not him. You're not him.

I stare at him for a moment in defiance, only to fall back into tears again, my spark diminished.

And just as the onslaught started and when I can't bear the presence any longer, the specter vanishes and I'm in a field. I get up, glancing furtively around and clutching my beating heart.

I'm on a hill, in front of a woman, who seems at a loss for words for a moment. Our eyes meet—hers a gentle blue, her face light and welcoming, and her hair a gentle glowing orange.

In the distance, I hear a car horn honking and a man yelling angrily at us from his window. I cringe, but ignore it, my eyes on the woman.

Then she smiles at me from her picnic blanket, an infant in her arms.

There's something instantly familiar and warm in her smile, one I'd know anywhere—of feeling just a bit safe and understood—someone who I could always come back to and feel loved by.

"Mom." I stare at her, speechless.

She nods affectionately. "I didn't know where you were." Her eyes become glossy as she takes me in. "You're different."

I swallow.

Then she pats the ground beside her and after the briefest hesitation, I move to sit. I sit there for a moment, feeling just a little peace in the sun and affection, as she lets me rest on her shoulder.

But I know that moment can't last forever. I couldn't live with myself anymore if I didn't say anything now.

After a moment, I choke, "I'm not ... I'm a girl ..."

I wait for her response, my heart caught in my throat.

She smiles and nods, tears streaming down her face. "I should have known. I'm sorry. You were always the sweetest little b—" She closes her eyes. "Child. But I'm so glad to see who you've grown into."

I swallow and she holds out her arms as I throw myself into them and cry like a baby.

She holds me and we both sob. I feel a strange tenderness in her arms. "I may not be the perfect mother, but I'd like to try again. I want to understand."

I clutch her harder and she squeezes me for reassurance. "It's okay, Mom. You tried. Everything—you did everything for me."

"I hope I did." I hear a tremor in her throat, then a pause. I love you for whoever you are or decide to be."

She makes a soothing sound as I cry. "I hope you find a lot of people who know how to support you."

I nod.

"If you tell me you're my daughter ... I'll do my best to love you as one."

I pull back and she smiles affectionately one last time. "I love you more than anyone."

I try smiling back, but I can barely see her, as I rub the tears from my eyes, and she fades to white with them.

I yelp through my tears, reaching into the thin air—that brief feeling of peace leaving me numb and cold.

"I can't do it alone," I whisper. "Will you be there for me when I get back, Mom?"

There's nothing but silence and a white world.

I should have known—but for some reason, I believe her words wouldn't change if I ever came back to her.

I realize that's just what I wanted to hear.

I sniffle, because I know her well enough that she'd actually be there—eventually, she'd support me.

And maybe that makes me feel just a little less alone. It gives me hope that I can have the courage to be honest with her. I owe it to the person who gave me everything.

Strength in Cowardice

Eu

I can feel the presence of Veiria, her mind a weak tendril extended to me, as a small outline of silver forms, a maroon light shining like a star where her brooch would be. She holds it with the outline of her hand, and I feel the influx of air around me.

The wind responds to her call, swirling around me in glittering flecks of ice and glass.

The wind sweeps away, revealing full armor of silver that's rather stifling. A royal blue, fur-lined cape drapes over my shoulders. And in my hands appears an icy silver-blue sword with a rose insignia. "Sir Eu" is inscribed on the blade in elegant cursive. *Really, Veiria?*

"Bless thee, Eu," comes the overly-dramatic voice of Veiria. "Be my knight so you can come and save me—to be my prince. Or suffer the consequences," she adds, stifling a giggle.

"Pfft, Veiria. You're such a romantic soul," I say, my lips curling up fondly. "But don't you think it's a little overkill to make me wear this thing?" I twist around, looking down with a frown as I try in vain to get comfortable.

Veiria doesn't answer and I sigh as I'm met with a far more annoying voice.

"Eu," says the sticky voice ahead of me. "Veiria's protector and hero. *Her beloved.*"

"Yeah, yeah, pleasantries," I mutter with a wave of my hand.

I approach the heartbeat resounding loudly in my ears. I can't even imagine how Veiria's faring in there, but I know she is. For now, I'll put on a strong face, even though my heart is hammering at the omniscient force.

"You can't even protect her. How can you call yourself a real man?" The voice mocks.

I close my eyes, remembering Veiria's smile. Her voice. Her laugh. The fears and the hopes in her heart.

I know that's not why she wants me. "Veiria's strong—stronger than you give her credit for. She doesn't need me to save her. She'll do it herself. I believe in her." I smile grimly at the heartbeat. "My fight isn't with you." I hold up the sword Veiria had given me through the tentative connection of her dream—a knight's sword for me to carry proudly, my grip awkward. "I don't even know how to wield this thing. It's way too heavy."

I cast it aside and the voice hushes. The sword sails through the air over the cliff face. "Whoops. I"m sorry, I can't pay for that. Honest mistake." I shrug and clumsily bow, before my blood boils in my veins and I writhe in agony, screaming and twisting on the ground. I grit my teeth. "Veiria wouldn't do this, you know?" Then the feeling abruptly ends.

She didn't, the voice booms directly in my forehead.

Telvin runs to my side and holds my aching body, as I continue to writhe on the ground in the aftershock, whispering in my ear kindly, but on the verge of panic, "Are you alright?"

I stare defiantly at the heartbeat, Telvin next to me. "Tell her we'll meet soon. I believe in her."

The beating heart vanishes like a mirage, and I see Veiria encased in the distant sky in her prison of amber.

"Well, that was something." I scratch the back of my head, still wincing.

Telvin cradles my head, placing it in his lap.

"You're sweet, Tel." I smile tightly and close my eyes in bliss as he grips my hand too tightly. "I could rest here all day."

"Don't do that. We have work to do!" he says shrilly. Then his tears fall on my face. "Don't ever do that. You just threatened your safety to be showy."

I wrinkle my nose playfully. "You're smart. You know it wouldn't have done shit."

I open my eyes to see him shake his head, wiping at his eyes with his sleeve. "No. You're precious to me, my love, but I hate seeing you hurt."

"Lay off, Eu." Meren lifts her chin. "You're hurting my little brother."

"Whatever you say, Ice Queen." I close my eyes and sigh.

I feel the tension leave the three of us, as she comes to sit next to us cross-legged, patting my shoulder awkwardly. "I'm glad you're alright. I'm still not entirely fond of you, but you've caught Telvin's eye, and that has to count for something. Good job."

The ground suddenly shakes and Meren jumps to her feet, rolling her eyes as she throws her body in front of us defensively and snaps her fingers wildly.

The glass shards of Neihdria appear from nowhere, slamming themselves into Meren's barrier.

She pants and turns to me. "At least you're a little smart." She smiles grimly, before she turns back to focus. "I'm glad you believe she can do it on her own." Then her eyes focus on maintaining the barrier and the three of us hush, as I stand shakily, Telvin grabbing my arm like a desperate mother hen.

The shards buffet the barrier in wave after wave, Telvin tucked in next to me and his eyes wide as he stares at Meren. "I didn't know she was this powerful."

Meren bares her teeth, her forehead seeming to pop with the effort and sweat collecting on her skin as she stretches her arms out in deep concentration.

Another rattle encases us from all sides, but especially one.

For some inexplicable reason, most of the shards seem to aim for Telvin, circling out of their way to ram into the side of the barrier. I hug Telvin's waist to my side protectively.

The shards rain down on Meren's protective force field as she pants laboriously, her gaze wild and challenging, in-between regular glances over her shoulder at Telvin.

I can do nothing but watch as the glass batters our cage in a hurricane, the Maroon Star glowing ominously in the backdrop, casting long shadows over everything, and scorching the world.

Then the sky darkens in twilight and Noctine drifts out, blocking out the star for just a moment. They hover, their arms spread in power and the air around us is sucked away, as the glass fades from existence in tiny rifts in time and space.

Noctine smiles with an ancient power as Meren keels over, her barrier flickering and then fading out.

Telvin squeals and struggles out of my arms, racing to her side and shaking her with tender hands.

I stare speechless at Noctine as they seem to rip out my soul and I stumble backwards.

"Well met, Eu," they say, before the ground shudders and begins to rupture.

Telvin freezes, his mouth agape. "We're out of time." He stares at me wide-eyed and my heart drops. "This is the end—for all of us, save Veiria."

I swallow, gazing from Telvin's frightened eyes to Meren's unconscious body slumped helplessly on the ground, to Noctine, levitating in the sky with an almost smug expression. "Decide how you'll end things, Eu. You'll continue in another life, but Veiria—she needs you now. Who will you be to her?"

My mouth is dry as I answer, "The friend she needs."

The world rumbles again, the grass below me sparking with tendrils of fire as I pull my hands back, the red star melting the earth and my skin with an apocalyptic glow.

The sound of a bell resounds in my head, chiming the end as I back away from the flames, Telvin yelping and fanning them away from Meren.

This is the end.

But not Veiria's.

Who were we?

Crescendo in the Theater

Veiria

The scene changes and I'm finally in something truly affirming—a laced wedding dress, a veil pulled down.

Eu stands before me handsomely—his curly dark hair matching his tux, and a smile plastered on his face. He gazes at me with his beautiful cinnamon eyes.

"You want me to take you forever."

"Yes!" I squeal.

Oliv— I turn on my heel, dragged toward a cake topper and a coffin in the shape of a groom.

"Shut up! Stop ruining everything!"

Come to me! An erratic chanting starts, almost mocking me with its off-key chorus.

I struggle and without thinking, there's a gun in my hands. I draw it with shaking hands, then lift it in front of me. I squeeze my eyes shut as I pull the trigger.

I don't hear the shot, but my chest wants to rip open, and I gasp, holding it.

"Veiria," Eu says softly. He turns my shoulders, and I open my eyes to look at his frown, breathing heavily. "What's wrong?"

"It's nothing." I give a pained smile. "I'm your girl, aren't I?"

"Of course you are, Veiria."

He grabs my hands and leads me towards the dance floor. As we get there, he holds my chin and I close my eyes, waiting for him to lean in for a kiss—to feel his soft lips on mine like in my dreams.

"You're having doubts."

My eyes fly open. "What?"

"You want to move on."

Suddenly it's frigidly cold.

"Eu?" My breath clouds and I shiver, but flickers of my dance with my alter-ego come back to me and a gentle melody plays as Eu pulls out a music box.

"She gave you her heart." He looks up with a deep sadness. "You promised her you'd move on."

The floor shatters beneath us and I lose my breath, falling into a huge amphitheater, an orchestra in the middle and masked spectators watching our descent in expectance.

"Eu! I'm sorry! Please!" I plead into the void, reaching for him. "I won't let go! I won't let go!" I scream over and over again into the void. "I can't move on without you! You're everything to me!"

My voice is drowned in a haunting opera and tense strings, as I reach out my fingertips in vain.

"Come back to me!"

The opera reaches a shrill crescendo, the voice turning sorrowfully tragic as we plummet to the floor of the amphitheater.

"Please," I pray, holding my hands together. "Please save him. He's my love—my one and only. The only person keeping me going." Then I cry out in sorrow. "I don't even care if he's not real, just let me have him!"

I squeeze my eyes shut, feeling hot tears sprayed across my face in the pressure of the wind.

The operatic voice turns dark and ominous, a low cello fading in, and I open my eyes to find Noctine in the audience with a sympathetic, knowing look.

They raise their arms forward and then spread them wide. It's as if to say, *just a little longer*, as a void opens beneath us in the darkness, and I see blue sky and white clouds.

"Thank you." I send my gratitude to them, I hope, with all my heart and plummet through the void. "I just need to say goodbye and then all of you can rest. I'll leave you at peace and unharmed."

They bow their head, I hear a gentle piano, as a copy of Eu plays the same melody from the music box, a cutout of myself beside him, sitting close to him so that we're almost touching, and then I'm lost in the void, the piercing crescendo and the soft melody gone. I reach through the clouds to the boy I desire to have just one last time.

Eu

The onslaught suddenly stops, the air deathly still and the red star pulsating and swapping rapidly between the moon and Yelyaa, the star I know.

The air and the color of the world seems to flicker, as I put my hand to my head, a splitting feeling wracking my brain.

Telvin collapses into my arms, his breathing labored, and Meren gasps, falling to her knees, her hands splayed as she heaves like she's going to vomit.

Noctine turns to us from their perch in the air. Their eyes bore into me with some deeper meaning. "I have to leave you. Veiria's in danger. I've decided she's worth it this time. She's ready to be set free."

I glance at them in confusion.

"Don't look so dour, Eu. You only have a few minutes left. Enjoy it." In an instant, Noctine vanishes and a pitch-black void opens up.

Out of it falls Veiria. For a moment, she sprouts transparent, glowing wings, bursting in the air around her like luminous tears, then she plummets to the earth like an angel fallen from heaven, a bridge appearing from her feathers.

She collapses, spinning. I run to her across the bridge as the world shakes and crumbles away behind me, and without thinking, I tense my legs and jump into thin air, the glass shattering behind me into a thousand incandescent fragments.

Veiria's eyes flicker open, and my heart is flooded with relief.

"Veiria, hang in there!" I reach out my hand.

"Eu! Eu! Help me!" She seems more frantic than I've ever seen her, her eyes panicked and my heart drops in my chest as I reach out to save her, forgetting about Telvin, about Meren, and about Noctine in this moment.

Saving Veiria is all that matters to me right now.

I careen towards her, wishing I could just get close enough to hold her and soothe her panic …

Veiria

"Eu!" I scream into the void, as I start careening downwards, glass and water spinning around me. *Save me*, I think like a prayer.

Panic rises in me, as the wind hushes my screams.

I feel a frantic hand grasp my wrist as I fall and snap my face up to his gorgeous, equally panicked smile and in an instant, my panic fades and time slows.

Eu pulls me into his arms as we continue to fall and without thinking, I laugh, pulling him closer until we're only inches away.

He looks confused and attractive and oh-so-kissable. "My hero," I giggle. I suddenly grow nervously quiet, only feeling the sound of my racing heart and forgetting everything but the moment. "I want to kiss you, Eu." I say it with such aching longing as I gaze at his perfect lips.

I feel his breath caressing my lips and see the uncertainty in his eyes.

He presses closer and I take that as affirmation, pressing my lips to his, my hands grabbing at the collar around his neck and his familiar dark curls.

My smile widens and I feel profound elation. It rises with a strange sadness I ignore. *My first kiss.* I want to scream it.

He pulls my hips closer to him, holding me delicately and I want to swoon.

He's so handsome.

I pull away, my arms still wrapped around his tanned neck as reality slips back in.

"My first kiss."

"I'm a profound kisser, thank you." He blushes red.

"Thank you, Eu."

The wind bites at my hair and I feel droplets as a body of water rushes up at me, a column of glass launching down from above.

"For giving me what I've always wanted. My dream."

"Of course, Veiria. But ... what do you mean by that?" His brow furrows.

"It's nothing. I don't really know even." I shake my head, aghast and joyous at once. "Probably just girl things." I wink at him.

He opens his mouth, his cheeks still hilariously red, but before he can say anything, the world comes to greet us and we're crashed into oblivion, glass striking the water and swirling as Eu is pulled away and I grasp into the abyss in confusion, before I'm plunged through a reflection of myself into darkness ...

The glass shatters and my joy quickly fades to an intense pressure as I grab my skull.

A thousand tiny whispers sound and blurry images flash in the dark.

He won't like the real you. Won't you tell him who you really are? What you really are?

They whisper and I shriek. "No, he loves me!"

Liar. It flashes through the darkness in electric yellow. *Your family hates you. Your friends would leave you, if you even had real friends. Veiria, don't you see that they only want a dream?*

"NO," I state resolutely. "He'll love me."

A real girl wouldn't seek all her affection from a man who doesn't know you. A real man likes a woman. You're telling me you're one?

"Shut up!" My voice turns weak, and I cover my eyes as I start to whimper. "Get out of my fucking head!"

There you are. The temper. What a Lady you are, Veiria. Or should I say, Ol—

"FUCKING SHUT UP!!!" I slam my fist to my forehead, my vision turns blood red and then I'm back.

My eyes open slowly.

Eu's lips are on mine, and I feel my cheeks get warm, until I realize his mouth is open and he's pumping his hands against my chest.

CPR.

I cough, spitting water, the sky an unfurling sphere of glass around us.

"Thanks, Eu-Eu." I slur my words, looking around in confusion."

"You had me worried. Again."

"Sorr—"

He gives me a death glare and I mumble, "Not sorry. Anyway, where are we?" I wince as I try and block out what I'm scared are memories.

There's a strange teenage boy gazing at someone familiar looking. The two pass each other in a school hallway, hardly giving each other a glance if not for the sidelong gaze of ...

...

Never mind.

I shake my head. I can't afford to be in my head right now.

Eu needs me, right? Or do I need him?

I sigh and then smile at him in attempted flirting, remembering our kiss.

He gives me a pained look and ignores me.

I don't think it's working.

I think I messed up.

"Eu ..." I reach out to him, dejection at the back of my throat.

Eu won't talk to me for the hundredth time since our kiss.

I sigh, pacing the lake as Eu starts spiraling in his head about how to get back up.

I messed up. I messed up. I messed up.

And I know in my heart that he didn't really want me, did he?

Did I take something away from him? I think Telvin might have been the one he really wanted, if only I'd noticed the signs sooner. I was convinced he wanted me ...

Lost in thought, I sit at the edge. And closing my eyes ... I hear a ticking in my head.

Tick-tick-tick

It gradually grows louder as I look at Eu and he slowly fades, looking back at me, our eyes meeting.

Eu

I pace the lake, panic eating away at my insides at how to save Telvin.

I saved Veiria, but at what cost? Then she kissed me

...

And I kissed her back.

I clutch my head, kicking a rock by the lake in my pitiful fury. I'm just as much to blame.

Then Noctine's voice resounds coldly in my head, and I snap my head up.

It's not your fault or hers, Eu. Forgive her and yourself. She's a girl falling through a dream, and she needs you.

I look back at her, as I see the sunset on the horizon and hear the faint ticking of a clock.

Guide her to the end. She's almost there, if you'll just let her see it.

I gaze at Veiria as she fades. "I can't do that." I look up at the fading sky and my heart plummets.

In another life, Eu. For now, there's just Veiria. It'll only hurt Telvin for a moment. You'll see him in time.

I nod, knowing that I'll of course help my friend in the final stretch. I try to ignore what Telvin must be suffering without me as I strengthen my resolve for Veiria. "Take me to her."

Sweet Dreams

Meren

I wake up to the feeling of pain searing my arms and legs. I blink, looking up to see Telvin attempting to drag my arm in vain.

"Telvin. Telvin!" My eyes jump open at another searing pain against my legs, as the flame licks at my skin.

I scream in anguish, recoiling my leg away, as the fire spreads, my skin peeling to ash. I turn my head and look at the flames consuming my body, with the cold realization that we're fading away—that it's our time to go.

Telvin throws his arms around me, and I can't help myself. I sob in the moment—at the pain—against my skin and in my heart.

I'm not real. I knew that from the beginning, but now, I sink back in defeat, closing my eyes to the pain and trying to block out my fear. Only now in the end have I given up on fighting any longer. There's no point in fighting when I've fulfilled my promise while I was still here.

"Don't worry. I got you, Meren. We'll leave together ... like how we started." Tears stream down his face fondly, consumed by the heat before they can reach my face.

I look into his face, my eyes wide and filled with my fear, his filled with love, the fear still licking at my heart, as much as I try to remember that it doesn't matter. Even so, I hug my brother, trembling.

"I love my sister," he whispers in my ear.

My throat bobs. "Telvin. I ... you were all I ever needed. *Be safe.*"

He wipes at his eyes. "We'll go together till the end. You think Veiria would want this?"

"It doesn't matter," I say in defeat, my voice cracking. "She can't change my future."

We hug tightly and I finally say it with a shaky breath, "I love you too, Telvin." I'll protect my little brother to the end, and he'd do the same for me.

Slowly, the flames lick up the rest of my body as I breathe silently in my brother's arms. He vanishes to light.

Make him happy, Eu, I think as my last wish.

Then my skin vanishes to fire, a light escaping me, as Veiria grants me one last wish.

Live on.

I know it can't be, but I still smile my gratitude, before my brother and I vanish in each other's arms, as if we were never there and the world wilts where we once were.

Tender Days Lost to the Hand of Time

Veiria

Tick-tick-tick …

My eyes flutter open to a gold disc on the horizon—the sun setting over a sea of tranquil clouds that ebb and flow by my feet, which are situated on a metal platform. I shift my head to the right, feeling the cool material with my fingers, as I locate the source of the ticking—clock hands on an island-like pocket watch suspended in the sea of clouds.

I sit near the top of the watch, where the words "END" are engraved in blood red.

I reach out my hand and flinch.

You aren't there yet, says a voice in my head.

I jerk my head around, but it's just me. Nevertheless, my hair remains on end, as I tense like my body will jump at the next hint of a breath. The wind ruffles my skin a little and I do jump, before taking a breath out and shivering.

As I step in a circle again, warily casting my gaze around, something materializes in my periphery and I spin around to see … well, Eu.

I stop in my tracks and smile tentatively as Eu seems to glance around, confused.

"Veiria?" His brow furrows. He gets up and starts walking towards me. I take a step back and he frowns, stopping. "What's wrong?"

"Is this real?" I ask quietly. "You won't hurt me? Or say the awful things in my head?" I retreat to the edge of the watch and the ticking noise stops, the hands frozen.

Eu puts his hands up in surrender. "Veiria, I swear you're safe. Please talk to me. We're friends."

For a moment, I feel the lash of rain and wind and I squeeze my eyes shut and squeal, cowering at a flash of lightning. "Are you really real? Because if you're not, I don't want you here. I've had enough heartbreak—enough pretending for a lifetime. I either want to live, or I just don't want to be here anymore."

I squeeze my eyes shut as the footsteps come closer, the rain lashing my hair wildly in a gale.

Then his voice is soft. "I want to see my friend smile. Please talk to me, Veiria. I don't want you to push me out."

I open my eyes, and the gale is gone, the sunset painstakingly melting into the horizon behind him like my twilight hour.

"Can you promise me you'll still be here when I open my eyes?" My voice shakes.

"I can't promise anything about tomorrow, Veiria, but I'll listen to you as a friend if you give me the chance."

I clench my fingers over my heart until they're white and look at him with eyes that sting. "I wanted so badly for you to be real."

"Veiria?"

"You wouldn't understand ..."

"Veiria." He moves over to the edge and pats the space beside him. "Sit next to me." I feel unwilling to move for a second, before I walk over to join him, dangling my feet into the clouds.

We sit for a few long moments. I try to ignore the fact that he's beside me, but I can't bear the thought of not looking at him now that I know that he's gone.

My heart seizes up at the small distance and his gorgeous, scrawny figure.

He looks at me and smiles and something gives in my heart. "I'm not the girl you thought I was … When I was younger, I think I wanted to be like the girl in front of you. I wanted so badly to be a normal girl."

"But you are normal, Veiria."

He must see the hurt in my eyes, because he stops. "I'm sorry, Veiria, I'll listen."

I take a deep breath, watching his delicate jawline and the breath through his steady, strong chest. "Can you hold me? I'm alright if it's just as a friend. I'm okay if that's what you want."

"Sure, Veiria." He scooches over, pulling me into the safety of his chest. "You're right, Veiria. I like Telvin, I'm sorry."

I nod with a strange numbness. "I know." I just didn't want to admit it. "I just couldn't let you go."

"I'm really sorry, Veiria. Please don't take it personally."

I close my eyes and smile. "Your girl is trying. I'll be your wing woman."

I can feel the reluctant laugh in his chest. "Appreciated. It means a lot, Veiria. I was scared of how you'd take it. You're a fragile little bird sometimes ... And I guess I've been struggling with this for a while." I look up as he shifts a little under me. "It's confusing liking both girls and guys. But Telvin's ..."

"Cute," I say spontaneously. "I mean, you two are cute together. Sorry, was that weird?"

"A little." He blushes. "So anyway, what did you want?" His voice sobers, like he's seriously listening.

I gaze at the rays of the sunset, feeling their rays and Eu's warm heart melt my frozen one. "I wasn't born ... the way I wanted to be. It's starting to come back to me, but I was treated like you. I hated it. Every day felt like I was forced into something I hated, especially when I grew older ... I was ugly, I kept my head down, I was forced to be with people I didn't want to, do things I hated. My body changed in ways that I knew were wrong but couldn't communicate. I was called words I hated, but ones that were normal to you. It was like, for all these years I had to put on this mask ... play this role of some stranger. All that time I felt wrong. I couldn't always put my finger on why, but I knew I wasn't myself. I knew I longed for things I couldn't have, but I just ... they just slipped away. I missed out on ... so much." I swallow and Eu squeezes me closer. "I'll never be able to grow into the woman I wished I was, have the girlhood I missed, have the body I wanted like any other girl, or have the experiences that I didn't get to live. They were stolen from me." I sniffle, my voice catching, and I wipe at my eyes. "I wish I wasn't put on this earth sometimes. I don't want to go through the agony of trying to be something that was a given for all the girls I wanted to be like. I don't want to have to live with that pain. I don't want to think about it." I know there's hurt in my voice, but I don't care. There's so much longing behind each word that my voice nearly cracks. "But now I'm here with you and every moment is torture, because you're so much of what I wanted to have. You're what the girls my age were promised—what they were told to want. And I can't be like those girls, because I wasn't born like them." I clutch his shirt tightly. "Can't you stay with me to the end? Couldn't I have been born like this?"

"I'm sure you were beautiful before."

"No … you don't understand. Everyone told me I … that I was handsome …" I look down. "And a b—" I purse my lips. "I can't do this, Eu. I can't say that, because it can't be true." I try and fail to smile and speak barely audibly. "I'm trans. Please don't think I'm sick. If I lose you …" I take a shaky breath—*then I'll go off the deep end fully. I'll break.*

I hold my breath.

Eu's quiet for what seems too long. Then he pulls back. "I love you just the way you are, however you look or will look." He brushes a strand of my hair. "The Veiria I know is a girl—a woman, and she's beautiful, heart and soul. I don't know exactly what that means for you, but I get the gist." He pulls me into a gentle, tender, loving hug. "You're a beautiful soul, Veiria. You'll be my friend always and I will always love and support you. I love you. Platonically, but I love you."

I feel hot tears on my cheeks. My mouth opens and I cover my face in my hands.

He strokes my hair and holds me protectively against his chest. "You're safe. You're 'my girl.' I want to see you have the life you want. Don't give up, because I know you'll get there."

I nod into his chest. "Thank you ... thank you so much, Eu. You'll be with me?"

"Always," he whispers.

"I can't do it." Something in my voice breaks.

"You can. I know you can."

I shake my head more forcefully.

He pulls me away and looks at me gently. "You can."

"No." My voice spikes back up earnestly and I stand abruptly, suddenly panicky. "I can't do it. I can't!" I cover my head.

"Veiria, you're scaring me. Everything's going to be alright." He stands there, his eyes comforting, but my heart won't rest.

I step away and the watch and the sunset and the clouds start to vanish as the watch hand shifts to 'END' and a bell tolls, ringing loudly in my ears.

My eyes go wide and panicked.

"Veiria, I'm here. I'm here." His voice slowly drowns out.

"Eu!" I scream as the metal beneath me quakes and just before he brings his arms around me protectively to hold me again, he vanishes in a gust of air and I stare around in furtive panic, crouching down and screaming in the darkness alone. "EU! EU!" I scream his name with all my lungs.

Alone.

"I can't do it without you," I whisper to deafening silence. "I can't do it alone, or at all." The world's too scary.

Deep in Her Heart

Veiria

As I open my eyes, I'm there again and I scramble to my feet.

Come here, Veiria. It echoes in the void.

I squeeze my eyes, as the heartbeat thunders, flashes of longing flickering under my eyelids, of days looking and wanting. Of being something I couldn't be. Wishing I could blend in with the ... be like one of the girls. No different.

See the truth. Save me!

"I can't!" I squeeze my eyes harder, but I know the truth.

Struggling but always being othered. Being different. Maybe I was okay, maybe I was a safe one, but I still wasn't one of them.

I was ...

I shake my head and scream.

"I'm a ... I'm a ..." I wipe my eyes as they rapidly start leaking tears and I sit in a puddle.

You're a boy. You were never wanted. You weren't like them.

"You're wrong. I'm a girl!" I choke on it, but my voice is breaking.

Liar. Deep voiced. Creep. You're dangerous.

"I'm not! I just want to live! I just want to ..."

You want to live a delusion.

"I want to live! I want to live as I *should have!*"

Where did your meekness go, Veiria? Your shyness?

"I want to be done with you." I cradle myself and rock on my knees. "I wanted to be just like them. To braid my hair. Gossip like any other girl. Maybe join an athletic team and be sisters. Go shopping at the mall. I wanted that special prom. I wanted the small conversations and connections that my old friends got, that I didn't because I was different. I wanted to be raised and taught as a girl. No one ever showed me how to do my makeup or take care of my period or tell me how pretty I was or ... or ... I want to live!"

You're gross and pathetic. You're a man in a dress that only wants a stereotype.

"That's not true." I rub at my eyes. "I just want to be treated as a girl. I don't care how. I don't want to look over, the girls I knew turning around because I'm different. Because I don't belong. I don't want to be ... I can't ... I'd rather kill myself than grow up a man." I stare into the taut air defiantly. "I'd rather not be here at all." My voice grows quieter. "But I'm scared. I can't do it alone. My ... my dad might kill me for real. I'm ... I'm my mom's son ... her ... her boy." I swallow. I stare between my knees, the water level rising to drown me and my heart. "And I have no friends. I never fit in with the boys. I was the weird one and I hated them back for the awful people they'd become for how they were raised. And eventually, I was pushed away from all my friends who were girls. There's nothing for me even if I did come back. I don't think they'd even let me go on hormones."

The water reaches my chin, and I don't resist as it seeps down my throat and I start sputtering water between coughs.

Then a light shines down from above and I look up. *Come with me, Veiria. The voice sounds like it's smiling. Come with me. You don't need anything to start anew.*

"But it's pointless." I want to give up, but still, I reach for the light. "I'm just so tired." I smile. "Maybe I wouldn't die as myself, but I can't go through the pain, but worse."

But it gets better. You'll live with it.

"Everyone will laugh at me. They'll call me a freak. They might kill me."

But there'll be people who'll come back into your life and love you for who you are.

"No, they'll hate me." My hand starts lowering.

You can't run away from everyone. The sad thing is people can say awful things. Will you let that rule your life as you always have?

I laugh despairingly. "That's quite encouraging."

You have a beautiful light. Being a woman is hard. And being a trans woman is hard. People will harass you, hate you, call you terrible things. It will be painful. Do you still want that?

"I want to be a real woman."

You think a real woman is what's on the outside. Haven't you always been one in your heart?

"I have ... But others ... But that's not enough."

You'll never be born the same as the women you want to be like with all your heart. You can't change that. But that doesn't mean you can't be true to yourself. Veiria ... who are you really in your heart? Who are you really deep down?

I close my eyes. Sorting through images of a bright-eyed child with the world ahead, as the world gradually closed in around her, suffocating her, caging her. Who would she be? Did she really deserve better?

You do.

Something in my chest grows lighter at the affirmations.

Valerie. The name in my heart. In that moment, I want to cry tears of joy.

I reach up into the light and grasp a hand ...

"I'm Valerie. Valerie Copper."

Welcome Valerie. I love you.

I'm pulled into the light and above the surface.

Into the world, or not quite, for I have one last memory to say goodbye to.

Goodbye to My Truest Friend

Valerie

I stand barefoot on a sunset beach, the surf licking at my toes.

I'm me. Just me. No illusion. It's a future me—the me I'd work towards. One on hormones. One who'd learned to love her body with the help of those same hormones, kind people, and kinder thoughts as she watched her reflection change, chose the person she wanted to be, and watched the people around her treat her differently, for better or worse.

This Veiria—now Valerie—she has a future and it's a hopeful one, where there's freedom on the horizon. There may be a battle, with herself and with the world, but even if people hurt her, that's better than living a lie. That's better than walking each day like she's already dead.

She smiles at the horizon, her heart bursting with hope at her future and at the boy who turns around to greet her.

"Hello, Valerie," he says with that same goofy, open smile, dressed in navy khaki shorts and a white t-shirt.

My heart stirs and I want to run to him in joy and heartbreak too, because my heart is cleaving in two. I don't want to say goodbye. "Hi," I say nervously.

"You're pretty this way. I told you you would be. One day you'll make it here."

"On the other side ... you won't be waiting for me." I swallow.

"You're not ready?" His mouth turns to a cute frown. I'll have to stop thinking of that—how cute he is. He isn't interested in me and that's okay.

I walk towards him with a new confidence, even if my legs are still shaky and I'd collapse without this one last goodbye. "I thought I needed you." I look into the warm eyes of a friend. "I thought I needed you to live—to feel sane and to not lose myself. I wanted desperately to be that girl who had everything, and I thought everything ... I thought my everything was devoting myself to a boy—to you. I thought I had to be this perfect girl. It's not and I don't. I know that. A girl isn't marriage or childbirth or validation of my womanhood from others or periods or exclusive cliques. It's not extravagant perfect proms or pretty dresses, even though I love those and that won't change. A girl is who I am in my heart." I clutch my heart and look earnestly at him. "I know that now. I'm scared to walk alone, but I know who I want to be."

Eu puts his arms around me comfortingly. "You're not alone, Veiria. I'm still your friend. Just close your eyes and I'll be with you."

I squeeze my eyes shut as tears well in my eyes. "Thanks, Eu-Eu."

"Plus, I think a world without me would be severely boring."

I giggle in his arms and hear the laugh resound in his chest. It gives me strength. "You'll be mine. My one and only friend."

"I want you to make lots of new friends. You can enjoy life without me. Right, Valerie?"

"Don't worry. I can, Eu-Eu. But you need to promise still."

He looks down at me between his arms. "You have my solemn oath. I will be your truest friend. It's a deal."

"Good." I struggle to hold my smile. "I don't want this to end still. I don't want you to go. I don't care that I trust my voice still, I don't care about anything. I wish I was really a goddess, if only so I could bring you back with me. So, you can stand by my side. I'd bring Telvin too, don't worry. And Meren. And your family."

"I'm sorry, Valerie, but I'm staying here ... in your beautiful dreams. I'm glad I was a part of them."

I put my arms around him now as I start crying into his chest. "I think I knew you. In real life. You didn't even know me that well. I didn't tell you anything and I'm so sorry."

"Shhh ... It's alright."

"No, it's not. It's ... you deserved better there."

"Valerie, I'm flattered, but I get it."

"I just wish ... Please don't hate me when I come back. I don't think I even knew you that well. You were just a crush. You probably thought I was a gay guy."

"Valerie. If I hate you there … just tell that guy he's a jerk and move on." He touches my heart and starts to fade.

"Don't leave me, Eu! Please, keep holding me until you're gone. Just a little longer!"

"Don't, don't, Veiria. It's okay. You're loved. You're safe. I'm in your heart always and I'll never leave." He then whispers, "I'll never leave my Veiria, my Valerie, my girl. Just remember that I'm rooting for you. That I'm by your side. And one day I want you to smile for me with all your heart." He tucks me into his arms, placing a gentle, goodbye kiss on my forehead. "It's not goodbye, Valerie …"

He fades further and the light of who he once was filters into my skin. "No! Eu! I take it back! I take it back! I can't do it!"

But he's gone and my skin glows as I hear a voice. "I'm here, Valerie."

I collapse to my knees as I choke on my tears, his voice fading too, and I scream long and hard into the sand. I scream long and hard for no one to hear as my tears are taken by the sand, the waves welling to my fingers, until a boat drifts next to me and I climb the small craft numbly, sinking to the planks and holding onto the mast for life as the boat sets sail to the horizon. I finally look up, my tears slowly and painstakingly drying as I leave the shores of my dreams and my memories of Bell, Diel, Noctine, Telvin, Meren … and *Eu* behind me. As I leave that place where I had everything I longed for all my life for a brief moment. I wipe my eyes, staring to the horizon and the distant shore reflected in my eyes.

I hold my head a little higher.

For Eu, I'll be brave.

Even if I forget him one day. Even if I only had him for an instant, he meant the world to me. I won't let his memory go to waste.

And so, I step onto that shore with a smile as the boat hits the docks, my feet firmly on the ground, and turn back, sending my gratitude to Eu.

My world … my memories finally fade.

And I welcome tomorrow with a smile.

Reminiscing on a Dream

Valerie

Valerie Eu Copper—that's the name I chose for myself. My name. I never thought something as simple as my own name could bring me so much joy.

Valerie—the name that came to me in a hazy dream, long since gone.

Eu—in honor of someone who is all but a distant memory. I'm not even sure if he's real, but I have a feeling that I wouldn't be here without him.

Copper—It's always been my last name. Sometimes I hate it, sometimes I don't mind it. But I decided to keep it, if only for my mom.

She/her—my pronouns. Something that people can spit in my face and refuse to call me, but that won't change the fact that this is who I am.

I walk through the school, my head up as I try to be proud, when I know I still have a long way to go before I feel that way.

But some things are different. These days, I no longer hide. It's terribly frightening and lonely in a way that's more authentic, if still cruel. But I'm me, and for once, I can walk through a room and not feel like an impostor. I can be myself without feeling like screaming, with some feeling of wrongness. Now if only I could get on hormones soon, so that screaming feeling would really go away.

But as long as I live with my parents and go to this school, that's an impossibility. So, I live a double life, being me when I can, hiding when I have to.

Granted, sometimes it never feels safe, but for the voice in my heart called Eu, I'll be strong.

I've started to grow my hair out as long as I can get away with, wear whatever affirming clothes I can find whenever it's safe to do so, I've been looking into HRT, though I dread the possible ten-year wait-list, and I've even created a private social media account where I'm out and try to pose with girly clothes in a way where I look cute and feel slightly less dysphoric in my body, not prepared for the onslaught of chasers flooding my DMs with their fetishistic comments and flirtations. But that's all I can really do right now—pick and choose where I'm out and where I hide, where I'm brave and where I'm better being safe.

I pass a corner, groups of students gossiping and rushing to classes or loitering in the halls between the bell. Some cast weird glances at me, while some are too preoccupied getting to class.

I sigh, shouldering my bag and heading to my locker with a new hot-pink bag I thought was cute.

Someone brushes by me—rather, two people—and they catch my eye.

I turn around.

A boy with tawny brown skin, dark curly hair, awkwardly worn clothes. And another boy, a little shorter with chestnut skin and dangling, wavy black hair in a comfy sweater.

Something tugs deep in my memories as I try to remember, only placing my name on the boy I had a crush on for months, Vincent, and another boy I swear I once knew or should know. I think his name is Timothy.

They're holding hands walking through the school hallway, laughing and close together. I think I saw them smile affectionately before they passed me.

Suddenly, something goes off in my head. Two names: Eu and Telvin.

I stare at them, my mouth slightly agape as I almost drop my things.

I wipe at my eyes in confusion as I feel something warm in my chest. My vision gets a bit blurry.

That's right. I knew them once. In my mind, but it was enough. I dab at my eyes and smile for them—that they made it here and that they didn't just exist in my head. They were real. Their love was real—is real.

Then I turn away from Vincent and Timothy, as they make their way down the crowded high school hallway, still holding hands.

My breath leaves me as I glance to my locker—another jolt through my memory, as if I'd seen a ghost.

Meren stands behind me, crossing her arms and leaning against my locker. "Good to see you ... Valerie." There's a tender look of nostalgia in her eyes.

"Meren," my voice seems to drop off a cliff in shock. "But I thought you were ..."

"Dead," Meren says quietly. "You wished I were here. Thank you." She closes her eyes and smiles, like she's still in another world ... in my dream.

Then I throw my arms around her, sobbing, "It's really you."

She hugs me back, gently. "All this time, you wished for a sister in your dreams. Don't think I wasn't coming for you." She pulls away and smiles. "You will always be my friend, Valerie. My family. It doesn't matter if they don't remember us." She looks at the two—Vincent and Timothy—something deeply broken in her eyes. "But I'll be here. *Always*. You can count on me, if you need anything."

I turn, casting my gaze back on them. "Thank you." *All of you.* For giving me a world where I can be happy.

~ End ~

Author's Note

You know, I sort of released this book for fun, or at least, that's what I told myself at first. It's been a passion project. A Maroon Star & A Silver Thread, as well as To Hold a Flower (my first book) were two books written for me first-and-foremost, publishing for others second. I wrote the initial draft of both six years ago.

To be honest, I almost didn't end up publishing this book. What decided it for me was the last four chapters. That and a few other scenes from the book were parts I felt were too important to never publish. Veiria's journey is deeply important to me. She may not be my first published openly trans character, but she's the first time I wrote a transparently trans journey that I felt was somewhat authentic (I wrote this book before Bluebirds, I just happened to publish that one first). Her journey to come out and come into herself was the first trans woman "coming out" I've written.

I think the chapter "Deep in Her Heart" is the closest I've ever come to describing the catharsis and joy of finding, choosing, and embracing who you really are. It's the closest scene I've ever written to the feelings of "finding" my own name. In my mind, I didn't choose my name, it came to me like a gift. Like something indescribable that made me feel alive and the world feel beautiful again. It was like a gift of pure love, and it was the happiest moment of my life. My name, Caroline popping into my head was what started making me feel alive ... gave me the courage to choose me and fight to live as the person I am. 'Caroline' gave me courage, peace, and freedom, the same way it did for Valerie.

I decided to publish this book on Trans Day of Visibility (March 31st). It's a special day for me as a trans person and it felt especially fitting for this book.

Veiria is far from perfect and shouldn't be taken as a moral compass. I know a lot of people probably won't like her because they find her immature or annoying, but that shouldn't diminish who she is. I generally like her and enjoyed writing her, despite understanding other peoples' annoyance with her. I hold her close to my heart.

I thought the themes of this book were relevant and meaningful. Especially early in transition, I got a lot of my validation and affirmation from men treating me like a lady and / or finding me attractive and I still sort of crave men worshiping me quite a bit (perhaps too much for my own good). Of course, I quickly found out the downsides of male attention firsthand (fetishization and objectification), but I didn't really tackle either of those much in this book. What "Star" was for was personified in the relationship of Veiria / Valerie and Eu / Vincent. Veiria is enamored with Eu both romantically and sexually as a sort of token / validation of her womanhood. She's trying desperately to entrench herself in rigid cisheteronormative ideals to fit in as a woman. But the truth is that she doesn't need male attention to validate herself and deep in her heart, she knows that. "Star" is her learning to stand on her own two feet and embrace herself for her.

"Star" is also a story about escapism—both through Veiria wanting an unrealistic ideal of femininity and more clearly through her escape from reality as a way to avoid and cope with her pain in her inability to be her authentic self. But escapism will never fix her problems, as she's never truly happy just living in her constructed existence.

I do want to give a few disclaimers:

1) If it's not safe for you to come out, please don't feel pressured to. I hate that trans people have to hide for our safety, but unfortunately we often do. It is implied that Veiria might not be in the safest or most supportive environment to come out, but she decides to and that's a risk and her choice alone.

2) I have a quote addressing "needing" to love yourself before loving another person. This isn't necessarily 100% my belief and of course, it depends on context. It helps a relationship and is healthier to love yourself first, but I think as long as you're making an active effort to work on yourself, then relationships where you haven't gotten there yet can work. What I was trying to get at was that Veiria was putting her entire personhood into Eu. A relationship with Eu isn't what she needs—she needs his friendship and support right now and she needs to move on and take a leap of faith and self-love for herself.

3) On cisnormativity and heteronormativity. Veiria idolizes and yearns to be cishet, the societal normal. In her dream, she imagines herself as cisgender (she's trans) and straight (she's bi). Veiria has no experience being out as trans in real life, therefore she hasn't developed or grown confidence in her trans identity yet. Her frame of reference for being a girl is through society's

narrow expectations of a cisgender woman. In regards to heteronormativity. 1) I do want to stress that men and woman can be friends and that many of Veiria's notions of attraction come from gendered roles in society and her upbringing. I've had my fair share of being shipped (often by adults) with my friends I purely viewed as platonic before I transitioned (fortunately, after I transitioned, people stopped doing that) and it's really uncomfortable and weird (that's addressed in Eu's agency and bi acceptance arc). Veiria's attraction to Eu shouldn't reinforce these gender roles. In fact, she does settle for platonic love in the end. My point is that she's been so conditioned into cishet standards (Eu has as well), that she earnestly and eagerly inserts herself into that role when given the chance to present in a way that's more true to her (while Eu is more uncomfortable and expresses a lack of agency earlier than her). The gendered expectations Veiria has internalized should in no way indicate straightness as being the default. Last of all: Veiria being a trans woman attracted to men is straight attraction and her attraction to women is lesbian / sapphic attraction. Veiria is a woman.

4) I kept a lot of the "dream within a dream" sequences intentionally vague and open to interpretation. Some of them are twisted and dishonest and not meant to be taken at face value. Some of them are "censored" in a way as Valerie deals with (or doesn't deal with /

acknowledge) her dysphoria. Note that everything is a dream and is some way influenced by Veiria's ideals, mimicking her desires and fears.

5) I don't like the "born in the wrong body" narrative. To me it was made by people who don't understand trans people as an easy explanation. I wasn't "born in the wrong body." My body is a trans body and I love it (disclaimer: dysphoria is real though and it does need to be treated). Now I and a lot of trans people do need various stages of transition, including medication, social transition, and sometimes more to reduce gender dysphoria and be our genuine selves (not necessary for all trans people; we each have our unique needs), but I don't think cis people can understand that we can come to love our bodies (with the help of gender affirming care / medication and social transition for many trans people). I love my trans body (on estrogen). My true self is the body I was born on being given estrogen to develop in the way that's affirming and true to me. I do need estrogen to feel myself and reduce my gender dysphoria, but I wouldn't trade that journey or my body for a cis one. As much as I wished at times to be a cis woman, as time has gone on, I've realized how much I love being trans and being on estrogen (estradiol) + an anti-androgen like spiro (spironolactone) (physically transitioning), plus socially transitioning as well has made me feel more myself and able to love

myself and my body without the crushing weight of gender dysphoria.

In terms of whether this book will have any sequels. As of now, it's a standalone. It's possible (likely even) that I'll write a sequel more in the contemporary genre (in real life with more real stakes and theming) where Valerie comes out and starts her journey (maybe even has a more genuine romance). It's also possible that I'll write a prequel exploring the relationship between Veiria, Meren, and Telvin that would be another fantasy and set in this same world in the past. Honestly, I feel like Meren should really be the heroine. If I wrote a prequel, she'd definitely get more of a spotlight.

"Star" may be the most fantasy book I write. Typically, I focus on very, very character-centric stories (very light fantasy and more recently, contemporary). "Star" allowed me a great deal of creativity, but it's also way, way more plot- and action-oriented than most of my other books. That said, it was a fun side project when I was having writer's block on my main series. This book was more a breath of fresh air and an experiment than anything, but it also let me explore some themes that are relevant to many bi and straight trans women early in transition.

On Eu: Eu was a comfort character for a while during early transition. On days I was struggling, I'd imagine him there with me to give me courage, like he does for Veiria. I'm not as much of a fan of Eu anymore as I was back then (to be completely honest, Eu started creeping me out just a tad in the Eu x Telvin romance), but he still has a place in my heart. He's the character who underwent the most changes between drafts.

I mentioned earlier, but Eu was the other character with a major arc. His arc revolved around agency and accepting himself as bi. Like Veiria, he was shoved into cisheteronormativity, sometimes seemingly forced or guided to be with certain people romantically and sexually (like the "star ball"). His arc is breaking away from those expectations. In doing so, he embraces being bisexual and being in a gay relationship, getting over his internalized homophobia (expressed when he meets Telvin) and becoming a healthier person, comfortable in his sexuality.

On Meren: My love for Driena (a character from my To Hold a Flower series) sort of bled over into my characterization of Meren in this book (especially in the Acellia section, coincidentally my favorite part of the book) and I sort of embraced that. Though Meren is distinctly her own character. I was wrapping up this standalone and drafting the third book in my series around the same time. Meren is my favorite character in this book. She reminds me of my own sister in some ways. I really think she deserves to lead her own story. She's probably also one of the coolest characters I've ever written (her, plus Telvin and Noctine). She's grounding for Veiria and closer to her than Eu ever was. Their friendship is healthier than her and Eu's and pulls Veiria back into reality a little. Meren and Telvin are the closest characters to a moral compass in this book, as they're the more mature of the four.

A Maroon Star & A Silver Thread also takes creative inspiration from and is a love letter to the world, characters, and story of *Xenoblade Chronicles 2*. I love the *Xenoblade* series. The first game is actually my favorite in the series, but creatively, the second game gave me a lot of inspiration and imagination that helped birth some of the creative decisions in this book. I loved the world and characters of Alrest in 2 and Star is sort of a vaguely inspired homage (the similarities are largely in aesthetics).

The chapter "Sacrificing the Things You Love" also has a visual and emotional homage to *The Legend of Zelda: Skyward Sword*. Beyond that, Star takes inspiration from *Madoka Magica*, *.hack//Sign*, *The Legend of Zelda: Link's Awakening*, *Celeste*, *Le Portrait de Petite Cossette*, and *The Star Touch Queen* and *A Crown of Wishes* (both by Roshani Chokshi), and in general, pieces of media with dream worlds and / or magic.

Alice in Wonderland and *Romeo and Julliette* are the only named references. Disclaimer: 'Hatter,' 'Alice,' and 'Cheshire' are characters belonging to Lewis Carol.

I got inspiration for Acellia from living by a beautiful bay—the water, gorgeous sunsets, and sound of seagulls.

Character List / Identity Clarification:

Veiria (she/her) - Trans Woman & Bi

Eu (he/him) - Cis Man & Bi

Meren (she/her) - Cis Woman & Undefined

Telvin (he/him) - Cis Man & Gay

Noctine (they/them) - Nonbinary (Transmasc) & Undefined

Reference

Carroll, Lewis, and John Tenniel. Alice's Adventures in Wonderland. New York, The Macmillan company, 1904.

Acknowledgements

Thank you for everyone who helped me grow and feel comfortable in my trans identity and womanhood. Thank you for your patience as I went through my self-discovery. For watching me as I went through the angst of a quite interesting (and much better) second puberty, confusing changes in how I saw the world from a new perspective and how people saw me, and slowly growing my confidence and self-respect in my identity as a confidently out trans woman. Especially to my friends in the book community on Instagram—for you being there for me the past few years without judgement and telling me how much it's meant to see me grow.

Thank you to my sister—my biggest supporter, who accepted me from the moment I came out. Thank you for everyone who tried to support, validate, and accept me—friends, family, coworkers and who made time to be kind. And if you didn't immediately, I'm grateful you came around. Coming out and the first several months of being out was the scariest thing I've ever done. Thank you for those of you who gave me the chance, patience, and grace for me to grow into the woman I am today. I still have a long way to go, but where I am already feels like a miracle.

Thank you to my cover artist, Chii / mihaellustrates for your absolutely gorgeous, magical cover art. You really outdid yourself with this one. It's so eye-catching and dreamy. Despite it being far outside the tone and style of the previous work you've done for me, it's absolutely perfect and beyond anything I imagined you could do. Thank you again and I'm always so happy to work on more projects with you. <3

Thank you to my editor and friend, Ellie (I.O. Scheffer). I'm happy to work with you again and I appreciate all your effort on my releases lately. Thank you for helping me improve some weaker aspects. As always, I highly recommend I.O. Scheffer's *Fearghus Academy* series (starting with *Fearghus Academy: October Jewels*); it's my favorite book series! It's a great series for queer and neurodiverse readers set in a magic school with exciting action, a lot of heart, and meaningful friendships.

Thank you to my friend and beta reader, John North. I really appreciate your feedback and it was very insightful. You're an amazing author and I love your *Gorgon* series! I would highly recommend *Gorgon: The Crimson Witch* for a bloody, anime inspired action book filled with themes of self-love and a growing bond between two sisters.

I made the mistake of getting another reader really last minute, so I can't promise I implemented all your suggestions, but nevertheless, I appreciate them and plan to work with you again and give your feedback more of the time and attention that it deserves.

Next, thank you to orchestral music. I've more openly embraced my love for orchestral music. It's part of who I am. It means a lot to me and has helped me through a lot. I love orchestral music because it's emotional, beautiful, and personal.

Thank you to the composers, Yuki Kajiura, Manami Kiyota, Kenichiro Suehiro, Keiichi Okabe, James Newton Howard, and Lena Raine, the vocal groups, Kalafina and Fictionjunction (both Yuki Kajiura projects), and the singers, AURORA (I feel like her song "Dreams" goes perfectly with the book's cover), Chappell Roan, and KEIKO (Keiko Kubota). My favorite composer is Yuki Kajiura. She's been my favorite composer for nearly the past decade of my life. I love everything she's involved with. I've gotten inspiration, comfort, emotion, and enjoyment from a variety of these and other composers and singers over the years.

Thank you in particular to Yuki Kajiura for writing music that's immensely personal and enjoyable to me. Her music helped me through a lot and it's special to me.

Besides that, the music to the *Xenoblade Chronicles* series was an inspiration for this book, so I'll thank the composers, Yasunori Mitsuda, ACE (Tomori Kudo and Hiroyo "CHiCO" Yamanaka), Manami Kiyota, Yoko Shimomura, Kenji Hiramatsu, and Mariam Abounnasr.

Also, I want to mention Lena Raine, the composer of *Celeste*, who's a trans woman (both the game's protagonist and creator are also trans women). *Celeste* is an impactful game about mental health, depression, and anxiety.

Veiria mentioned her favorite composer composing beautiful music for flute. My favorite composer, Yuki Kajiura writes the most serenely beautiful flute music in a lot of her scores, pieces, and songs. It's so gorgeous. <3

I also mentioned opera in the book. While I want to get more into opera, the "opera" I like is more opera-esque anime music that's stylistically similar. I especially love whenever Yuki Kajiura collaborates with the opera singer, Yuri Kasahara in her scores. It's breathtaking.

Also, thank you to my close friend and former roommate, Scout Hughes who took my author photo.

~ Other Books by Caroline Sophia Hamel ~

~ *To Hold a Flower* Series ~

"To Hold a Flower" – Book 1

"The Essence of Longing" – Book 2

"The Illusion We Craved" – Book 3 (Planned for 2026)

~ *Sweet Girls & Bluebirds* Series ~

"Sweet Girls & Bluebirds" – Book 1

"Sweet Girls & Nightingales" – Book 2 (Likely 2025)

"Sweet Girls & Songbirds" – Book 3 (Planned for 2026)

~ AMS&AST Related Works* ~

Prequel Novel **Name TBD** (Unknown Release)

Sequel Novel **Name TBD** (Unknown Release)

A Garden of Pleasures (Spinoff Erotica) **Name Not Final**
(2025, if I end up publishing it)

*None of these three are confirmed.

About the Author

Photo Credit: Scout Hughes

Caroline Sophia Hamel (she/her) is a trans woman from the Pacific Northwest writing stories on empathy, identity, mental health, and queerness. She loves emotional, character-driven stories, books, and anime, as well as orchestral music, J-Pop, and queer artists.

Caroline published her first book at the age of 22. She is passionate about creating a space for those who need it.

-

If you would like, consider leaving a review for A *Maroon Star & A Silver Thread* on Goodreads or another book site. I'm an indie author, so any and all reviews are appreciated and greatly help my reach. Thank you for reading.

www.ingramcontent.com/pod-product-compliance
Lightning Source LLC
Chambersburg PA
CBHW071344300726
48976CB00006B/1763